"What brings you to Shelter Creek?"

Wes looked at her with a steady gaze she remembered far too well. "I've wanted to come back here for a very long time. I couldn't, until now."

"You couldn't. Because you were what...a secret agent on a mission? Prevented by some invisible force field from crossing the Sonoma County line?" *Oops.* She hadn't meant for her resentment to show.

"I would have come back sooner, if I felt I could."

"I see." She wasn't going to get into this with him. He'd made his choice all those years ago, and over and over again with every year that went by without a word from him. "Well, enjoy your visit."

"I'm hoping to stay here. In Shelter Creek."

Emily swallowed hard. It was hard to talk when her lungs seemed to have lost the ability to process oxygen.

D0591859

Dear Reader,

Emily Fielding, Shelter Creek's only veterinarian, had been working with the Shelter Creek Wildlife Center since its start. She helped Maya and Caleb trap a mountain lion in *Reunited with the Cowboy*, rescued coyote pups with Liam and Tricia in *Her Surprise Cowboy*, and tended to injured animals on Aidan's ranch in *Rescuing the Rancher* after a wildfire swept through his property.

I always knew Emily would have her own story. She had a father whom she adored, who'd left her his practice when he retired. His were big shoes to fill, and there were clients who didn't believe Emily could fill them because she's a woman. Emily also had a heart that had been broken and had never quite healed, even though she pretended that everything was fine.

Emily needed a hero who would be patient with her and who would love her for who she was. Wes Marlow was that man and I adored him from the moment I saw him walking down Main Street in Shelter Creek. I hope you like him, too, and that you enjoy this sweet story of love lost and then found.

Warm regards,

Claire McEwen

WESTERN

Second Chance Cowboy

—

CLAIRE McEWEN

HARLEQUIN

WESTERN

HARLEQUIN®
WESTERN

Recycling programs for this product may not exist in your area.

ISBN-13: 978-1-335-45445-4

Second Chance Cowboy

First published in 2021. This edition published in 2021.

This edition published by arrangement with Harlequin Books S.A.

For questions and comments about the quality of this book, please contact us at CustomerService@Harlequin.com.

Harlequin Enterprises ULC
22 Adelaide St. West, 40th Floor
Toronto, Ontario M5H 4E3, Canada
www.Harlequin.com

Printed in U.S.A.

Claire McEwen writes stories about strong heroes and heroines who take big emotional journeys to find their happily-ever-afters. She lives by the ocean in Northern California with her family and a scruffy, mischievous terrier. When she's not writing, Claire enjoys gardening, reading and discovering flea market treasures. She loves to hear from readers! You can find her on most social media and at clairemcewen.com.

Books by Claire McEwen

Heroes of Shelter Creek

Reunited with the Cowboy
After the Rodeo
Her Surprise Cowboy
Rescuing the Rancher

Visit the Author Profile page
at Harlequin.com for more titles.

For Arik, Shane and Chauncey the dog.
We stayed home all day, every day, while
I wrote this book. I can't imagine any other
people (or dogs) whom I could spend that much
time with and still smile and laugh every day.
I am so grateful for our little family.

CHAPTER ONE

EMILY FIELDING SLUMPED on the bench outside the Creek Café. She could move no further until she'd had a few sips of her coffee. The first taste of the rich brew burned away the outer layer of her fatigue, but sitting down like this was a mistake. The bench had its own gravitational force, strong enough to keep her aching body from ever rising again.

She leaned her head back against the café wall and closed her eyes. At least it was Friday. All she had to do was get through today. Saturdays were easier because she only worked a half day at her veterinary clinic, unless some poor animal had an emergency.

"You're not really going to sleep here, are you?"

Emily forced her eyelids open. Her friend Vivian was standing a few feet from the bench, grinning down at her. Vivian's dark hair was pulled back in a ponytail and she was wearing a navy blue sweatshirt with the logo of the Shelter Creek Wildlife Center on the chest. "Of course not." Emily tried to smile, but it came out as a yawn and she clapped her hand over her mouth. "Just refueling before I go into the clinic."

"Let me guess. You had a late-night call?"

"An early-morning one. A breeched calf out at Pacific Pride Ranch."

"Oh, no." Vivian was a wildlife biologist, but she lived on a cattle ranch with her husband and understood the dangers of a complicated birth.

"We got him out, but it was a little sketchy for a while there." That was putting it mildly. Delivering that calf safely had taken every trick Emily knew. "I managed to get back home afterward for a shower and nap, but I'm still sleepy."

"And now you have to work all day?" Vivian shook her head in dismay. "You work way too much."

Vivian was probably right, but there wasn't much Emily could do about it today. She shrugged off her friend's concern. "I'll be fine. Who needs sleep when there is coffee?"

"Of course you need sleep! Have you had

any luck finding another vet to come work with you? Didn't you say you'd placed an ad?"

"I did, but no one has answered it." Emily pushed herself up to sit a little straighter. "I guess there aren't a lot of veterinarians who want to work in a tiny town in the middle of nowhere."

Vivian waved her hand in a vague gesture encompassing the quaint downtown around them. "How can they not want to live here?"

Emily glanced around. Shelter Creek woke early on a sunny February morning. Shop owners on either side of the café were getting ready for the first weekend tourists. Minnie Layton, who owned Wild Poppy Fashion, was hauling a rack of sale clothing out onto the street. She was chatting with Sally Smith, owner of the yarn shop next-door, while Sally cleaned her front display window.

Over the years, as tourists discovered the sleepy ranching town just a few miles inland from the Pacific Ocean, the cottages and run-down storefronts had been restored. Their clapboard walls were painted in pale greens and blues, whites and yellows. Flowers bloomed in every available patch of soil, and picket fences framed pretty gardens. Wine tasting rooms and restaurants had sprung up, along with boutiques and galleries.

Emily relished another sip of coffee. "It's a great place to live. Hopefully, I'll find someone to work with me soon."

"Speaking of work, I'd better head into the café before all the muffins are gone," Vivian said. "Maya and I are meeting this morning and I promised her a treat."

"Gotta keep the boss happy," Emily teased. Maya Burton ran the wildlife center, so technically she was Vivian's boss, though she was also a great friend to both of them. "Tell her I'll be by this afternoon to check on that gray fox."

Vivian nodded. "I hope it's okay. The poor thing seemed really lethargic last night."

"The antibiotics probably hadn't kicked in yet," Emily reassured her. The fox had been caught by a local farmer who'd seen it limping across her field of organic kale. Emily had drained an abscess in its paw yesterday and now the little guy was recuperating in the wildlife center's hospital. "Call me if it's still sleepy when you get there."

"Will do. Hopefully it will be grumpy and upset. Then we'll know it's on the mend." Vivian took a step toward the café, then paused. "I won't see you this afternoon. I'm only working until noon so I can take the kids shopping in Santa Rosa. Get some rest tonight. Okay?"

"I will... I hope," Emily said. "See you at book club on Wednesday night?"

"Absolutely. Don't forget, we're having a dessert buffet. Promise you'll make your amazing mocha brownies?"

"Sure." Emily raised her cup. "They have coffee in them."

Vivian laughed at Emily's lame joke and headed into the café. Emily reached into her jeans pocket for her car keys and jiggled them in her free hand. What was her first appointment today? It might be Mrs. Crawford's two Persian cats, big fur balls with pretty blue eyes and razor-sharp claws. Their annual checkup usually resembled a wrestling match. It might require a second cup of coffee. For her, not the cats.

Heaving herself up from the comfortable bench, Emily shuffled toward her white truck with the clinic's black logo on the door. Hopefully, there wouldn't be any emergencies today. Maybe she could even get home by six and crawl straight into bed. She took one more look around downtown Shelter Creek, so pretty in the clear morning light, and froze.

A tall man in a black cowboy hat was walking along the sidewalk across the street, looking idly at the shop windows. His face was angled away, but still, he looked so familiar. Emily's ribs tightened around her lungs. Something in his profile, the tilt of his jaw, reminded her of Wes. But that was impossible. Wes had left Shelter Creek when they were in high school. And he'd certainly never worn a cowboy hat.

As she watched, the man turned farther away from her to peer into the hardware store window and she took in his broad shoulders and his long legs in black jeans. He was wearing a worn denim jacket. There was something about this man… An old ache pulsed in her chest. Would Wes have become someone who dressed like a cowboy?

Emily pictured his crooked smile and the sparkle in his eye when he used to come riding with her at the stable where she boarded her horse, back in high school. But Wes had never reached out, never come back. Why would he be here now? Emily took a gulp of her coffee. Maybe she was having hallucinations from lack of sleep.

The man glanced toward her, as if he sensed her watching him. Instinctively Emily ducked down behind her truck. Squatting on the sidewalk behind the cab, she put a palm to her forehead. This was ridiculous. There was no reason to hide. This guy couldn't be Wes. And even if it was, what was she so afraid of? She wasn't the starry-eyed kid she'd been back then.

Her truck was parked in front of Hubert's Collectibles, and fortunately, Hubert, owner of Millicent, a teacup poodle who'd been to visit Emily for a tummy ache last week, didn't open his shop until eleven. Otherwise he might be wondering why the town's vet was cowering next to a parking meter.

She should stand up. She should get to work. She set her coffee down and crawled a few paces forward so she could peek around the front of the truck. The man had moved on. He was walking at a faster pace now, moving past Emily's friend Eva's art gallery. There was something about his walk, the swing of his arms, the way he kept his body so straight and his weight slightly back… If she didn't know better, she could swear it was Wes.

Emily picked up her cup and stood up slowly. She'd worked for years to forget Wes Marlow. Not that it had worked, obviously, since she was thinking of him now. But at least memories of their high school relationship had faded, and the hurt he'd caused had turned to tough scars long ago.

She should go. Just get in her truck and drive to her clinic. Instead, Emily started walking, keeping pace with the man, staying just behind him on the opposite side of the street. He was leaving the more touristy shops behind now, passing the auto parts store and the vacant lot with the dusty oak tree in the corner. The next building was the vast Tack and Feed Barn, located, as its name implied, inside an old barn. The man went inside. Emily waited for a few cars to pass before she dashed across Main Street and followed him in.

He wasn't near the entrance. Maybe he'd gone straight to the back of the shop. Emily set her cup on a shelf by the door and walked the first aisle, running her hand along the rack of fancy dog leashes. The comforting scent of leather, grain and dust brought her to her senses. What was she *doing*?

Heat rose in her cheeks. Good thing there was no one in the front of the shop to see her making a fool of herself, chasing after a cowboy. But since she was here, she might as well visit the saddle she'd had her eye on forever. Someday she'd buy it, or one like it, when she finally got a horse of her own again. Emily walked deeper into the barn until she came to the cool, dim tack section. She found her saddle and traced her fingertips gently over the floral design etched into the leather.

"Are you finally going to buy it?"

Emily jumped back, her heart in her throat. "Lloyd, you startled me!" Lloyd Layton, owner of the Tack and Feed Barn and brother to Minnie, who owned Wild Poppy Fashion, was leaning on one of the old posts that supported the barn.

He chuckled. "You look like you've been caught trying to steal it." For once Emily wished he'd turn down the volume of his warm, booming voice. She was supposed to be sneaking around, not attracting attention. "You know, Em, I won't have this one around forever. Someone was looking at it pretty seriously just last week."

Glancing regretfully at the delicate silver lacing at the edge of the seat, Emily sighed. "I don't need it. I don't have a horse."

"You will, once you slow down a little at that job of yours. Buy it now and you can display it in your living room until you're ready."

She had a little extra in her bank account, but she'd only recently finished paying off her vet school loans. "I don't know, Lloyd. It's such an impractical saddle. I won't need something this pretty."

"Suit yourself." Lloyd held up both his hands as if proclaiming his innocence. "I'm not trying to make a sale, here. I just don't want to see the look on your face when you walk in here one day and this saddle is gone." He smiled. "Though, you know, if you keep at this, you might just break the world record for time spent contemplating a purchase. So that's something."

Emily grinned. "That certainly is." She gave the saddle one last glance. "I'll think about it." She shot him a wink. "A little more. Meanwhile, I'd better get to work." She'd forgotten for a moment about the man she'd been following. *Good.* It was her lack of sleep that had her acting on such a strange whim. "Take care of my saddle."

Lloyd's laugh rang out behind her as she stepped back out into the pet section of the feedstore. And there he was, the man she'd followed, standing directly in front of her, examining a selection of dog bones. A small squeak escaped from deep in Emily's throat. This close she could see that under the brim of that black cowboy hat it *was* him. Wes Marlow. The boy who'd gone missing and broken all their hearts.

Wes looked up at the sound, and for a moment he didn't move a muscle. Then he took a step in her direction, peering down at her from a height he didn't have back in high school. "Emily?"

"Wes."

His eyes were still the green she remembered, but it was impossible to read the expression in them. He had a slight smile on his face, but he didn't look happy. Instead he looked wary.

Well, he should look wary. If she hadn't set her cup down she'd be tempted to dump her coffee right on top of that fancy hat of his.

But the changes to his face distracted her. He still had thick, black hair, long enough to hang in shaggy edges below the brim of his hat. But the dark stubble lining his jaw was unfamiliar, and his face had lost any boyish softness. It was more defined, more lined, more lived-in.

Emily swallowed, trying to hold down the panic that suddenly flooded her system. She'd followed him in here on a vague instinct. She hadn't considered what she'd do if the mystery man really was Wes. *Words. You need to think of words.* "Why are you here?"

He gestured toward the rack of dog treats. "Getting a few things for my dog."

That wasn't what she'd meant by her question. But maybe small talk would give her a chance to recover. Her ears rung with a buzzing sound and her hands had started to shake. "What kind of dog?"

He cleared his throat. "A husky."

"Oh." He had a husky. It was just about the only thing she knew about Wes Marlow right now and she used to feel like she knew him better than anyone else. But that was a long time ago. She straightened her shoulders and plastered what she hoped was a neutral expression on her face. "What brings you to Shelter Creek?"

He looked at her, right at her, with a steady gaze she remembered far too well. "I've wanted to come back here for a long time. I couldn't, until now."

"You *couldn't*. Because you were what… a secret agent on a mission? Prevented by some invisible force field from crossing the Sonoma County line?" Oops. So much for neutral. Maybe she hadn't buried her hurt feelings quite as deep as she'd thought.

His smile curled into something more genuine. "I didn't notice any force field on the way in."

"Oh. Good to know." Emily waited for Wes to elaborate more, to finally explain why he'd waited so many years to come back. He was silent, smiling at her, studying her, as if taking inventory of the changes in her.

Picking up the nearest dog bone, pink rubber with white spots, Emily fidgeted with the toy, trying to hide her shaking hands. She didn't want shaking hands. She didn't want any reaction to him whatsoever. So what if he was back now? He'd made his choice all those years ago, and over and over again with every year that went by without a word from him. She set the pink bone back on the rack, accidentally squeaking it in the process. She started at the unexpected noise, her face blazing as Wes chuckled softly.

"You all right there?"

Emily tried to muster the remains of her dignity. "I'm fine. But I have to go. Enjoy your visit."

"Stay."

"What?" For a moment she thought he was asking her to stay and talk to him, and the flutters in her stomach undermined all the years she'd spent trying to feel nothing.

"I'm hoping to stay here. In Shelter Creek."

Emily swallowed hard. Her lungs seemed to have lost the ability to process oxygen. "As in…live here?"

"It's what I've always wanted."

"Could have fooled me." She took a few steps back, trying to find a spot in the store with a little more air. "What exactly are you planning to do here?"

"Work, I hope."

"Work?" Images filled Emily's mind, of running into Wes while out grocery shopping, seeing him at Shelter Creek's many holiday events. Saying hello in passing, just like any other resident of her town. The pastry she'd eaten earlier swam in her stomach.

And her parents. She had to tell them. Her dad was recovering from a heart attack. Seeing Wes unexpectedly might trigger another one. "What kind of work?"

"I'm a veterinarian."

The dog treat rack between them seemed to move. Everything else went slightly out of focus. "Wow. Good for you." Emily had never fainted, but she might now. She had to get out of here.

"It's good to see you again, Emily."

"Yes, it is." What was she saying? "I mean, it's good to see you. Also." She flapped her hand in an awkward wave as she turned away, forcing herself to walk calmly out of the store. To keep her balance. To keep her breakfast where it belonged.

As soon as she was safely on the sidewalk, she put a hand on the outside wall of the feed-store to support herself. The rough texture of the wood under her palm grounded her. She pulled in a few deep breaths. *A veterinarian?* He had to be aware that she was a vet, too. They'd spent so much time helping her father at the clinic when they were young. She'd always planned to follow in her father's footsteps.

What was he going to do? Set up a practice here? Steal her clients? Was he serious? After sneaking away in the middle of the night without a word to anyone all those years ago, he was going to just move into her town? Except it had been his town, too, for a few years there.

Breathe. Focus. Those questions would have to wait. Right now she needed to make sure that her father didn't get a shock that might put him back in the hospital, or worse. She had to get to her parents' house and give them a heads-up that Wes Marlow was back in town.

WHAT HAD HE *EXPECTED*?

Wes picked a dog chew off the rack, examined the unappetizing rawhide, and put it back again. No dog toy could distract him from the disappointment curdling in his stomach. He'd known that coming back to Shelter Creek would be complicated. But he hadn't prepared for the horror splashed over Emily's features, or the way she'd tried to get away from him as fast as possible.

Somehow he'd been delusional enough to imagine that he'd arrive in Shelter Creek, get settled and then go to find Emily, dressed well and driving his nice truck. He'd show her how successful he was. He'd explain himself in an articulate speech, prepared and rehearsed. She'd forgive him, and welcome him home.

Ha. She'd caught him completely off guard and he'd made a mess of it. And there hadn't been any welcome in her wide, blue eyes.

But maybe Wes had set himself up for the disappointment he felt now. He'd held this town up as such a perfect place for so many years. Treasured it in his mind like a talisman to reach for whenever it felt like he couldn't keep going. Every cramped room he and his brother, Jamie, had shared, every low-paying job he'd had, every run-down neighborhood they'd inhabited had been bearable because it had been a step toward the day he could come back here and belong, not as some nice family's charity case, but because he was a hardworking professional who could bring something to the community.

Wes ambled toward the cash register, still lost in thought. So his first meeting with Emily had been awkward. That didn't mean that coming here was a mistake. Yesterday, after four days on the road from Houston, the sight of the sun slanting through the redwood trees—the hazy rays of light dappled with summer dust—sure hadn't felt like a mistake.

Wes had stopped the car and he and Rex had run out into the forest, bounding on the thick layer of fallen needles that carpeted the ground. While the dog wandered, Wes had looked up at the redwood branches reaching impossibly high into the blue sky. He'd breathed in the earthy scent and felt like he was finally home.

But being here wasn't going to be as simple as that moment in the forest. He'd hurt Emily, the girl he'd held so close in his heart for so long. He'd hurt her parents, who'd been so kind to him. They might not forgive him. They might not want him here. Yesterday was the last blissful moment of a fantasy he'd clung to for years. Now he had to deal with reality. And Emily's reaction to him just now was a warning that reality might not include the happily-ever-after that he'd always imagined.

CHAPTER TWO

EMILY PULLED UP in front of her parents' house and glanced at her watch. She'd driven here so fast she had about ten minutes to spare before she started work. Would her parents be up yet? Squinting through the passenger-side window, she could make out her mother at the kitchen sink. Probably just putting the coffee on. Good. Her mom might need the comfort of a warm drink when she heard Emily's news.

Jogging up the front walk, Emily knocked softly at the door, but her parents' standard poodle, Mavis, wasn't going to let her arrival remain a quiet affair. Big woofs resonated through the solid oak, along with her mother's hurried shushing.

"Mavis, it's me," Emily tried to reassure the dog. "Be quiet!"

The door opened and Mavis came bounding out like a fancy floor mop.

"Goodness, Mavis, settle down." Meg Fielding wrapped the lavender fleece bathrobe that Emily had given her last Mother's Day more tightly around her. "Emily, we don't usually see you at this hour. Would you like some coffee?"

Emily had downed the rest of hers on the drive over, but this was a day when the answer to "more coffee" was always going to be yes. She nodded and followed her mother inside, calling Mavis to follow. In the kitchen, Meg filled two mugs with coffee. The mugs had dogs on them, of various breeds. Meg handed Emily the Chihuahua, which seemed fitting because, faced with her mother's inquiring gaze, she felt about as small as a Chihuahua. Not up to delivering news that would resurrect a painful part of her family's past.

Her mom offered Emily milk for her coffee and they sat down at the kitchen table. "So," her mom said, getting right to the point. "What brings you here before work?"

"Is Dad awake?"

"I am now, thanks to Mavis and all her ruckus." Her father walked through the door, dressed in his usual jeans and a T-shirt. "She's better than a burglar alarm."

"I don't know about that." Emily smiled at him as he leaned down to kiss her cheek. "I still managed to steal some coffee." _

He peered at her more carefully. "No offense, but you look like you could use it. Late night?"

"Calving season." That was all Emily had to say. Her dad had run the Shelter Creek Veterinary Clinic until he retired and left the practice in Emily's hands.

"Oh, I remember those nights," her mom said. "I don't miss the phone ringing at all hours."

"Aw, come on, Meg." Her dad caught her mom by the hand. "It was an adventure, right? Especially when we were first married, and I'd drag you along to assist."

"Back before I knew better." Meg pulled her hand away, but there was love in the teasing smile she gave her husband.

Her parents had always been in love, but ever since her dad's heart surgery, it seemed like he and her mom had a new appreciation for each other. Emily understood. She had a new appreciation for them, and terrifying firsthand knowledge of how easily life could change in an instant. Which was why she was here today. She couldn't let Wes Marlow's sudden arrival in Shelter Creek come as a dangerous shock.

Her father sat down with his coffee. He had the Saint Bernard mug this morning and her mom had a collie. Perfect. Tom Fielding was so big and hearty, rescuing every animal that crossed his path. Meg was so pretty and refined.

Emily stared at her Chihuahua mug, trying to think of how to say what she had to say. Words weren't her strong point. Today, facing Wes, she'd only been able to summon a few. For her entire adult life she'd imagined what she'd say if their paths ever crossed again. Phrases like *How could you?* and *Why?* Instead she'd just asked him about his dog.

Emily glanced at the clock on the microwave. She'd better hurry or she'd be late for her first appointment. She took one last fortifying sip of coffee. "I came by to tell you about something that happened this morning that really surprised me."

"Was it a calving issue? Would you like me to give you a second opinion on something?" Her father's eagerness betrayed how much he missed his practice.

"Tom, you are not going out on any calls right now." Emily's mom put her hand over his. "You promised you'd take it easy, and focus on exercise and eating well. I want you to be healthy so we can still go on our anniversary vacation."

Her father sighed, but smiled at his wife. "You take good care of me, Meg." Then he turned back to Emily. "So was it calving?"

"It was people, actually. Or, one person, really." Emily gave up on trying to find the right words. "I was downtown getting coffee, and I ran into Weston Marlow."

Her parents both set their mugs on the table in the same instant. "Wes?" Her mom looked at Emily with wide eyes. "Visiting Shelter Creek? After all these years?"

"Not just visiting, according to him. He wants to stay here."

Her father sat back in his chair, frowning. "I never expected we'd see him again."

"I didn't want you to just run into him somewhere," Emily bumbled on. "I didn't want you to have a shock, like I did."

"You did the right thing, coming here," her mother assured her, casting a worried glance at her husband.

"I'm not made of glass, you two." Tom patted his wife's hand reassuringly. "I'm not going to break." He looked at Emily. "Did you talk to him?"

Emily told them the whole story, emphasizing the time she'd spent crawling behind her truck, spying on him, to get them both laughing. After the chuckles had ceased, her father sipped his coffee, looking thoughtful. "He became a veterinarian." He smiled at his wife. "Meg, maybe we had a little influence on the kid, after all."

"Of course you guys did!" Irritation welled up on her parents' behalf. "You opened up your home to him. You treated him like your own son. You did so much for him." Emily's emotions put a quaver in her voice. She gulped her coffee and stood up. "I have to get to work. But I'm glad you two know he's here, so you're ready if you see him around."

"I'll walk you out," her mother said.

Outside the front door, Meg pulled Emily in for a hug. "Are you okay, dear?"

Flustered, Emily pulled back. "Of course. I was just worried about Dad, you know? I didn't want him to be startled and end up back in the hospital." She glanced at her mother, suddenly suspicious. "Why are you asking?"

"Because Wes broke your heart when he left."

Emily opened her mouth to protest, but her mother held up her hands. "I'm not blind, you know. I saw how sad you were. You two were very close…you were going to attend prom together, remember? You and I had so much fun picking out a dress in Santa Rosa."

Remember? She'd never forget. She'd skipped prom, telling her parents she had a headache. Really she'd spent the night crying and staring out the window and wondering where Wes had gone. She'd tried so hard to hide her feelings, because her parents were grieving, too. It scared her that they'd been hurt by Wes's actions. She'd felt her parents were so invincible, until she saw how shaken they were when Wes ran away.

Plus, she'd never told them that she and Wes were dating, or that the ring she'd started wearing on her finger senior year was the promise ring he'd given her. She'd never known how to tell her parents that she was madly in love with the boy they'd taken from the foster care system and nurtured as their own son.

"I'm fine, Mom. Just surprised to see him this morning. I figured he was gone forever. Anyway, he's not my problem anymore. Not *our* problem. So don't you and Dad go getting involved with him again, okay?"

"You have a good day at work." Her mom held out her arms and Emily stepped in for another hug, noting that her mother had not answered her question. She gave her mom a kiss on the cheek. "Is having Wes in town going to upset you guys? If it does, I'll go find him right now and tell him to leave."

Her mom stepped back, but kept Emily's hands in her own. "Oh, honey, Wes was a troubled boy. We did the very best we could for him. It hurt that it wasn't enough, and of course we worried about his safety for many years. But your father and I have taken comfort in the fact that we gave him a safe, healthy home for as long as he wanted one." She smiled gently. "And maybe that really did mean something. Why else would he want to come back to Shelter Creek?"

Emily gaped at her mother. She had spent all the years since Wes left assuming he'd disliked it here.

He'd certainly started out disliking Shelter Creek. The cool city kid stuck in a quiet rural town. But he'd become happy here as time went on. Or at least, she thought he had. After he left, she'd wondered if he'd tolerated them all until he couldn't stand it any longer. It would explain why he left in the middle of the night without a word to anyone.

It was all too complicated for this early in the morning. She needed work, and animals, and the straightforward problems they presented in her clinic. She knew how to think about animals. She knew how to solve their issues and heal their pain.

"I'll talk to you soon." Emily squeezed her mom's hands one more time and headed to her truck. She had about three minutes to get to the clinic, which was basically impossible. She'd have to call and tell Lily, her receptionist, that she was running behind.

She slid into the driver's seat, made the call and then drove down the block, away from her parents' quiet, shaded street. They lived right on the edge of town, with green hills on one side of the road and people's front yards on the other. Everything looked just like it always did this time of year—lush, green and bursting with life. It was all completely normal and she should feel normal, too. Running into Wes today wouldn't change anything. She'd had fifteen years to accept that they meant nothing to each other. That wouldn't change, just because he was back in Shelter Creek.

CHAPTER THREE

NOT MUCH HAD changed on Manzanita Lane
since Wes had last walked the cracked and
pot-holed pavement. Houses were still painted
in pretty colors and had front yards full of
flowers. The road still gave way to farmland
and pasture, which in turn gave way to grassy
meadows and patches of oak and bay trees
that huddled close to the creek as it wound
its way west toward the Pacific Ocean. This
little street at the edge of town was home to
the four happiest years of his life. Wes had
thought about it so many times, wished he
could come back here so often, that the sound
of his boots on the pavement seemed almost
unreal.

Even if he hadn't run into Emily this morning, he'd planned to pay her parents a visit.
It was a reckoning long overdue. But just because he'd been resolved to speak to them
when he left the inn fifteen minutes ago,

didn't mean he could find the courage now. He and Rex had already circled the block three times.

Rex didn't mind. The gray-and-white husky was so excited to be out in the country he had barely lifted his nose from the ground. His tail wagged nonstop at delights Wes's human senses couldn't perceive.

Rex was a lot more comfortable transitioning from the city to Shelter Creek than Wes had been the first time he came to this town. Wes had shown up here with a chip on both shoulders, an angry young teenager who'd been kicked out of his grandparents' home in Los Angeles and landed in the foster care system. Those first few weeks, he might as well have been set down on another planet. Here you could lie in bed at night and listen to coyotes and owls. Here you could start walking out into the hills and likely not meet another person for days. Here he felt about as big as a dime and about as hard, too, unable to bend or break or let anyone in.

But Tom and Meg Fielding had been too kind to resist. From Meg's homemade meals and compassionate care, to Tom's fun, blustering love of animals and nature, everything about them had slowly brought Wes out of his shell. After a few months, he'd fallen in love with his life here. After a year or so, he'd fallen in love with their daughter. A love that felt like a betrayal to Tom and Meg's generosity, so he'd insisted to Emily that they keep their feelings hidden.

What would he say to them now? There'd been so much else he'd kept hidden. His worries and fears, all battened down under his tough-kid exterior. And then he'd left without a word, and stayed away so very long.

Guilt had him planning to pass by their white picket gate one more time. But as he drew closer, he saw Tom Fielding standing there waiting for him, and knew it was too late to run away again.

"That's a nice dog you've got there." Tom stepped through the gate and stopped in front of Rex, holding out his knuckles for the husky to snuffle. Rex's tail became a blur of wagging fluff. Animals had always loved Tom. The old veterinarian glanced up at Wes, his blue eyes still piercing under his gray brows. "Were you going to come in and say hello? Or just walk on by again."

Tom's demeanor seemed friendly, but his

words landed hard. Wes knew he'd been caught with his cowardice on full display. "I was working up the nerve. It's been a long time."

"Emily stopped by this morning to let us know you were here in town. Meg and I were hoping to see you. Why don't you come on inside and we can catch up?"

That was encouraging. When Wes had imagined seeing them after all these years, he'd envisioned a scolding full of harsh words that he well deserved. "I've got Rex with me."

Tom shrugged. "We've got a standard poodle with a big attitude. Mavis can hold her own with this guy." He tilted his chin toward the front door. "You like coffee? We've got a fresh pot."

"Sounds good. Thanks." Wes followed Tom up a stone path that felt more like thin ice. Tom had always seemed like a giant to him, a larger-than-life figure. Now they were equal height, and Tom's age showed in his silver hair and the slight stoop of his shoulders under his blue polo shirt. They'd been cordial so far, but there was a chasm of time and hurt between them. It was up to Wes to find a way to bridge it.

"Meg?" Tom pushed open the front door. "We have a visitor!" A dog started barking, somewhere in the back of the house.

At the first sight of Meg in the doorway, Wes's throat closed and he swallowed hard. Her warm smile was just as he remembered— kind. The lines around her eyes mapped all the joy and worry she'd felt over the years. Her hair was white now and hung past her shoulders, and she had the top part of it pulled back neatly. She wore dark blue pants and a pretty, blue flowered shirt. Her hands came to her hips as she stepped onto the front patio. "Weston Marlow, just when did you become a cowboy? And where in the world have you been all this time?"

There was a quaver in her voice, and knowing he'd put it there brought up the shame that had kept Wes away from Shelter Creek all these years. "I've been a lot of different places," he managed. "I always wanted to come back here."

"And who is this?" She smiled down at Rex, who'd sat next to Wes and was leaning on his leg.

"Rex. I can leave him outside, if you'd prefer."

"Let's see what our dog has to say about

it. Excuse me." She disappeared for a moment, then a huge gray standard poodle came bounding out the front door, barking excitedly. "This is Mavis," Meg said.

Rex, good boy that he was, stayed seated while the poodle quit barking, sniffed at him and then danced her welcome.

"Enough, Mavis. Sit." The poodle sat immediately at Tom's command. "I think they'll be fine together. Let's go inside and have that coffee."

Wes took off his hat and Meg ushered him and Rex into the living room. The scent of lemon floor wax and firewood stacked on the stone hearth took Wes back in time. The furniture was new, the old worn denim couches he remembered replaced by more formal pieces. Still, when Wes sank into the armchair Meg indicated, it felt like home. Rex lay down on the colorful rug at his feet and put his head on his paws. Mavis the poodle flopped onto a dog bed near the fireplace, keeping a watchful eye on Rex.

Meg and Tom left for the kitchen to get the coffee, though more likely to confer about what in the world to do with him. Wes looked around the room. The clock on the mantel was the same, as were the figurines in the china cabinet. The room was nicely decorated but cozy—a place where you could put your feet up on the leather ottoman and get lost in a good book.

The moment he'd first entered this house, his third stop in the foster care system, he'd sensed that this place was different. Not a group home, or the kind of foster home that felt like a boarding house, where kids came and went and all the stuff the foster parents gave you had been used before.

Meg and Tom's home had been simply that. A home. Their family was just a regular family that happened to have space for one more. His first night here, Meg had asked him to help put the food on the table and he'd inhaled the rich aroma of her good home cooking and wanted to cry with relief. As if in response to the memory, tears stung now and he blinked them away.

Tears were self-pity and that never helped. He had to focus on what he'd come here to do—give Meg and Tom an apology. He owed Emily that, too, though from the look on her face at the feedstore earlier, he wasn't sure she'd ever give him a chance.

Even if she did, could he do it? Or would he stand there, stumbling over his words like he had this morning? She'd been so pretty when they were young, but she was absolutely beautiful now. Fierce in her movements, like she was going to get a lot accomplished and you'd better get out of her way. Her hair had thickened and darkened and tumbled in honey waves down her back. Her face was fresh and scrubbed of makeup, of artifice. Fine lines recorded a history he wished he could learn.

Meg came in with her coffee and an extra mug for him. "Do you still take milk, no sugar?"

His emotions clogged up his throat this time. She'd remembered such a small detail about him. He nodded and took the coffee. It was in a mug with a dog on it, a basset hound who looked kind of sheepish. Just about the way he felt right now, actually.

Tom and Meg sat side by side on the couch, their coffee mugs in hand. "Thank you for having me in to visit," he told them.

"How does it feel, coming back to Shelter Creek?" Of course Meg would start by asking how he felt. Her heart was as generous as he remembered. Wes cleared his throat.

"Strange. Familiar, but not really. The whole town looks sort of fancy now."

"We get a lot of tourists nowadays," Tom said. "Folks have prettied the place up for them."

There was a lull and Wes knew it was up to him, the uninvited guest, to keep the chat going. But did he make small talk? Or jump right into his long list of apologies? He opened his mouth. Closed it again. Took the easy route. "So, Tom, do you still have your clinic?"

Tom shook his head. "I retired a few years ago. Emily took over the business."

Uh-oh. If he'd had a plan when he'd started driving here, which he really hadn't, it was that Tom would find a way to forgive him and invite him to work in his practice. But with Emily at the helm…it wasn't clear if she ever wanted to speak to him again. Let alone hire him.

One thing at a time. He had to get to the real reason he was here. "I owe you both an apology," he blurted out. "For leaving in the middle of the night, after four years of your kindness."

Meg looked at him and he thought those

might be tears glimmering in her eyes. Great. Show up here unannounced and make her cry. He was off to a good start. She didn't say anything, though. Just waited for him to go on.

"I told you, I think, about my little brother, Jamie, and how he went to live with my uncle in Pittsburgh."

"We wanted him to come live with us," Tom said. "But the social worker told us if there were family members who would take him, he had to stay there."

"That's the law," Wes couldn't hide the bitterness in his voice. "But in this case, the law failed. I got a letter from Jamie, when I was still living here. He said our uncle and aunt were hurting him, keeping him out of school and treating him like some kind of servant. He begged me to help him get free."

Meg gasped and set her coffee down on an end table. "Wes, you should have told us."

"Looking back, maybe I should have. But I was pretty sure you'd want to get the social workers to look into it. Jamie was afraid if you did that, Social Services would give my uncle and aunt a warning. Try to educate them about good parenting and all. He knew they'd just hurt him worse if they found out he'd complained."

Wes leaned over to pet Rex's head, taking comfort in the dog's soft ears and thick fur. It was too hard to look at Meg or Tom and see the pain in their eyes. "I didn't want to go. I wanted to stay here and live with you. But I couldn't leave Jamie there. So I packed my stuff and I left. Hitchhiked into Santa Rosa and caught a bus across the country."

Had the clock in here always ticked this loud? Meg and Tom were holding hands now, their fingers curled together in solidarity. They'd stood together through whatever hurt he'd caused that night, and they'd stand together now.

Idly he wondered if he'd ever have a relationship like that.

Tom broke the thickening silence. "What happened next?"

Wes swallowed hard and went on, "When my bus arrived in Pittsburgh, I waited until dark. Then I walked across town to my uncle's house. By the time I got there it was probably about two in the morning. I climbed up to Jamie's window and helped him pack some things and we ran away."

"Where did you go?" Concern etched a furrow between Meg's brows.

"We ended up in Houston. I didn't really have a plan, but when Jamie and I got to the bus station that night, the Houston bus was about to leave. They had room for two more. I knew Houston was a big city where I might be able to get work, and we had no connection to it. Who would think to look for us there?"

Tom shook his head slowly, like he couldn't quite take it all in. "Where did you live?"

"We rented a garage apartment from a family that didn't have much more money than we did. They were new immigrants—they didn't speak a lot of English—so they didn't ask many questions about where our parents were."

"But what about school?" Meg was a former teacher. Of course she'd think of that.

"When school started in the fall, I'd turned eighteen. Legally an adult, right? Jamie was going into fifth grade. I told the lady in the office that my parents had passed away and I was Jamie's guardian. When they asked for school records, I told them he'd always been homeschooled. It was a big, crowded campus in a rough neighborhood. They didn't worry too much about a quiet kid like Jamie who got all his homework done."

"And what about you?" Meg's kind gaze met his. "Emily told us you became a veterinarian."

Wes glanced at Tom, strangely shy to admit the influence his former foster father had on him. But Tom was looking down at his coffee cup, seemingly lost in thought. "I did. At first I just worked, trying to get us on our feet. Mainly at restaurants, busing tables, washing dishes. But eventually I took a test and got my GED."

"Good for you," Meg said.

"Then I went to a community college and transferred to University of Houston. It took me five years, because I couldn't attend school full-time, but eventually I got my degree. And then, when Jamie started college at Texas A&M, I got into vet school there. They've got a great program." Pride swelled his chest. "I've been practicing for over three years now."

Tom finally looked up. "That's quite a journey. I'm proud of you, Wes."

"Thank you." Wes took a deep breath, ready to say the words he'd imagined saying so many times. "You set an example of who I wanted to become."

Tom leaned back on the couch and folded his arms across his chest. "I'm honored," he said quietly. And then he added, "It feels good to know that we might have made a difference for you."

Of all the things Wes had wondered about the harm he'd caused Tom and Meg, it never occurred to him that they'd doubt their own influence or impact. "You have no idea. You two, and Emily, were the only real family I'd known. Of course you made a difference."

"It was hard to know, when we never heard from you." Emotion heightened Meg's voice. "We didn't know if you were alive or dead. We heard from Social Services that your brother had gone missing, too. We could only hope that you were together, and that you were okay. That's all we knew. That's all we've ever known." She stood abruptly. "Excuse me." She walked out of the room.

Wes could barely meet Tom's gaze. "I'm so sorry," he said. "Maybe I shouldn't have come back here."

"Or maybe you should have come back a

whole lot sooner. Or at least sent a postcard," Tom said dryly.

His hope for some kind of prodigal-son moment was foolish. Wes saw that now. A pipe dream he'd held on to to get him through all those hard years. "I'll go. I don't know how long I'll be in town for, but I'll make sure to let you know before I leave."

"I thought Emily mentioned that you wanted to stay in Shelter Creek."

"I did." Wes looked down at Rex, who was sprawled on the rug, completely oblivious to the tension around him. "I think that was a mistake. Y'all don't need me around here, digging up old trouble."

"Maybe," Tom said. He leaned forward, put his elbows to his knees and regarded Wes steadily. "Or maybe you're just running away again."

The words hung between them, each one sharp and clear as ice.

"I don't want to cause more harm," Wes tried to explain.

"You said you've always seen Shelter Creek as your only real home. If that's true, then you should stick around for a while and see if that's really the case."

"But what about you? And Meg? And Emily?"

"We all still care, Wes." Meg had come back into the room and was leaning on the door frame between the living room and the hallway. "The love we felt for you didn't end just because you left. But there's hurt there, too, that needs healing. Just like with animals, healing takes time and effort and it isn't always easy. But if you're willing to give it a try, it can happen."

Wes shook his head, not in denial, but at the enormity of what she was saying. "I don't know how to go forward."

"If you want work, go talk to Emily," Tom said. "She's looking for help with the practice. There are way too many animals in this community for one vet, though she tries to be there for everyone who needs her."

Wes tried to suppress his rueful smile. "I'm the last person she wants knocking at her door looking for a job."

"Are you a good veterinarian? Can you provide references?"

"Yes, sir."

"Are you experienced with large and small animals?"

"I am."

Tom drummed his fingers on his knee. "It's Emily's practice now. It's up to her what she wants to do. But I know she's been advertising for a second veterinarian, and you might be what she needs."

"I'm not what she wants."

"Maybe, maybe not." Meg shrugged. "Why don't you ask if she'll take you on a trial basis? That way she can see if she wants to work with you. And you can see if you really want to stay here in Shelter Creek."

Their generosity in even suggesting this plan was so much more than he deserved. "Thank you," he told Meg. "I'll see what she says."

"I just want to know one thing," Meg said. "Why didn't you ever contact us? All these years…" Her voice trailed off and she went to sit beside her husband again.

This was the part Wes most dreaded telling. How to explain what had no clear explanation? He took a sip of coffee and tried to gather his thoughts. "For the first few years, I was scared to. No matter how much I missed you, I worried that y'all were so law-abiding you might feel compelled to tell Social Services where I was. I didn't trust a system that might put Jamie back in an abusive home."

Meg glanced at Tom, then back at Wes. "That poor little boy."

"He was terrified of my aunt and uncle," Wes told her. "He had nightmares about them for years after I got him away."

"Where is Jamie now?" Tom asked.

"London." Wes smiled with the upwelling of pride that information always inspired. "He attended business school after college and he's working for a big bank right in the heart of London now." He shook his head. "I still can't believe it. My baby brother is a big fancy banker now."

"You must be so proud." Meg's smile felt like a warm blanket draped over Wes's shoulders.

"Proud and relieved." He shrugged. "Seeing him off on that flight to England was the first time I felt like I was free to pursue what I wanted. And what I wanted was to come back here." He remembered their previous questions. "I know I should have reached out once Jamie was eighteen. Once there was no chance anyone could take him away from me.

I thought about it so many times. But I was ashamed of how I left you all."

"You're here now, though," Tom said. "So shame couldn't have been the only reason."

Wes nodded. "The rest is a little harder to explain."

"Try," Meg said gently.

Wes clung to her kindness and stepped out on shaky ground. "When I came here to live with you, I had a thick skin. A shell that kept me somewhat safe, you know? And you all cracked that open and taught me how to care and how to feel. When I left here, I had to re-build that shell again.

"It got me through a lot of tough times. I worked many jobs, didn't sleep much, pushed myself to the limit to make things happen for Jamie and me. I think I was scared that if I got in touch with you, that shell I'd rebuilt might crack, and I'd lose all my nerve."

Meg nodded, her eyes soft and bright with unshed tears. Tom was studying his coffee again like it might have some answers in there. Wes stumbled on, "I didn't have room for a lot of feelings. I just needed to keep going until I felt like I'd done right by my brother. Until I was sure that we were both going to be okay."

"That's a long time to go without feeling things. Without feeling loved." Meg looked away, her eyes blinking rapidly.

Wes swallowed hard. She'd zeroed in on what he hadn't seen for himself. Maybe that was why he'd been so drawn to this place. It was the last place he'd felt loved and cared for. He reached for Rex, burying his fingers in the thick fur around his neck.

"I may not understand all of it completely," Tom said. "I may not like it, either. But I do understand what it's like to be in survival mode. I worked my way through vet school. Those years are a blur. And I wasn't trying to raise a sibling while I was at it."

Wes had been proving himself for so long. To be taken at face value, to be given grace like this… He swallowed again, and stood. He hadn't come here to cry like a baby in their living room. "I appreciate you hearing me out. I don't want to take up your whole morning."

"Come and see us again," Meg said. "And if you decide to leave town, you'd better say goodbye this time."

"Of course."

Tom reached out and Wes shook his hand. "Sounds like you did well for yourself and your brother."

"Thank you." This man had been the only father he'd known, and Wes had to force himself to let go of his hand. He'd lost the right to cling to him when he climbed out his window that night so long ago.

"Go see Emily. The worst that can happen is she says no," Tom said.

Wes grimaced at the thought. "I don't suppose you can put in a good word for me?"

He was half joking and Tom knew it. His answering smile had a wry twist, but still lit something warm inside Wes's chest. "You're on your own there."

"As it should be." Wes turned to Meg. "Thank you for the coffee, for listening to me today and for everything you did for me when I was young."

"Do not make me cry again, Wes Marlow." She wagged a finger at him, tears shining on her lashes. "Now go. Take that dog of yours for a hike. Get to know the area again. But come back for coffee sometime."

"I don't want to impose," Wes said. "I walked

away. You all have no obligation to me, what-soever."

"You were never an obligation," Meg said quietly. "You were a joy. You were what we wanted. You were family."

The lump in his throat had grown into a boulder. Wes nodded, and went to the front door, Rex following close at his heels.

When Wes stepped outside and shut the door, the house behind him was silent. Rex trotted up the garden path toward the road, looking back to make sure Wes followed. Clapping his hat on his head, Wes wondered if Tom and Meg felt a little like he did. That him coming back here had mixed the past in with the present, and it wasn't clear yet whether that was actually a good idea.

CHAPTER FOUR

HER DESK WAS a mess. Emily flopped back in her chair, sending it rolling away from the papers stacked six inches high. Files to review, payments to authorize, decisions to make.

She scrubbed her palms across her forehead in a useless attempt to get her brain to focus. Nope. Wasn't going to work. Between her lack of sleep and running into Wes this morning, she'd been as scattered as these papers on her desk all day.

The phone call with her mother just now hadn't helped. Apparently Wes had visited them today. He'd explained to her parents that he'd run away to save his little brother. Then he'd raised him on his own. All the years since Wes left, Emily had sustained herself with anger and indignation. But how could she stay angry when he'd been off doing something so heroic?

But she *was* angry. Maybe that made her

a bad person, but he could have sent a post-card. Even just a few words. *I had to help someone. I'm sorry.* Anything would have been better than all that silence. All those years of wondering...of worrying...of simply not knowing.

This was ridiculous. Why was she letting someone she hadn't seen or heard from since high school steal any more of her time and energy? There was so much work to get done. She glanced at the empty coffee mug on her desk. Nope, that was a bad idea. It was six in the evening, and coffee now would steal the sleep she so desperately needed tonight.

The thought of sleep inspired a jaw-aching yawn. Maybe she'd just go home and crawl into bed. She could come in early tomorrow and deal with all this work, as long as there were no other late-night emergencies on the horizon.

As if on cue, there was a knock on the clinic door. Lily, the receptionist, and both the technicians had already left for the day, so Emily pushed herself up from her chair and shuffled across the waiting room to answer. In a small town like Shelter Creek, people didn't always make an appointment, especially if their animal needed emergency care.

Emily twisted the bolt on the door and pulled it open.

Wes was standing on the doorstep, cowboy hat in hand. Emily took a step back as some traitorous part of her heart lit up at the sight of him. She straightened her shoulders. Whatever her heart was up to, that was just muscle memory, nothing more. "Wes, what are you doing here?"

"I saw your parents today. Did they tell you anything about our conversation?"

She hadn't expected to have to talk about this with him so soon. Emily took a deep breath, welcoming the cool evening air flooding in from the open door. "They told me why you left. About your little brother. That's terrible, what happened to him."

"It was bad." Wes gave her a tentative smile. "He's doing well now, though. He just graduated from business school."

"That's nice." It was a lot to take in. Wes had left her to basically become a parent. "It's impressive that you raised him yourself."

He shrugged. "We all do what we have to do."

"Most teenagers don't have to do what you did."

He grinned then, that irreverent, mischievous grin she remembered from when they were young. "That's probably a good thing."

Emily couldn't answer. That smile, that self-deprecating humor, it was what she'd first fallen in love with. It paralyzed her now.

"I wasn't always the best guardian to him," Wes went on. "I never had any idea what I was doing."

"You must have done something right." She was managing to make small talk, but a lot of her mind was busy trying to process this. Her long-lost love standing on her doorstep, dressed like a cowboy from his hat to his boots.

"Your parents mentioned that you're looking for another vet."

That pulled her out of her thoughts. "You want to work *here*?"

"We always said we'd grow up and work together someday."

"We said that a long time ago. A whole lot has changed since then." She studied him, trying to understand why he was suddenly interested in their ancient dreams. "You really are serious about wanting to live in Shelter Creek?"

He nodded, his earnest gaze searching her face. What was he looking for? What could he possibly hope to find? "I've always missed this town, Emily. I've wanted to come back for a long time."

Old hurt rose up through the layers of her skin. "But you didn't."

He looked down at his hat for a moment. "I know I walked away. I never reached out. You have a right to be upset."

"Upset?" She was tempted to slam the door right in his face. "Wes, you left in the middle of the night after living with us for more than four years. You never said goodbye. You never wrote or called to tell us you were okay."

"I'm sorry, Emily. I was wrong to leave you like that. I should have at least sent you a note. I've always regretted that I didn't."

She'd wanted those words for so long but now she had no idea how to respond. He regretted not writing. But did he regret leaving *her*? Had he missed her?

Wes held his hands out, palms up, as if

pleading. "I was a kid, Emily. I was doing the best I could."

"I'm sure you were. But what about the decade and change where you weren't a kid? We've had internet and email and social media for a long time now. You could have reached out. You knew where to find us."

Wes's gaze didn't waver from her face. "I had a lot of reasons. None of them sound too good now. I was ashamed of how I left. I didn't want to feel the things I might feel, if we were in touch."

What things? her pathetic heart wanted to ask. She wanted to know if he'd hurt the way she had. He was here now. Maybe he'd held on to some of the feelings they'd had? Or maybe, as her mom had suggested on the phone, he was hoping to find family. Community. Some roots after so many rootless and difficult years.

She studied him. The familiar thick, wavy black hair. The green eyes. Irish roots, that was what her dad had always said about Wes Marlow. He'd been a mystery to her when he'd shown up as her parents' foster kid her freshman year of high school. He was even more mysterious now, showing up here out of the blue.

She glanced down at his neat, dark jeans and cowboy boots. "You look so Western."

He grinned. "Life in Texas can rub off on a guy. Plus, I spent a lot of time working on ranches over the years."

Wes was a real cowboy? He'd been such a city kid when he first moved here. "Did you get your veterinary degree in Texas?"

"At Texas A&M. How about you?"

"UC Davis."

He peered past her into the clinic. "You've fixed the place up."

"After Dad retired, I figured it could use a face-lift." Reluctantly, Emily stepped back and waved him in.

Once inside, he turned in a slow circle, taking in the pale lavender walls, the neutral upholstery, the gray tiled floor. Suddenly he grinned and she remembered with a pang how they'd laughed together, way back when. "You made it kind of girlie."

Her hands went to her hips, instantly defensive. "I'm a girl vet. Why not?"

"It's nice. I was just wondering what all the

old-timers in Shelter Creek thought the first time they walked in and saw the pink walls."

"They're lavender, and they didn't say anything." They had, actually, but she wouldn't admit it to Wes. A lot of the ranchers in the area hadn't wanted to work with Doc Fielding's "little girl" when Emily had first taken over her father's practice. But they hadn't had too much choice since she was the only vet in town. The lavender walls had been an act of defiance, when she'd realized that some folks were going to judge her, and find her lacking, just for being a woman. It wouldn't really matter how she acted, or what color she painted her waiting room, they'd still think she wasn't up to the job.

Wes peered into the office that had been her father's. "Doing a little paperwork?"

The sarcastic note in his voice raised her defenses. "Look, I don't know what you hoped to find, coming back here after so much time…"

The phone rang then, and they both waited, letting the call go to voice mail. A teary voice came on. "Emily, are you there? Please pick up."

This was why Emily still used an old, manual voice mail machine. She reached over the reception desk for the phone. "Hello, this is Emily."

It was Haley Erwin, who ran the boarding stable southeast of Shelter Creek. "Two Socks got into some barbed wire. It's looking pretty bad. Can you come over?"

Two Socks was one of Haley's own horses. A big gelding, over sixteen hands, with an unpredictable personality. "Okay, Haley, keep him calm. Can you get him into a clean environment?"

"I have him in the wash area by the barn."

"Perfect. Try to disinfect the cement around him as much as possible. I'll be there in twenty minutes."

Now she wished she'd made that pot of coffee she'd been dreaming about before Wes showed up. Emily turned to him. "I've got to go. A horse and barbed wire, never a good combination."

"Let me come with you. I can help out."

"No." The word came out strangely loud and Emily's face heated. Her parents had sent him here. She should be considering him for the job. But how could she work with Wes?

If he noticed her rudeness he didn't flinch.

Instead the expression on his face was calm, his slight smile kind. "Are you sure? I'm an experienced vet. After I got my degree, I worked in a large animal practice."

"Really?"

"When I lived here I used to love going out to the ranches with your dad. It made me want to work with large animals. To try to solve problems out in the field, like he did."

The angry girl inside wanted to throw it back in his face. To ask why, if her father had been so important to him, Wes had left without a word and hurt him so badly. But he'd explained. Her parents had accepted his story. Plus, now wasn't the time. A horse was in pain.

His offer *was* tempting. Two Socks had given her so much trouble on past visits. And from the sound of Haley's voice, she wasn't going to be very calm or helpful. Emily could call a friend for help. Caleb Dunne was great with horses; maybe he'd have time to come with her. But Wes was right here. The fact that she didn't want to spend time with him paled in comparison with a horse who needed help now. "I'm not paying you. And this is not some kind of audition for the job. This is just because you happen to be here, and this horse can be difficult."

"I've got it. Do you have what you need for sutures?"

"Of course. My truck is fully stocked." Emily went to the closet in her office to grab the thick down coat she kept there for surprise evening calls. "Let's get going."

Wes followed her out the clinic door. At her truck, he went toward the driver's side, then clapped a hand to his forehead. "Sorry, automatic reaction."

Emily shook her head in disbelief. Such a *guy* thing to do, assuming that he was in charge when he'd only shown up here a few moments ago. "This is my case," she reminded him as she unlocked the truck. "You're coming along to assist."

"I get it." He slid into the passenger's seat and buckled up.

Emily took a shaky breath. Just sitting next to Wes opened the floodgates to a wave of memories. The way he used to stumble out of his room in the mornings with tousled hair and a sleepy smile just for her. Their first kiss, so hesitant and careful, one evening when they'd taken her dog out for a walk. Sitting at the kitchen table studying for an exam, feeling the energy radiating from him, just as she could feel it now. Could she even drive with him in the cab? Could she think straight on this case if he was with her? "Maybe this is a bad idea."

"You said the horse is tough to work with. I can help with that. I promise."

"I hope you're right." She started the truck and turned toward downtown Shelter Creek. She'd need to cross town to get to Haley's property. They were quiet for a few moments and she tried to get used to the idea of Wes Marlow, in the cab with her. Assisting her on a call. "This is surreal."

"Right?" Wes gestured to the town around them. "There have been so many changes here. Look at all these restaurants and art galleries. And wine tasting rooms. How'd everything get so fancy?"

She'd been thinking about Wes and he'd been thinking about Shelter Creek. It hadn't taken five minutes for him to start taking up way too much space in her mind. She should never forget how easily he left her behind. How she'd already spent way too many days of her life thinking about him. "I meant, it's surreal, driving in a truck with you. Seeing you. You look the same, except all grown up."

"Ah." He gave her a look she could feel, even though she kept her eyes on the road. "You look the same, too. Except better."

That had her glancing his way. "Better, how?"

He suddenly looked flustered. "Just…better."

Maybe she was shallow but it was gratifying to know that he might be wrestling with a regret or two. Still, there was no way she was going down that path with him. "You're right, the town has changed. A lot of the ranching land around here has been turned into vineyards. Thus the tourists, the wine tasting rooms and the art galleries."

"It looks nice. I'm looking forward to trying out some of the new restaurants. Want to grab some dinner after this?"

Emily could barely contain her disbelief. Did he think he could just show up in town fifteen years later and act like nothing had happened? Like they were buddies who would "grab some dinner"? "No, thank you."

After a few awkwardly quiet minutes, they reached the driveway to Haley's stable. Emily slowed and waited for an oncoming car to pass.

"I remember this place," Wes said. "You used to board your horse here."

"Shadow. He was such a good guy."

"What happened to him? He was in his teens back then, right?"

"Yeah. He lived to be twenty-eight. Then he got a case of colic that even my father couldn't fix. We had to put him down." It was still hard to talk about losing her beautiful old horse. Emily turned down the drive. "I miss him."

"That must have been hard. You've never gotten another horse?"

She shook her head. "I don't have time for that now."

She guided the truck past the first neat red-painted barn, the outdoor arena, then the indoor one. By the biggest barn there was a paved wash area. It was getting dark out, but Haley had the area lighted. Emily could see Two Socks, standing on three legs. Haley, in her sixties now, her long salt-and-pepper hair pulled back in a ponytail, walked toward them, waving.

Emily rolled down the window. "Hi, Haley," she called. "Is it okay if I park right up here by Two Socks?"

Haley clasped her hands as if in prayer. "Thanks so much for coming, Emily. Park wherever you want."

Emily pulled her truck carefully alongside the paved wash area. Getting out of the cab, she caught the look of surprise on Haley's face when Wes exited the passenger side.

"Haley, this is Wes Marlow. He used to live here in Shelter Creek. He's a vet, too."

"I remember you. You're the foster boy who used to come here with Emily back when Shadow was here." Haley beamed a smile at Wes, oblivious to the potential impact of her words. "Glad to have your help. Two Socks isn't cooperating much this evening."

Emily glanced at Wes, but if "foster boy" bothered him, he didn't let it show. He shook Haley's hand and glanced at Two Socks. "That's a nice-looking horse."

Haley beamed. "He's a good boy. But he sure knows how to find trouble."

The wash station was a paved area with a drain in the middle and metal fencing on three sides. Two Socks was a big chestnut gelding, with two white socks on his forelegs that gave him his name. Haley had turned on some floodlights on the outside of the barn, so it was easy to see the horse's green halter, the lead rope tied to a hitching post and the nervous flicking of his ears.

"Hey, Two Socks, how ya doing?" Emily stopped at the fence and held out her knuckles for the big gelding. Two Socks put his ears back and raised his head, tugging at his rope.

Emily took a step back and Haley took her place. "Easy there, boy." Haley ran a hand down his neck to calm him. "Steady."

Two Socks stopped pulling, but his ears stayed back, and he eyed Emily with obvious suspicion.

Squatting down outside the fence, Emily could see the wound on the horse's left hind leg. The front of the leg, from hock to hoof, was covered in blood. "He's really scraped up the front of his cannon bone. Haley, do you have any treats he loves? That might help him relax a little more."

"Sure. Just a minute." Haley gave her horse one more pat and walked off to the barn.

"Let's keep our distance until she comes back," Emily told Wes. "This horse doesn't like strangers."

"Can I try?" Wes held out a hand to Two Socks.

"No, Wes, trust me, he'll just get riled up and this will be even harder."

"Suit yourself. Some people say I have a way with horses, though."

"Just do as I say, please?" Maybe he was good with horses but Emily wasn't taking any chances with Two Socks. If Wes got the horse riled up, she'd never get that wound bandaged.

He shrugged. "Okay. You're the boss."

Haley returned with an assortment of carrots, apples and alfalfa cubes. She offered Emily and Wes each a piece of carrot. "Why don't you both give him a treat?"

Emily went first, smiling as Two Socks removed the carrot delicately from her outstretched hand, keeping as far away as possible in the process. "It's okay, big guy," she told him. "I'm here to help you."

She started for her truck but couldn't help pausing to watch Wes with the horse. He stepped up and offered his carrot. After Two Socks had taken the snack, Wes didn't pull his hand away, just turned it over and held it there in a lightly curled fist. Two Socks snuffled his knuckles and took a step toward him. Then the big horse lowered his head and let

Wes scratch along his blaze, his forelock and down his neck.

"Would you look at that?" Haley glanced at Emily. "I've never seen Socks be so good with someone he doesn't know."

Emily certainly hadn't, either. She pushed down the tide of annoyance rising inside. She hadn't really wanted Wes to be right when he said he worked well with horses. If he was a good vet, he'd be a good candidate to work with her. And she probably couldn't turn him down because she'd had precisely zero applications for the job.

She opened the cabinet on the side of her truck and pulled out a clean plastic container. She put a packet of sutures in, her scissors, needles, numbing solution, wound wash, disinfectant, anti-inflammatory and an oral sedative. All the while, Wes was hanging out with his new best friend, Two Socks. He'd even untied the horse and was smiling as the gelding rubbed his forehead on his shoulder.

Emily brought the supplies back to the wash area. "He seems relaxed. That's great. Let's take a closer look at his leg."

Emily took a flashlight from her pocket and kept a safe distance while she beamed it onto the wound. It was easy to see the puncture near the top, and the flap of torn skin below, where the wire must have scraped down the leg as Two Socks struggled to free himself. "Ouch. That must hurt quite a bit."

"How bad is it?" Haley came closer to see for herself.

"It's not that deep, thank goodness, but it's big and messy. We'll have to clean the wound really well. Then I'll put in a few stitches to close the skin, and bandage it all up. You can keep him in a stall for now, right?"

Haley nodded. "Yes, I've got a stall available. I'll keep it neat as a pin for him."

"Okay. I'm going to give him a mild sedative so we can clean this wound."

"Are you sure you need one?" Wes spoke softly as he continued to stroke Two Socks along the forehead.

Emily glared at Wes. Was he questioning her choices in front of a client? "It's mild."

"If you numb the leg, I can do some massage on his neck to help calm him. That might be enough to get the job done."

Emily swallowed back the retort on the tip of her tongue. "Wes, I need to get a few more things from the truck. Will you help me, please?"

His eyes narrowed. He knew she was lying, but he nodded. "Haley, can you stay with Two Socks and keep him nice and calm for us?"

"Sure." Haley took the lead rope from Wes and Emily turned on her heel, not waiting to see if Wes followed her to the truck. But sure enough, he was right behind her.

"What supplies did you need?"

"This isn't about supplies and you know it!" Emily had to force her voice to stay calm. "Don't question my judgment in front of one of my clients."

"I wasn't questioning you. I was offering help."

"Help? A massage?" She stared at him, not knowing what to think. "Wes, I don't think your horse massage is going to help me much when my face is a few inches from Two Socks's leg and I'm trying to stitch him up."

"You'd be surprised what acupressure and massage can do."

Emily's face heated. "Please don't talk down to me. I've read up on acupressure. It has its uses, but your suggestion endangers all of us.

If Two Socks panics, he could kick me. And he might injure himself more."

Wes held up his hands in a gesture of surrender. "I shouldn't have suggested it. It wasn't my place. I'm truly sorry. Bring on the sedative."

"I will." But he'd sown a seed of doubt. If he really could keep the horse calm, they'd avoid the risk of the gelding dropping to the ground during the procedure, which was possible, even with a mild sedative.

Her pride wanted her to be right. But this wasn't about her being right. It was about what would be best for the horse. "What if you did this massage thing while Haley held his foreleg up, so Two Socks can't kick me?"

"As long as you numb the wound really well, I think it will work."

As much as she didn't want to admit it, her instinct was nudging her to give it a try. But Two Socks was Haley's horse. "Let's check with Haley."

They walked back to the wash area and Emily explained the idea to Haley. "I can't guarantee that it will work. If it doesn't, we'll have to try the sedative."

"But you think it *might* work? I'd certainly

prefer it if we didn't have to make him all woozy."

Emily shrugged. "I think it's worth trying. But, full disclosure, Wes doesn't work with me, and I haven't seen him do this before, so I don't know how it will go."

"Wes, you're sure you can keep him calm?" Haley put her hands on her hips. "I love this horse, so be honest."

"I really think I can." Wes was all quiet confidence.

"Then I think we should try it." Haley positioned herself by Two Socks's left foreleg. "Just tell me when you need me to lift his leg."

"Not yet." Emily reached for the anti-inflammatory. "Wes, since he seems to like you, will you give him this?" She took the lid off the syringe and handed it to him. "It's apple flavored."

Wes let Two Socks smell the medication. Then, murmuring quiet encouragement, he inserted the syringe into the corner of the gelding's mouth and prompted the big horse to lift his head. When he squeezed the solution into the back of the horse's mouth, Two Socks complied. No fuss, no head tossing, no backing up or avoiding. He just swallowed the medicine as if it was horse candy.

Wes handed Emily the empty syringe, his smile laced with just a touch of triumph. "He's doing great," he said.

"He is." Emily tried to hide her astonishment. Two Socks had never been this cooperative with her. "I'll get the anesthetic ready. Haley, I'm just going to block the nerves around the wound so I can stitch him up."

"Sounds good," Haley said.

While Emily readied the injection, Wes ran his fingers along the gelding's thick chestnut mane until he located something. "Pressure point," he said quietly. His strong fingers started rubbing the spot in gentle circles, and after a moment, Two Socks let out a long sigh. His ears went from high alert to floppy.

"He really likes it." Haley grinned. "Just look at him."

Emily gaped at Wes. "I'll be honest, I've never seen him look this relaxed."

Wes smiled quietly back to her. "Everyone likes a massage now and then."

It came back to her in a rush, the way he used to give her shoulder rubs sometimes, after they'd been studying. Emily pushed the uncomfortable image away and turned to Haley. "Can you lift his leg and put it on your knees? Hold it tight. And let me know if your back starts to hurt."

"Will do." Haley leaned into her horse's shoulder and ran her hand down his foreleg. Two Socks was a little reluctant. Giving her that leg meant he had to put weight on his injured one. But after a moment he gave in and lifted his hoof. Haley stooped and braced his foreleg on her thighs. "Okay, go for it."

Emily disinfected the area above the wound with alcohol and gave Two Socks a shallow injection to numb the lower leg. The horse flinched slightly as the needle went in, but that was all. He stood quietly while Emily quickly cleaned and disinfected the wound. Then she readied the sutures. "He's going to let us know if this stings," she said quietly. "Is everybody ready?"

"Ready," Haley said.

"Wes?"

"He's fine. Trust me," Wes murmured back.

Trust me. Emily wanted to laugh out loud at the words. But that wasn't an option, so she rolled her eyes instead and knelt to stitch the wound. Two Socks didn't budge. In fact, he didn't even seem to notice. When she was finished, Emily dressed the leg and wrapped it securely. When she stood up, relieved to be finished, the big gelding looked half-asleep, leaning his head on Wes's shoulder, mesmerized by his horsey massage.

Haley was the only one suffering. She set Two Socks's leg down carefully and straightened her back. "Oof. It's possible I'm getting old."

"Maybe you need a back rub, too," Emily said, unable to resist poking at Wes. "Please keep the bandage on and our patient as quiet as possible in his stall. I'll come by and check on him tomorrow."

"That's perfect, thank you so much, Emily." There were tears in Haley's eyes. "I can't believe this happened. We replaced our barbed wire fences last year, but this coil of wire was hidden in the grass in one of our pastures. I didn't know it was there."

"Maybe you can send someone out to ride all your fences and make sure there isn't wire anywhere else," Emily suggested. "Just in case."

"I'll do that." Haley put a hand to Wes's arm. "Welcome back, Wes. And thank you for helping out tonight. You and Emily sure make a fine team."

Wes grinned over Haley's head at Emily. She glared back. "Thank you," Wes said. "I'm glad we could help."

"And, Wes, if you ever feel like teaching a clinic on how to do that horse massage, I bet I can get you a bunch of participants."

"Good to know. I might take you up on that."

Emily waved to Haley and started for the truck, a dark cloud settling on her shoulders. *A clinic.* Wes had been in Shelter Creek less than a day. He'd been on one vet call and someone already wanted him to teach a clinic? Her first months as a veterinarian had been all about defending her qualifications because she was a woman. She'd had to convince people to let her treat their animals and Wes just waltzed in here and got offered a clinic? She slammed her door a little too hard when she got in the cab. That wasn't a good move. She was being irrational...she knew she was.

Wes got into the passenger side of the cab and shut his door. Emily waited while he fastened his seat belt, and then started the truck back up Haley's driveway to the road.

"Nice woman," Wes commented. "And that is a beautiful horse. I hope his leg heals up well."

"I'll follow through with her every day this week to make sure it's fine." She sounded a lot more snippy than she meant to.

"Is everything okay?"

She could feel Wes looking at her in the dark cab, and what was he even doing here? Showing up in her life again like nothing ever happened? Like he hadn't disappeared and scared her and hurt her? Hadn't left her wondering where he was for *fifteen* years?

"Of course everything's okay. You show up at my clinic asking for work. Then you question my choices while we're with a client. Yeah, I'm just fine. Wes. Couldn't be better."

"I didn't mean to undermine you. I could see what the horse would respond to. I'm pretty sure he would have panicked on a sedative."

"How could you possibly know that?" Emily turned onto Main Street.

"I guess I understand horses. I can't really explain it. I just knew that Two Socks hates feeling out of control and the sedative would exacerbate that feeling. I could sense the tension emanating from his neck muscles, and I was pretty sure he'd respond to the massage and acupressure."

Emily glanced over at him. "You're saying you have some kind of sixth sense with horses."

"I guess. But I apologize if I overstepped. I won't teach a clinic for her if that bothers you."

"It's not about the clinic." She was lying, and embarrassed that he'd seen through to her jealousy. Now she felt like a jerk. "Of course you should teach it."

"So what's got you so upset? Is this all about the sedation?" When she didn't answer his voice softened. "Come on, Emily. Be straight with me. What's wrong?"

She was weak around him still. Unable to resist his calm cajoling. "It's not your fault, really. It's just the way the world is. As a woman, it took me a long time to be accepted as a veterinarian. Especially with ranchers around here. There are still clients who make it clear they wish I were a man." She glanced his way and he nodded as if to let her know that he'd heard.

"That must be really frustrating. I don't know what it's like to be a woman, but I do know what it's like to be underestimated. I spent a lot of years around people who assumed I was going to fail, just based on who I was."

She looked at him in surprise.

"I was a foster kid. Even Haley remembered that about me, all these years later. Every time I showed up at a new school, teachers had their expectations set on low before they even met me. Sometimes it felt like a lot to overcome."

"You never said anything about that when you were living with us."

"You were beautiful, beloved Emily, of the happy, supportive Fielding family. How could I expect you to understand?"

When she looked at him in dismay, he grinned at her. "And I was crazy about you. Trying to impress you. I wasn't going to let you know that most people thought I was a total loser."

She shook her head, trying to absorb his perspective on the kids they'd been. They'd reached the center of town. Many of the shops on Main Street were still open. Couples were strolling in and out of the restaurants. Friday night was usually busy but not like this. Emily slowed and stopped to let a couple, walking hand in hand, cross the street in front of them. A man Emily didn't recognize crossed, too. He was carrying a bucket full of flowers.

"What is he doing?" she asked when he stopped in front of them and waved a bouquet of what looked like pink roses.

"Don't you even know what day it is?" Wes grinned at her as he rolled down his window. He waved the man over. "I'll take them," he said.

Emily stared at Wes in confusion. Why was he buying flowers? She just wanted to get home. She was so tired, and this day, whatever day it was, had gone on forever. It seemed like weeks ago that she'd spotted Wes walking down the street, but it was only this morning.

Money changed hands through the truck window and the rose seller thanked Wes, then ran back across the street. Wes turned and offered the pink roses to Emily. "Here. Happy Valentine's Day."

She gasped. "It's Valentine's Day?"

He put his fingers to his forehead and shook his head slowly in mock disbelief. "Don't tell me you didn't even know."

"I was up most of the night dealing with a calving. I can barely stay awake, let alone worry about some silly holiday." Her cheeks were pinker than those roses. Luckily, it was dark in the truck. "Seriously, I don't need a valentine!"

"Everyone needs a valentine." Wes set the roses on the console between them. Emily checked to make sure everyone was out of the crosswalk and continued driving on toward her clinic.

The flowers were really pretty and they made the truck smell sweet. Wes's gesture was charming and annoying. Was he trying to remind her that they'd been sweethearts once upon a time? She didn't need any reminders.

Oh, no. The realization settled in her stomach. Valentine's Day. She'd completely forgotten to celebrate the holiday at work. She should have had some chocolates and decorations for her staff at the clinic today. She usually did something nice for them on a holiday. She'd been working so much, she'd been so tired lately, she'd totally forgotten.

It was all too much. She needed sleep. She needed time to process all this. She definitely didn't need some fake valentine from a guy who couldn't possible feel anything for her. "Wes, don't be silly. I don't want flowers."

"I owe you some, don't I? I left right before prom. I was definitely planning to get you flowers that night."

"That was so long ago. Let's just forget about that night." She tried to ignore the roses, now a reminder of when things were so much sweeter. When she'd been the kind of girl who couldn't wait to go to the prom with the boy she loved.

Wes stared out the window, the only sign of tension the restless tapping of his fingers on the sill. When they pulled up in front of her office, he spoke. "I'm sorry that things went wrong tonight. I was trying to prove to you that I could be an asset to your practice."

Emily put the truck in Park and reached for the door handle. "I don't see why you want to work with me. We don't exactly have a simple relationship."

"Shelter Creek is my dream place to live." He reached for his door handle, then looked over at her with a slight smile. "You're my dream coworker. You always have been."

He was all charm, and that young woman who'd wished for prom and roses wanted to believe him. "Yeah, right," she scoffed. "You don't know me. I could be a nightmare coworker. The truth is, you want to work with me because I'm the only gig in town. If you're going to resort to flattery, get out of my truck."

He obliged and she hopped out, too. Her whole body cried out for sleep, but there were still a few things to do at her desk before she could go home. "Thanks for your help tonight, Wes. But I'm not sure us working together is a good idea."

He came around the back of the truck. "I won't flatter. That was dumb. But just listen to me for a moment. Please?"

Emily crossed her arms over her chest and waited.

"Like I said earlier, there were a lot of reasons I didn't reach out over the years. And there was fear, too. Fear I couldn't shake. That you wouldn't want to hear from me. That you hated me."

"I did hate you, for a while." But she didn't, anymore. How could she, when she knew why he'd left? And all he'd been through over the years? But without all her old anger wrapped around her, she felt suddenly exposed. Like every old emotion had emerged from its hiding place.

He cleared his throat. Maybe he felt a little vulnerable, too. "Just take the roses home, okay? Put them in some water. Let them be the start of an apology I've owed you for so long now. Please?"

She liked that. *The start of an apology*. He wasn't trying to put a little bandage on such a big hurt.

Wes pulled a set of keys from his pocket. "Thanks for letting me tag along. I hope I was somewhat helpful."

That was the problem. He *had* been helpful. And he had been right about Two Socks. Plus, she desperately needed another vet, and one who was great with horses would be a big asset in this ranching town. But Wes? Being near him every day would be like voluntarily walking through an emotional minefield. "What will you do if you don't work with me?"

"Hope I can find some work close by? Or start my own practice and give you a little competition?" He shrugged. "I don't know. I didn't think everything through. I just dropped my brother off at the airport, went home and started packing."

"So you came here on an impulse."

"I came because I finally felt like I could."

Everything around them, the night, the breeze, her heart banging in her chest, stilled at his words. She didn't know what it was he hoped for. She had no idea what she wanted, either. But she knew she couldn't work at such a frantic pace much longer. And that she didn't want Wes to disappear, again. "You can start Monday," she told him. "For a one-week trial. If that works out, we can try it for a month. That's all I can offer."

"It's more than I have the right to hope for," he said. "Thank you. I promise you won't regret giving me a chance. What time should I be here on Monday?"

"Eight in the morning." Doubt in her decision mixed with the scramble of thoughts in her mind. Now she was the one acting on impulse. She should have told him she needed time to think. That she needed sleep.

"Thank you, Emily. I promise you won't regret this." He took a step back, as if he was going to leave before she changed her mind.

When his hand went to the brim of his cowboy hat, and he tipped it in her direction, it was a reminder of how little she knew him. Her California city boy had become a Texas cowboy, and walked a bunch of unfamiliar roads in between. "I'll see you Monday."

Emily watched him get in his truck. He gave her a wave, started the engine and drove away. She watched his taillights until he turned a corner out of sight. He'd promised she wouldn't regret giving him a chance, but Emily was pretty sure she already did.

CHAPTER FIVE

"Rex, you know you have to be really good today." Wes looked into his dog's icy blue eyes and wished one more time that he could bring the husky with him. He always had when he worked in Texas. But Wes knew he was already pushing his luck by asking to work with Emily. He had a lot to prove this week and couldn't be distracted by his dog.

Rex flopped over on the deck for a belly rub, waving his big white paws in the air.

"You ham." Wes rubbed the dog's stomach and looked around the backyard of the cottage he'd rented on the eastern edge of town. The high fence that ringed a decent-sized grassy yard had been the main reason he'd chosen this place. Luckily, the house was kind of nice, too—an old wooden cabin with what had to be the original enamel range in the kitchen and a claw-foot tub in the bathroom. Plus, and most important, the landlord allowed dogs and had agreed to a monthly lease.

Wes gave Rex another pat and went through the door into the kitchen. He took the toys stuffed with dog treats, and the giant bed he'd bought for Rex to lounge on, and brought them back outside. He'd spent the weekend building a doghouse out of plywood that he'd set in one corner of the deck. There was a soft bed in there, too, though so far his dog hadn't shown much interest in his daytime shelter.

Rex took the fake bone and started gnawing, eager for the snack hidden inside. Wes quietly shut the back door and hurried out the front to get to work.

Once he'd parked his truck in the clinic parking lot, Wes took a few deep breaths. This was it. His chance to prove what he could do. His chance to show Emily what he'd become. To see if the dream he'd harbored for so long could possibly come true.

All those years in between them, and he'd never forgotten her. In the few quiet moments he'd had, in between his multiple jobs and caring for his brother, he'd pull out his memories of Emily and pore over the details like they were a secret treasure. She'd been quiet and studious when they were young, but when she laughed, it was wholehearted and pure and shattered all the cool he'd tried so hard to maintain.

He used to be one of the reasons she smiled and laughed. He'd loved that he could break through her intense, intellectual mind and get her to relax. He'd give a lot to make her laugh again—but could he? He'd hurt her so badly when he left. He'd been such a coward afterward. Afraid to reach out. Afraid that if he heard her voice he'd crack and crumble. Sure that the brittle strength he'd summoned to get himself and Jamie through so many hard times would disappear if he let himself feel how much he missed her.

He'd known that coming back here was a long shot. That earning her trust again might be impossible. But he had to try. If he failed, maybe he'd finally be able to let go of all these long-held dreams and move on. If he succeeded… He couldn't even think that far ahead. He just had to focus on getting through this day without messing up too badly.

Opening the door to the clinic, he inhaled the familiar smell of disinfectant, with an undercurrent of dog. A young woman with short brown hair was seated behind the front desk.

"May I help you?" she asked, her smile as cheerful as her cat-shaped earrings.

"I'm here to meet Emily."

"Oh! You're the vet who's going to be working with Dr. Fielding this week. Welcome!"

"I'm Wes Marlow. And you are?"

"Lily Robinson. Have a seat. I'll see if she's available."

Wes sat on a padded bench in the waiting area. Lily went into the back of the clinic, then returned to answer the phone, Wes listened in. It was someone concerned that their cat was off his food. Lily transferred the call back to someone named Trisha, a veterinary technician, then took another call. Her demeanor was bright and professional. The office felt calm and welcoming, though Wes still wasn't used to the lavender color scheme. But if he ignored it, and the fancy decor, he could put himself right back in time to when he and Emily would come here to help her father. They'd made a little money cleaning cages and tidying up, but mostly they'd loved watching her father and his technicians at work. The way Tom assessed an animal, diagnosed it and made it better had seemed like magic to both of them. Was it any wonder they'd both gone into veterinary medicine?

He and Emily had been friends those first couple years. Two teens put together unexpectedly by her parents' desire to help out a kid in need. Theirs had been an uneasy connection at first. Wes had thought Emily resented him when he first arrived, but later she'd confided that he'd intimidated her with his tough exterior, city style and rough manners.

Tom and Meg had polished him up in no time, and eventually his and Emily's shared interests had grown into a friendship. They helped each other navigate school and homework and the small-town high school social scene. They became inseparable buddies who, on a warm evening walk during the summer after junior year, confessed that they were completely crazy about each other.

"You made it." Emily came toward him dressed in jeans and a dark green sweatshirt, her hair pulled back in a simple ponytail. His memories of his high school sweetheart merged with this strong, confident woman who was motioning for him to follow her. "Come on into the back. I'll introduce you to the staff and show you around."

He followed her, smiling as Lily caught his eye and mouthed *good luck*. They went past Emily's office and on into the three exam rooms, all spotlessly clean and painted in calming pale colors similar to the lobby. Cute photographs of animals were enlarged into portraits on the walls.

"Hang on." Wes put a gentle hand on Emily's arm to stop her as she was leaving the third exam room. "Did you take those pictures?"

She nodded and he thought the skin over her cheekbones flushed a little. "I did. Yes."

"You stuck with photography all these years?"

Her eyes widened a bit, like she was startled he remembered the hobby she'd taken up during their senior year of high school. Then she raised her shoulders, shrugging off his interest. "Not so much anymore. I took those while I was still working with my father. Since he retired, there hasn't been a lot of time."

Wes nodded, taking one last glance at the

close-up photo of a kitten. It was lying on its back, holding a small felt mouse between its front paws. "Great shot. You could have a side hustle taking photos like that."

She rolled her eyes. "I don't need a side hustle. Come on." Then she paused and the look she gave him over her shoulder was softer, almost shy. "Thank you for noticing, though. And for the compliment."

"It's sincere. I'm not just trying to butter you up so you give me a job."

And there it was. Faint but radiant. The smile he remembered. The humor that crinkled cute lines around her big blue eyes. "I'm glad. I avoid butter. It's bad for you."

Wes smiled back, relishing the brief moment of connection before she led the way into the back of the building. There was the surgery room and a couple of exam tables, with supplies neatly housed on shelves and tucked into labeled cabinets. It had never been this organized back here when they were kids. He should have guessed Emily would run a tight ship.

A blonde woman about their age came out of the storage closet with a big basket of towels. When she caught sight of Wes, she stopped suddenly. "Oh." Her gaze flickered to Emily for a moment, then back to him. "You must be Wes."

"Wes, meet Trisha Dale. Formerly Trisha Gilbert. She was a couple years behind us in high school."

"I remember you," Trisha said.

Wes didn't remember her, so he just nodded.

"Trisha is a good friend of mine and used to be my chief technician. She's filling in today since my head tech, Molly, is out sick."

"I look forward to working together," Wes said.

"Sadly for us, Trisha spends most of her working hours at the Shelter Creek Wildlife Center these days, rehabilitating animals." Emily finished with a loud sigh of mock despair.

Trisha grinned. "With Emily's guidance and advice, of course." She set her basket down on the counter behind her, and when she turned back toward them, Wes could see that she was pregnant. She put her hands on her rounded belly. "I hope you stick around, Wes. I'll be taking a break from work once this guy is born. Which means they'll be re-lying on Emily more than ever."

Wes gaped at Emily. "You work in a wild-life center on top of running this practice? Do you sleep?"

"Not much." Emily smiled at Trisha and Wes wished she'd beam the same warmth onto him. "Trish, I give it maybe six weeks before you're passing that baby to Liam so you can go visit your animal friends at the shelter."

Trisha laughed. "We'll see. I'll have my hands full as a mother of two. It might not matter how much I miss those animals. Any-way, it's nice to have you here, Wes. I'd better get moving. We're a little behind schedule."

She took her basket to a tall cabinet at the end of the room and began folding the towels and placing them on the shelf.

"We have field appointments this morning," Emily explained. "Luckily, Trisha agreed to come in and help us get things set up here. Then I have Dan, another tech, scheduled for this afternoon. So we should be okay."

"I've never run my own practice before," Wes said. "I've always been the associate vet.

I'm sure the scheduling and the business side of things keeps you busy."

Emily nodded. "You have no idea. I didn't, until it was all on my shoulders. I've made plenty of mistakes, but somehow this place is still standing."

"More than standing, I'd say. It seems pretty organized," Wes told her. "No offense to your father, but it never looked this neat when we were kids."

"Not his strong point, for sure." Emily motioned toward the front. "Let me show you the schedule for today. I'm sure Lily has printed it out for us by now."

In the reception area she showed him the printout. Looking over her shoulder at the schedule sheet, Wes inhaled a faint floral scent from her hair. It was calming and soothing and some part of him wished he could spend a few moments just breathing her in. That they could get out of here and lie on their backs in a big field and watch clouds sailing above them in the sky like they had when they were young. Maybe then they could talk all this out. Maybe then he could try to tell her more about the years he'd struggled, about why he'd stayed away, and why he couldn't wait to be free to come back here.

But no. He had to be professional. He had to take his cues from her and she was all business.

"We're going out to check on Two Socks," she was saying. "I went on Saturday to change the bandage, but yesterday Haley changed it herself. I want to double-check that she's got the hang of it."

"Sounds good." Wes scanned the paper. "This is a really packed morning."

"Welcome to my world. I'm the only vet in the immediate area. And spring is coming up. So we'll have calving, lambing and foaling on top of all the usual stuff."

It was going to be a lot for two people. How she got it done on her own, he had no idea. He figured he'd find out today. "Looks like we'd better get started."

She grabbed her coat and he followed her to the truck, this time remembering to let her take the wheel. They drove for a moment in silence before Emily spoke. "Can I ask you something?"

"Of course."

"Do you *really* want to work with *me*? I

mean…" She paused, and as he watched her she pressed her lips together like she wanted to stop whatever she was going to say. "I guess I need to know what you want out of this."

This was Emily. Straightforward. No games, ever. So he'd be as straight as he could, too. "I have always wanted to see you again. I have always wanted the chance to say I'm sorry for the way I left. For maybe hurting you."

"Maybe?"

"I don't want to assume anything. Maybe you were just fine."

"Yeah, that's right. I was fine. Absolutely."

He studied her profile, trying to figure out whether she was being sarcastic. "You seem fine." A faint, wry smile tilted the corner of her mouth. It took away any hope of holding back. "I'll be totally honest. In my perfect world, you forgive me, we like working together and we live happily-ever-after."

"Veterinary practice is stressful. That happily-ever-after part seems like a stretch."

That was her, letting him know that this situation between them was purely professional. He owed it to her to keep it that way, if that was what she wanted. "I bet we'll work well together. We always got along when we knew each other before. Even before things between us got serious."

She nodded once, keeping her eyes fixed on the road ahead. Wes waited for an answer but it didn't come. He used to be able to read every expression on her face, but she was chewing gently on her lower lip in a gesture he didn't recognize and he couldn't begin to decipher. Worried? Thoughtful? Hungry? He had no idea.

They were almost to Haley's stable. It was probably best that they were going to be so busy today. Being near Emily again had opened a seam in his heart and old feelings were pouring out like water through a cracked dam. What would Emily do if Wes said what was really on his mind—that he'd always loved her? She'd probably shove him out of the truck and drive off. And rightly so. Even in his own mind the words made him sound like some kind of stalker. Plus, he was grown enough to know that his feelings for her were all based around the girl she'd been. That might have nothing to do with the woman she was now. But man, did he look forward to getting to know her again.

Emily glanced his way. "Just to remind you, I'm still taking applications for this vet position."

She sure was determined to keep him in his place. But humble pie tasted good when she was the one dishing it out. "I'm on trial. I realize that. Have you had a lot of applicants?"

She shook her head. "Nope."

He nodded. "I see. So I'm here today because you're getting desperate."

She laughed then, just a short sharp sound, but he relished it anyway. "Something like that."

Wes grinned at her brutal honesty. "At least I'm clear on where I stand in this hiring process."

Emily turned down Haley's driveway and glanced his way, still smiling slightly. "And don't think that just because you work your magic on Two Socks again, you're all set. We've got all kinds of animals on the agenda today. You need to be great with all of them."

"No pressure or anything."

"You were gone a long time, Wes Marlow. You need to prove that you deserve to be here, riding in this truck with me."

"How long will it take, this proving thing?

Are you thinking a month? A few? Or are we talking years?" He shot what he hoped was a charming smile her way. "Just wondering."

She parked the truck near the barn and cut the engine before she looked his way. When she did he saw a hint of mischief in her eyes that sparked a glimmer of hope in his heart. "Longer than a week, I can guarantee that." She released her seat belt and jerked her head toward the door. "Come on. Let's go check on your first Shelter Creek patient."

CHAPTER SIX

EMILY WAS GRATEFUL that Wes had such a good bond with Two Socks. Her head was in such a muddle that she was happy to let him remove and replace the dressing on the horse's leg. She told him she was observing his work, but really she needed a moment to pull her thoughts into some cohesive order. All weekend, while she'd been here checking on Two Socks, catching up on her paperwork at the office and helping out at the wildlife center, she'd been wondering what possessed her to even consider working with Wes. Horse whisperer or not, he was a confusing complication, and that didn't make him a comfortable work partner.

But what choice did she have? He was a good vet. She'd called a few of his references this weekend and listened to them all rave about his skill with animals and clients, his vast medical knowledge and his professionalism. And despite refreshing her job announcement and trying to connect with some veterinarians on a networking website, there was no one else asking to come work with her in Shelter Creek.

Wes hadn't been wrong when he joked that she was desperate. The truth was, she was exhausted. She'd been working nonstop for the past few years and she craved some time off. To get it, she needed someone she could rely on.

Though Wes certainly hadn't proven to be reliable in the past.

She'd spent Sunday evening with her parents. Over lasagna and salad they'd encouraged her to use this trial week to listen to her instincts about him. To trust her own judgment. She'd wanted more guidance than that from them, but they seemed determined to stay out of it. Maybe they were being cautious, trying not to get hurt by Wes again. Or maybe they were determined to let her make her own decisions.

She'd never hired another vet before, but she was pretty sure that an ex-boyfriend who'd broken her heart wasn't an ideal candidate.

As if he could read her thoughts, Wes

straightened from where he'd been crouched by Two Socks's leg and gave her a warm smile that sent her pulse skittering. *No.* Her pulse was just fine. Perfectly normal. Emily pulled her phone out of her pocket and pretended to check something on it to give her heart a moment to settle.

"Want to come take a look?" Wes waved her over and Two Socks didn't even flinch at the gesture. He seemed completely relaxed with Wes doing the bandaging. "I bet in a week or so Haley can start taking him on some walks."

Haley, who'd been holding Two Socks's lead rope, beamed at Wes. "I'm so happy with his progress."

Emily walked a big circle around the gelding's hind end for a better view of the wound. Wes was right, it looked great. All the inflammation was gone, the scrapes were scabbed over and the stitched area wasn't swollen at all. "Wow. Well done, Two Socks and Haley. I agree with Wes. Another week of rest and then he can start moving around more."

Wes's smile wasn't just because she'd agreed with him. She could tell from the quiet satisfaction in his expression that he was truly gratified to see the horse doing better. "This is a great way to start the day, Haley. He's made an amazing recovery."

Haley ran her hand along her horse's neck. "Well, it's thanks to both of you."

"Just be careful not to push things too fast," Emily cautioned. "Keep him in his stall. He can walk in the aisle of the barn a bit, or for a few yards on paved surfaces, but that's it for now."

"Will do." Haley pulled a piece of carrot from her jeans pocket and fed it to Two Socks. "I'm so glad he's going to be okay."

After they said goodbye to Haley and were back in the truck, Wes turned to Emily. "I like it when things go right. That doesn't always happen in our line of work."

She nodded, steeling herself against this more gentle side of him. It seemed like he'd become a genuinely nice guy and she didn't want that. Didn't want to feel good feelings, because what if good feelings led to great feelings? Feelings like the ones that had been crushed when he went away?

"We've got a long day ahead. I'm sure there will be ups and downs." But it turned out to be a morning of mainly ups. The sick calf they visited at a ranch out on the coast wasn't sick, after all. It was having trouble nursing effectively, so they worked with the rookie owner on how to feed it from a bottle. Sheep vaccinations were easier than usual, because there were two of them doing the vaccinating. They had one more visit before they had to be back at the clinic for afternoon appointments there. It was one that Emily wasn't looking forward to.

"This next ranch is Fred Corrigan's. Do you remember him?"

Wes shook his head.

"My dad used to call him the most ornery rancher around Shelter Creek. He owns a dairy farm and he's getting up in years. It's too much work for him these days and that makes him even grumpier."

"Doesn't he have any kids to help him keep the business going?"

Emily shook her head. "Sadly, I think he scared his kids away from the family business. His son works at a tech company in San Francisco and his daughter started her own ranch out by the coast. She raises dairy *goats*."

"Ouch. That must have been a blow to dear old dad."

They pulled up by the big white barn. Even from the truck, the stench of cow was thick. Too thick. Emily peered through the windshield. The air near the barn was thick with buzzing flies.

This was the day Emily *had* to talk with Fred about hiring some help. Or retiring. Every time she'd come out here recently, she'd found his ranch getting more run-down. Now it had clearly reached a tipping point. A filthy dairy ranch wasn't safe for anyone.

Emily got out of the truck, realizing that she should have mentioned something to Wes about what she'd noticed here on previous visits. He came around the side of the truck, took in their surroundings and slapped on the straw cowboy hat he'd brought with him today. A hat that made him look far too handsome. He glanced her way, and she opened her mouth to say something.

Before she could, Fred shuffled out of the barn and waved. He had arthritis and his walk seemed more stiff than usual. His stooped back and hesitant gait pulled at Emily's heart, even though he rarely had a kind word for her.

The old rancher glared at her as she approached him. "I just about fell asleep, standing around waiting for you, young lady."

"We are running five minutes behind schedule today, Fred. I can see how that might feel like a lot of time to wait when you've got so much to do. Let's get started."

Fred looked from Wes to Emily, his brows lowered in suspicion. "Who's this cowboy?"

"This is Wes Marlow. He's a veterinarian visiting from Texas. He's considering a move to Shelter Creek. Wes, this is Fred Corrigan."

"Nice to meet you." Wes offered his hand and Fred reached out to shake it.

"Texas! It's too hot out in Texas. You're smart to come out west. Are you going to work with this young lady?"

"We'll see what she says after a trial period."

Fred jabbed a gnarled finger in Emily's direction. "Of course you'll have him stay. You could use some muscle on jobs like this."

Emily opened her mouth to answer but Wes jumped in first. "I've seen Emily work. She's plenty tough. I'm sure she's capable of any job out here."

Fred shrugged. "She tries real hard, but we

both know that doctoring livestock is best suited for a man."

Wes took a slight step forward. "I think your views on women are a little outdated, Fred."

Her skin felt so hot there might be smoke coming out of her ears. Emily didn't like Fred writing her off because she was a woman, but she also didn't need Wes Marlow jumping in to rescue her. Or both of them jabbering away about her, like she wasn't even here. "Hang on," she interrupted. "We've got a bunch of heifers who need exams and vaccinations today. Fred, you've never had cause to criticize my work. There's nothing you've needed done that I haven't been able to do. End of discussion."

They both stared at her, and if she weren't so mad she might have laughed. They reminded her of a couple of rams butting heads, who'd suddenly run right past each other. "Now let's get started. Wes and I have to get back to town for some afternoon appointments at the clinic."

Fred glared at her and jerked his chin toward the bar. "Well, cowboy, let me show you my prize heifers."

Wes fell into step beside him and off they went, Fred talking far more animatedly to Wes than he'd ever spoken to her.

Fred was still living in another era. He'd certainly been born in another era. Looking around at the faded paint and leaning fences, Emily wondered if Fred had lost his love of ranching, or if he simply couldn't keep up with it, now that he was older. It was sad to see things falling apart. She'd been worried about him the last time she was out here, but at least the barns had been clean. The closer they got to the old white building, the thicker the smell of manure and urine became.

Walking behind the two men, Emily could hear Wes continuing to defend her. "I'm happy to get to work with Emily. I've known her a long time. She's one of the best veterinarians I've ever worked with." Great. He felt so sorry for her that he was telling fibs, trying to boost her currency with her client.

It wasn't just that Wes felt sorry for her, though. Every rancher they'd met today had accepted Wes and his competence as a veterinarian without question. Emily had faced so much more scrutiny when she started— so many comments about her size and her strength and her experience. She still got those questions and judgments. But Wes— over six feet tall, obviously strong and looking all tough in his cowboy outfit—just got a *nice to meet you*, attentive listening and respectful nods when he spoke.

Well, she'd learned a long time ago that she'd meet up with a lot of sexism if she wanted to be a large-animal vet. But still, it burned. And somehow Wes trying to defend her stung far worse than anything Fred had said. Everyone knew Fred Corrigan was mean and inappropriate. But having Wes feel sorry for her, and try to make it better for her, was pure humiliation. The other night he'd said he understood what it felt like to be underestimated. But he was underestimating her now.

She had to let it go. They had work to do. They'd reached the barn and the stench almost knocked her over when they stepped inside. Flies were circling in small tornadoes above piles of cow manure. The barn hadn't been cleaned in at least a couple of days.

Fred seemed oblivious to the mess. He was pointing out one of the heifers tied in a row along a railing inside the barn. Wes was making a show of listening attentively, but he glanced back at Emily, a worried expression in his eyes. She was the one in charge, so she'd have to bring up the subject of the filth around them.

"Fred, I'm sorry to interrupt. The heifers look great, but what's going on in this barn? It's usually a whole lot cleaner."

Fred didn't snap back at her the way she'd expected. Instead he had the awareness to look chagrined. "My hired hands quit the other day. All three of them. Said they could get better pay and nicer treatment over at Jace Hendricks's place."

Jace was married to Emily's friend Vivian, whom she'd seen at the coffee shop last Friday. Just before she first saw Wes. "Have you advertised for any more help?"

"Nope." Fred shook his head emphatically. "I'm starting to think hiring folks is more trouble than it's worth. They just up and leave again."

Probably because you're so mean to them. Emily didn't voice that thought. Fred had been grumpy and bossy for decades; he wasn't going to change now. She looked around thoughtfully, trying to ignore the smell. "Have you spoken with Annie Brooks? She's head of the Ranchers' Guild. I bet she could figure out how to get you some help."

"That woman?" Fred snorted. "Always meddling, that one." He crossed his arms over his skinny chest. "I can handle things myself."

"A dairy business is a whole lot of hard work," Wes said gently. "No one could handle all of it themselves. You need some extra hands around here, Fred. Let Emily and me help you figure out what to do. Even if it does mean calling this meddling Annie Brooks."

Annie was a tough-talking sheep rancher whom Emily adored. They were in a book club together, The Book Biddies, and it was true that Annie got involved in a lot of people's business. But when she did, things always turned out for the better.

Fred rambled on, "It *is* a lot of work. That's part of the problem. All these young ranch hands, they don't know what it means to work hard. They want breaks and time off and health care and all these extras."

"Those extras will probably keep them working here longer." Emily took a step closer to Fred. "I think it's something to consider.

You need to keep up with what other ranches are offering their workers."

Fred turned to his new best buddy, Wes. "What do you think?"

"You never know, Fred. If you offer those things, they just might stick around. They might even do a good job." Wes used a joking tone that Emily would probably never be able to get away with around Fred.

"Humph." Fred looked at them shrewdly. "I doubt it."

"You won't know until you try," Emily reminded him.

Fred looked from her back to Wes. "You really think this will work?"

There he went again. Needing to hear a man say the same thing she'd just said. Wes obliged. "I think it's good business."

"Fine," Fred mumbled. "Emily, you can call Annie. But that won't help the state of my barn today."

Now Emily could laugh. "Fred, are you kidding? You know how Annie is. I'm going to step outside right now and call her. I'll bet you she'll have people here cleaning this barn within the next hour or two." She gestured toward the heifers. "Meanwhile, how about we do the exams for these ladies in the pen outside. The one that attaches to the cattle chute?"

Fred bristled. "My heifers are well-behaved. You've never had to use a chute with them before."

"It's never smelled like this in here before, Fred. Come on. It's a beautiful day. Let's bring them outside."

Fred looked at Wes. *Of course.* Wes nodded in response. "I have to agree with Emily on this one, Fred. Let's lead these beauties out into the fresh air."

Emily's shoulders relaxed a notch as she walked to her truck to get her cell phone. It was good to get a break from the stench and the sexism in the barn. Fortunately, she was able to reach Annie on her first try. She explained the state of Fred's ranch. They both suspected that if the barn was in such a shambles, the rest of the ranch couldn't be much better.

"I need to get inside his milk room and take a look at his equipment," Annie said. "If things aren't clean, he could cause some kind of health crisis." She paused thoughtfully. "I know a great dairy farmer south of here, on the coast. Maybe I'll have him meet me there and take a look."

"Don't get Fred all defensive, Annie, or he might not work with us."

"Oh, you leave Fred Corrigan to me. I was friends with his late wife, God rest her soul, and I will invoke her name if he gets out of line. Irma was one tough lady and I suspect her passing last year is one reason Fred's ranch seems to be falling apart."

Annie was a master at getting people to do the right thing. Emily felt the tension in her shoulders relax a little. "Thank you, Annie. I'm really glad you're willing to step in here."

"You have enough on your plate, honey, between your practice and your work at the wildlife center."

"Annie, can I ask you something?" Emily didn't usually make time for personal conversations during her workday, but her subconscious must have had other ideas.

"Of course."

"Did the ranchers around here ever give you a hard time because you're a woman?"

Annie burst into peals of laughter on the other end of the phone. "All the time. Until my sheep outproduced theirs, my wool won prizes at every state fair and I took charge of the Ranchers' Guild. Then they started to watch their words a little more."

Emily nodded, forgetting her friend couldn't see her.

"Is old Fred giving you a hard time?"

"I've got a guy with me today. Another veterinarian, who's sort of auditioning to work with me. All the ranchers accept him so easily. Fred was over the moon to finally have a male vet around."

Annie sighed audibly. "I'm sorry, Em. It should be different in this day and age. Remember, you're a fantastic veterinarian. I don't trust just anyone with my prize sheep."

It helped to talk to someone who worked in the same world she did. Who'd been dealing with it for a lot longer. "Thanks, Annie."

"Anytime. Now you get back out there and don't let Fred get to you. He's lucky to have you looking out for him and getting him the help he needs. I'll be there soon, along with a crew of folks to start cleaning up."

Emily hung up the phone and headed for the pen where the heifers were. If only Annie could solve all of her problems. Especially what to do about the way she felt right now.

Because no matter how grumpy she felt with Wes, she was still looking forward to working with him for the rest of the day.

CHAPTER SEVEN

WES GLANCED AT Emily's profile as they drove back to Shelter Creek. Her jaw was set firmly, as if she might be clenching her teeth. Her thick sandy hair was pulled back in a ponytail but the strands in front had escaped. They were lighter than the rest of her hair, bleached by the sun. There was a faint spray of freckles on her cheeks and he remembered trying to count them, way back in high school.

And on top of all her beauty, she was a great veterinarian. He'd been impressed all morning, but especially in the last couple of hours, working with Fred Corrigan. Emily had been tough, not letting grumpy old Fred push her around, and miraculously, getting him to accept some help with his ranch. Wes wanted to tell her how much he admired her, but Emily had been silent ever since they got into the car. It wasn't a tired silence, or a peaceful silence. He was pretty sure it was the grumpy kind.

Finally he couldn't stand it anymore. "What's wrong?"

She glanced at him, her blue eyes cool as ice. "Nothing's wrong. Just thinking." Her gaze went back to the road.

"Emily, I know it's been a really long time but I used to know you. And I remember this kind of mood. If I messed up, I wish you'd say something."

"You were fine. You're obviously a good vet, Wes. I can't complain about that."

"That's somewhat reassuring. So, what can you complain about?"

She glanced at him briefly. "I don't need you coming to my rescue with Fred Corrigan, or anyone."

"When did I come to your—" Then he remembered. "Oh. You mean when he was going on about having a man around?"

"Yeah, that. You even lied about us. Now he thinks we've known each other for ages."

"It's kind of true." Wes watched her knuckles go white on the steering wheel. Wrong answer. "I was just mad that he was treating you so badly."

"He was being a jerk but I handled it. I've *always* handled it. And I don't need you jumping in as if I *can't* handle it. I've never needed you before and I don't need you now."

Ah. So that was what this was about. "Of course you don't need me. You've created a successful practice, and you're obviously a great vet. But I can still stick up for you if someone gets out of line. That's what good people do."

"I can fight my own battles. I don't need some man thinking that he has to make it better for me."

But he'd wanted to make it better. Wes wasn't sure he'd even had a choice. After listening to just a few words of Fred's disrespect, he'd *had* to jump in. "If I was a woman would you want me to stick up for you?"

That stumped her for a moment. She shrugged. "Probably."

"But you don't want *me* to stick up for you?"

"Not just you. Any man. I've been handling that type of sexism my whole life."

"But don't you think when a man stands up for a woman it sends a strong message?

That I'm not going to sit around and tolerate it? That I'm not going to join in?"

"But you *did* join in. You and Fred were talking about me like I wasn't even there!"

Wes blew out a breath and thanked the good lord that he hadn't had any sisters. He felt a little like a fly caught in a sticky web. There were no good moves to be made here without the spider jumping on him.

"What if someone threatens you physically? Can I stick up for you then?"

Emily shrugged. "If I'm losing the fight, sure."

He smiled. "So I have to wait until you're getting beat up? Remind me never to get into a barroom brawl with you."

"Who gets into brawls?" She looked over at him, brows arched. "You?"

"No, not really. Maybe once. Or twice." He held his palms up in a helpless gesture. "You're changing the subject. I'm just trying to figure this out. You don't want me defending you against sexist comments at work. If a situation turns violent you may want me to jump in, but only if your combat skills prove to be inadequate. What about if a dog attacks you? What do I do then?"

She was smiling now. That was a good sign. "Help me, of course."

"Good to know. What about if this truck gets a flat tire? Can I offer assistance?"

"Sure." She glanced at him long enough to give him a wink. "Though I can change my own tires."

"I'll keep that in mind. But if a client acts like a jerk to you, you want me to just let them?"

She sighed. "I want you to let me handle it. Don't speak for me. If you do, it feels like you don't believe I can deal with it. It undermines me."

"Got it." He reviewed the conversation with Fred in his mind. He *had* jumped right in to try to fix things for her. Though she'd jumped right in after him and put both him and Fred into their place. "I'll try to keep my mouth shut in the future. If I mess up again, tell me."

She grinned and there was evil lurking there. "Oh, trust me, I will."

Wes pretended to cower into his corner of the truck and she laughed outright. He could listen to that sound all day. So bright and soothing, like water in a fountain. "Is it sexist if I offer to buy you a sandwich? It's far past lunchtime."

"Um…" She glanced at the dashboard clock. "I guess we have time."

"Don't tell me you usually work right through lunch."

"I've got a packed schedule!" She shrugged. "Besides, that's what granola bars are for."

She had been living like a workaholic for too long. "You can't exist on granola bars and do the kind of physical work we do. Plus, that's just kind of sad. You live in a town with one of the best delis I've ever been to. I dreamed about their turkey with avocado on sourdough bread for over a decade. Are you really going to tell me that you don't ever go there and get lunch?"

They were at an intersection and she rolled her eyes at him, but turned toward Main Street. "The Redwood Deli it is. And yes, I admit, I haven't had one of their sandwiches in a long time."

"This is why you need me to help you with your practice. So you can eat a real lunch a few days a week." He looked out the window as they drove past the park, with its towering redwood trees standing sentinel by the creek that gave the town its name. "Granola bars," he muttered. "Please."

Emily's eyes narrowed but she was pressing her lips together to disguise her smile. She guided the truck into a parking spot. "Let's go get your sandwiches," she said as she shut off the engine. "I hope they are as good as you remember them."

They were better. Wes sank his teeth into another satisfying mouthful of turkey and pickles and lettuce and avocado and felt another one of his dreams come true. How often, living on his tiny wages, eating cereal for dinner, had he dreamed of sitting here in this park, under these majestic trees, eating this sandwich? Now, here he was and the moment was even better than he'd imagined.

His years of poverty had been behind him for a while now, but they were always there, under the surface, reminding him how lucky he was to have enough. To have more than enough.

Emily bit into her sandwich across the picnic table. "Mmm," she said, swallowing and dabbing at her mouth with a napkin. "That is amazing."

"It's nice to stop for lunch, right?" Wes

pointed up to the redwood trees above them. "This has to be the best lunch spot on the planet."

"Where did you eat lunch in Texas?"

"It depends. Usually work took me out into the more rural areas, so I packed a lunch. Peanut butter and jelly, mostly."

She grinned. "That's what I ate when I was a kid."

"It's cheap, doesn't have to be refrigerated, and it works."

"So there's a very practical side to you." Emily shot him an appraising glance. They might be joking around about lunch but she was trying to figure him out. Good. Because he was trying to do the same, with her.

"I'm very practical. I had nothing for so many years that now I'm pretty careful with what I have."

"Except when it comes to deli sandwiches," she said, taking a bite of hers.

"Ah, but not just any deli sandwich. This one. The one I remembered all the time I was gone."

The humor left her eyes. "Glad you remembered something."

Wes set his sandwich down. "I remembered you. Why do you think I came back here?"

Emily swallowed her bite in a gulp, her eyes wide. "I guess that's what we're both trying to figure out." She waved her sandwich at him. "I can't believe I haven't gone to this deli more often."

"Maybe that's why I came back to Shelter Creek. To get you to eat a good lunch once in a while."

"Do not push your luck, Wes Marlow." Her smiling gaze caught his and he felt it like summer sun on his skin.

"Is that Emily?" A man in a sheriff's uniform was striding through the park toward them. Wes noticed his car parked on the street. Emily turned around, then waved to the sheriff. "Adam, what's going on?"

The man stopped by the picnic table and looked Wes up and down. "Wes Marlow, back in Shelter Creek."

Wes squinted at him, trying to remember. Dark hair, dark eyes, a big, good-looking guy who filled out his uniform...

"I'm Adam Sears. We went to high school together."

Wes suddenly placed the name with a much

skinnier, smaller version of the man in front of him. "I remember you. We were on the track team together, right?"

"We were. Welcome back. I think I have something that belongs to you."

"What?" For a confusing moment Wes tried to think of what he could have left with Adam so many years ago. Then he heard a bark from the sheriff's car and it all came clear. "Rex?"

"I found him running along the road. I think he was looking for you."

Wes stood. "I wonder how he got out?"

Adam laughed. "He's a husky. Those dogs can climb any fence if they've got a mind to."

This wasn't good. "How did you find me here?"

"Shelter Creek is a small town. I called the cell phone on Rex's tag and got your voice mail. I remembered you, and figured you must be visiting Emily's parents, so I called them. They said you were probably with Emily today, but I could leave Rex with them. I was on my way to their house when I spotted Emily's truck."

"Nice detective work, Sheriff." Emily held up a hand and Adam high-fived her.

"I really appreciate all your effort," Wes said. The delicious sandwich soured in his stomach. Rex could have been hit by a car, or lost in the woods.

"I'll call my parents and let them know that we have your dog." Emily pulled out her phone.

Wes started for the sheriff's car, Adam beside him.

"So you're back in town after all this time? Sure glad to know you're okay." Adam shot him a bemused look. "You gave everyone around here a pretty good scare back then. They had missing person posters up, search teams out looking, the works."

Wes stopped in his tracks. It had never have occurred to him that the whole town would have been involved when he ran away. But of course they would. Meg, Tom and Emily would have left no stone unturned, trying to make sure he was okay. "I left town to deal with a family problem. I never thought everyone would go looking."

"This is Shelter Creek. Of course everyone would look for you. This town is like that, in case you didn't notice in the years you spent here."

Wes had been young and scared and trying so hard to fit in. He hadn't noticed much beyond that. He'd loved it here, but part of him always felt like an outsider. Still, when he left, they'd all tried to find him. Wes turned the idea over in his mind with a sense of awe.

"Where'd you pick up that accent of yours?"

Wes grinned. "A whole lot of years in Texas."

Adam nodded. "I guess that explains the cowboy hat, too. What brought you back here?"

"The weather."

Adam glanced back at Emily. "Uh-huh. I figure you have a few more reasons than that."

Wes grinned. "Maybe." They reached the truck and Rex let out a yip of recognition, his nose poking through the partially open rear window. "Thanks so much for picking him up," Wes said. "He's a good dog. He's just used to being with me all day. I guess he got worried."

"You might need to leave him with a dog sitter." Adam opened the car door. Rex leaped out and into Wes's arms and he staggered back under the unexpected weight, rubbing the dog's fuzzy ears and accepting a few kisses on the cheek.

"That's enough," he told Rex. "Party's over. Now sit." Rex sat obediently.

"That's a well-trained dog," Adam said.

"Unless he's been told to stay in the yard, apparently." Wes motioned toward Emily. "Want to come sit with us while we eat?"

Adam shook his head. "Nah, I've got a lot to do. But it's great to see you. What are you doing Wednesday night? There's all-you-can-eat pizza and cheap beer at Dex's Ale House. I'm going to shoot some pool with a few buddies. You probably remember a couple of them. Caleb Dunne? Jace Hendricks?"

Wes tried to place the names. Jace Hendricks was the rancher that Fred had mentioned earlier today and it *had* sounded familiar. "I'm not sure."

"They were on the high school rodeo team."

"Oh. The cool kids." Wes and Adam both smiled. Everyone had looked up to the kids on the rodeo team at Shelter Creek High School.

"Now that you're such a cowboy, you should fit right in. Let us buy you a beer."

"Sure. Assuming there are no veterinary emergencies, I'll be there."

Adam looked startled. "You're a vet? Like Emily?"

"Yes I am. I'm working with her this week."

The deputy shook his head in wonder. "You two were always together in high school. What are the chances you ended up in the same career?"

"We both liked helping her dad." Wes glanced back toward Emily. She was still talking on her cell phone. "I'd better get back. We don't have much more time for lunch."

Adam followed his gaze. "I don't think I've ever seen Emily around town grabbing lunch." He winked at Wes. "Must be the weather."

Wes laughed. "It's definitely the weather."

Adam clapped a hand to his shoulder. "Great to have you back, safe and sound. Hope to see you Wednesday."

"Thanks again for the invitation. And for finding Rex. I'll make sure he doesn't have a chance to get out again."

Adam gave him a thumbs-up and got into his car. Wes returned to Emily, Rex trotting at his heels.

Emily set her phone down as they approached. "My parents say hello. So this is your dog?"

"Rex, meet Emily."

Rex sat and held out a paw, a trick Wes was especially proud of.

Emily glanced at Wes, eyebrows raised, and shook Rex's paw. "Nice to meet you, Rex. It seems that someone has taught you well." She ran her fingers over the fur on the big dog's back. "Did he climb out?"

"I've never left him in a yard during a workday before. He's always come to work with me. If I have to leave him for just a few hours, he's fine in the house. He watches the animal channel."

Emily nodded and Rex licked her knuckles. "He probably panicked. You're lucky Adam found him."

"I know." He watched Rex relax with Emily. She really had a way with animals. She'd found just the right spot behind Rex's ears and the dog's eyes were half closed in bliss.

"Why did you name him Rex?"

"You know why." He started whistling the theme of a film they'd watched together.

"Rex Harrison? From the old *Doctor Dolittle* movie?"

"Of course. Doctor Dolittle talked to animals. And Rex sure can get chatty sometimes." On cue Rex lay down and let out a contented yowl. "See?"

"He's a gorgeous dog." Rex rolled onto his back and Emily leaned down to rub his belly.

"I'm glad you think so, because I have a question. Any chance he can come to work with us for the rest of the day? He's used to being in a clinic. He'll just lie down in a corner and keep an eye on things."

Emily's brows rose. "Are you sure?"

"Pretty sure."

She gave Rex's belly another rub. "You're going to be nothing but trouble, aren't you, big dog? Just like your owner."

"We might be trouble, but we keep things interesting."

"Is that what you call it?" Her glance was a hundred percent skeptical. "He can be on trial, just like you. But neither of you should get your hopes up that this will become a permanent thing."

Wes couldn't help it. His hopes were already up. Today was fun. They worked well together and they could talk stuff out. Even when she'd gotten mad at him about how he'd handled Fred Corrigan, they'd managed to joke about it. Wes glanced at the remains of his sandwich, sitting on the wrapper on the picnic table. He looked up at the redwood trees arching green and brown so high into the sky. His hopes were up all right. He'd be pretty disappointed if things didn't work out for him to stay in Shelter Creek.

CHAPTER EIGHT

"So LET ME get this straight." Vivian grinned at Emily over her margarita, or, as the older ladies in The Book Biddies Book Club liked to call it, a cougarita. "After I saw you the other morning at the coffee shop, you thought you saw a guy who used to live with your family, except he disappeared one night, never to be heard from again."

"Correct." Emily was sitting on Maya's grandmother's living room carpet, leaning against the couch to support her aching back. It had been a long day.

It was Wednesday night, book club night, and she was enjoying a quick chat with the younger generation of Book Biddies, who also happened to be her friends and her colleagues at the Shelter Creek Wildlife Center. Maya ran the center, Vivian was the program director there, and Trisha was in charge of wildlife rehabilitation. Emily provided veterinary services and helped out however she could.

"So…" Vivian went on. "You hid behind your car and crawled along the sidewalk so you could check him out without him seeing you?"

"Yes." Emily grinned at the memory. "It was so ridiculous."

"And then what happened?" Maya scooted down onto the carpet from the couch to be closer to the conversation. "It *was* Wes, right? I heard a rumor he'd come back to town."

"I followed the guy to the feedstore, and yes, it was him. We talked for a couple minutes and he told me he was back in town, hopefully to stay. And that he'd become a veterinarian. That's when I just about had a nervous breakdown and I left." Emily reached for her plate of sweets. Thank goodness it was dessert night at book club. She had some serious emotional eating to do.

"Is he the guy you mentioned on the phone?" Annie Brooks was sitting in an armchair near the fireplace and must have overheard their conversation. "The one who was working with you at Fred Corrigan's when we spoke on Monday?"

"Yes, that was him." Emily chased a bite of Trisha's lemon cake with a sip of her ice water. No alcohol for her, in case she got an emergency call.

Maya regarded her thoughtfully while swallowing a bite of her chocolate chip cookie. "I thought you hated Wes Marlow."

"I don't hate him. I was angry and hurt for a long time. And of course I worried about him, too. But that was all so long ago." Emily tried to find words to explain, then gave up. "I'm not really sure what I feel about him anymore."

"You were so close in high school," Maya said. "When I think of you during those years, I picture Wes right there with you."

"We thought we were in love. We had all these plans to go to college together, and vet school together. Then we'd both work for my dad. I was so young and naive I totally believed it all."

"That must have hurt like the dickens when he left," Annie said.

Her old-fashioned language got Emily smiling. "Yes, it hurt like the dickens, for sure."

"I always suspected you had a broken heart in there somewhere," Maya said.

"What do you mean?" Emily looked at her friend. "You couldn't have known in high school, right? We kept it a secret."

"You *told* everyone you were just friends." Maya winked at her. "But that doesn't mean we couldn't all see how crazy you were about each other."

"What?" Trisha gaped down at Emily from her seat on the couch. "I had no idea you had such a romantic past."

"Well, it's not romantic anymore." Emily swirled the ice in her glass. "I'm just trying to figure out if I want to work with him."

"You definitely need someone to work with you," Maya said. "Though I'm biased, since if you get some help at your clinic, we can see you at the wildlife center more often."

"He seems like he's a good veterinarian," Emily said. "Plus, the truth is, if we don't work together, he'll probably set up his own practice and we'll end up competing against each other. That won't be fun. Especially because I'm sure a lot of ranchers would flock to him since he's a man."

"Flock. Ha," Annie said with her usual bone-dry humor. When her joke was met with silence, she sighed. "Flock? Flock of sheep? Ranchers? Oh, never mind."

"I get it, Annie," Trisha assured her. "Emily, I hate to agree with you, but I think you're right. You might lose some clients if he opens his own practice."

"Aha. So this is a case of keeping your enemies close," Vivian said.

"Except he's not my enemy." Emily shrugged. "The truth is, he's great with animals, especially horses. He's smart and funny and really seems to want us to get along and work together."

"He sounds like your perfect partner." Maya's grandmother, Lillian, their book club host for the evening, had been listening quietly from her seat near Annie. "Maybe it's best to let go of whatever happened in the past and work with him. You've been running yourself ragged these past couple years. Wouldn't it be great to share the practice with someone you trust?"

"But how can I trust him when he just walked away from my family without a word?" Emily set her glass on an end table close by. "I'm so confused."

"He made that choice a long time ago," Lillian said. "People change. You can't let old wounds hold you back, especially if you stand to gain from this situation."

"Think about it," Maya said. "You could have some free time to do whatever you want. More time to work with wildlife, or to hang out with us, or to take those cute animal portraits you're so good at… It could be great!"

"I know what the problem is." Monique, another book club member, had come closer to listen. She was leaning on the doorframe that separated the living room from the hallway. She was a hairdresser, and her locks were strawberry blond this week, curling elegantly around her shoulders. "The problem is that he's really handsome. A total hunk."

"How do you know that?" Vivian waved her hand as if to erase the question. "Never mind. You always know everything that goes on in this town."

"One of the perks of owning a salon," Monique said. "Plus, he's been jogging past my shop in the evenings with that pretty dog of his. I have to admit, I've been enjoying his flybys, so I asked around to find out who he was. Turns out I wasn't the only one who'd noticed the handsome new man in town. There are a few young ladies who have their eye on him." She smiled her Cheshire cat smile. "And a few older ones, too."

Jealousy oozed through Emily's veins and made her resent Wes all over again. She didn't want to be jealous. She didn't want to be anything but neutral when it came to him. She shoved the jealousy back into whatever dark corner of her brain it came from. "He can have them all. I just need a coworker I can count on to take over a bunch of my cases. I have no idea how my dad survived as the only vet around here all those years."

"A lot fewer people lived in Shelter Creek back then," Annie reminded her. "And there are a bunch of new ranches also. Vivian and Jace live on land that was abandoned for decades. Trisha and Liam's new place was just a hobby farm before they took it over. And now Jade's boyfriend, the one who was in the fire, has moved his sheep over to that ranch south of town. No wonder you're so busy, Emily."

"Speaking of ranchers, how did it go with Fred Corrigan?" Emily was ready to get the spotlight off herself and her dilemma with Wes.

"What happened to Fred?" Lillian asked. She and Annie were roughly the same age and had known, or tolerated, Fred for decades.

"Emily went out to vaccinate his heifers and found his ranch in total chaos," Annie said. "She called me and I went out there with some other folks to clean up and see what the problem was." She sighed. "The truth is, I think Fred needs to retire. His health isn't that great and his heart isn't really in his work anymore. I called his daughter, the one who has a goat dairy? I told her she better get up to see him and figure out what to do. In the meantime, I've got a few of my hands over there, working for him."

"How did you convince them to work for Fred?" Emily knew that no sane ranch hand would want to go from working with kind, competent Annie and her sweet husband, Juan, to dealing with grumpy Fred.

Annie leaned forward conspiratorially. "Do not tell a soul. Fred is paying them, but I'm still paying them, too."

Emily gasped. "That's so generous. Can you afford to do that?"

Annie shrugged. "When I married Juan we merged our ranches and our assets. We have more than enough. And Fred...well, what does he have? His wife has passed, his bad attitude scares everyone away... I can't bear to see his animals suffer as a result. But it's only temporary. Hopefully, his daughter will come to her senses and move her goats up to his property. Then she can combine her business with his and they'll be all set."

"Ladies, are we ever going to talk about the book?" Emily looked up to see another book club member, Kathy, standing behind Lillian. She'd been in the kitchen chatting with Eva and Priscilla, the other Book Biddies, who now filed into the living room, cougaritas in hand.

"Yes, we need to do that," Lillian said. "Otherwise we really might just have to officially change our name to The Booze Biddies. Now, did anyone read it?"

They talked about the novel for a while, and then, as the discussion wound down, and most of the women had gone to the kitchen to put their glasses in the sink, Maya leaned over to Emily. "Do you want to go to Dex's after this? Caleb is there playing pool with some of the guys."

"Yes, please come," Vivian added. "Trisha can't. She has to get home to take over watching Henry so Liam can go out with the boys. But we'd love to have you with us. Jade is going to meet us there with Aidan. It will be fun to catch up with her." Jade Carson was a local firefighter who'd been caught in a wildfire out on Aidan Bell's remote ranch. Now Aidan lived near Shelter Creek and the two of them were dating.

"I don't know," Emily said. "I have a lot of work tomorrow."

"But you need to get out." Maya put her hands together in a prayer-like gesture. "You need to blow off some steam and have some fun. Plus, it will take both of us to beat Vivian at pool. She's a shark."

Emily looked at her friend in surprise. "You are?"

Vivian grinned. "I'm full of deep secrets like that. Now, come on. We'll make you forget about Wes for a few hours. You need a break from your troubles."

It would be nice to go out, Emily realized. She almost never did. Sleep was precious when it was so often disturbed by an animal emergency. And playing pool might distract her from thinking about Wes. Though probably not. It was already Wednesday. On Friday she had to tell him if she was willing to extend his trial period for another month. Did she want to work with him for four more weeks? If she decided not to, could she keep going on her own without hitting a wall of exhaustion? There were still no responses to her job postings. Her mind was spinning from too many questions with no good answers.

"Okay," she said. "Let's go play some pool."

CHAPTER NINE

WES PUSHED HIS way out of the bar and hit the icon on his phone. "Jamie, is that you? How's it going in London?"

"Hey, bro. It's going pretty good. Did you make it out to that little town?"

"I made it." The last time they spoke, Wes had been at a park outside Phoenix, letting Rex stretch his legs.

"And how's the girl of your dreams?"

Wes jogged a few paces away from the entrance to the bar. The big gravel parking lot gave him some privacy as long as his cell signal held out. There was an oak tree off to one side of the lot and he headed toward it. "The girl, Emily, is all grown up and she's a veterinarian, too. She's letting me work with her on a trial basis."

His brother whistled low. "Sounds like your strange, small-town fantasy might be coming true."

Wes took the bait. "It's not strange to want to live in a pretty little town near the California coast. It sure has better weather than Texas."

"What are you doing right now?"

"I'm at a local bar with a few guys I knew in high school. We're playing some pool, having a couple beers." It was great to reconnect with Adam. The poor guy was going through a rough time, trying to figure out how to raise his two kids on his own. It was hard to believe he was a single dad. Adam had dated his ex-wife, Tanya, since high school and now, all these years later, their relationship had fallen apart. It made Wes wonder. If he'd stayed, and he and Emily had remained a couple, would they have lasted?

Then it hit him. If it was nine o'clock at night here, that meant it was five in the morning in London. "You're up early, bro. Is everything okay?"

Jamie was quiet for a beat too long. "Yeah, everything's fine. Just getting used to it, you know? Maybe I'm not quite on London time yet. I couldn't sleep."

Worry coiled in Wes's stomach. "How's the job? Have you gotten to know any of your coworkers yet? Maybe you could invite some of them out for a beer this weekend."

Jamie's laugh traveled the miles between them. "You never stop worrying about me, do you? The job is fine. My coworkers seem nice, and we hit the pub last night after work, so I'm ahead on the social game. I'm eating my vegetables, too, if that makes you feel any better."

Wes grinned. "It does, actually. I'm glad things are going okay." A couple of cars pulled into the lot and he heard women's voices chatting and car doors slamming. He watched from the shadows of his oak tree while they crossed the lot. One of the women was tall, with long wavy hair. Was that Emily?

He wished his stomach didn't do that flip. It wouldn't serve him well. He needed to maintain a professional relationship with her. He had to ignore the feelings he'd carried around for all these years and convince her that they could work together. If anything was meant to happen with her again, it would only happen once she trusted him and knew she could rely on him. After she respected the man and the veterinarian he'd become.

"You still there?"

He must have spaced out on Jamie. "Sorry, I got distracted for a minute."

"I should let you go back to your evening," his brother said. "I may as well get out for a run since I'm awake so early."

"But we'll talk soon." There was something in his brother's voice, a tired note, which had Wes a little worried. It was probably nothing. Maybe Jamie was just homesick. That was understandable considering he'd recently moved to a different country.

"Yeah. But tell me one thing before you go. Do you fit right into your small cow town? Does everyone wander around like you, wearing hats and boots and all that stuff?"

Wes laughed, picturing Jace and Caleb inside, playing pool, and wearing exactly that. "Some folks do, yeah."

"You really are out in the Wild West," Jamie said. Despite summers they'd spent living and working on dude ranches, Jamie had never bought into the Texas cowboy aesthetic.

"And I think you're already getting a British accent. Do I say cheerio before I hang up?"

"Please don't," Jamie pleaded. "I'll call you next week."

"Call anytime," Wes told him, wishing he could see his brother's face right now. Maybe it never went away, that feeling of needing to protect him.

Jamie hung up and Wes put his phone back in his pocket. Walking toward the bar, he glanced up at the sky, clear and crisp after rain this morning. There were so many stars without the lights of a big city to dim them. Wes pulled in a deep breath and sent a prayer up to those stars to watch over his brother.

Walking back into Dex's, the noise hit him instantly. The place was big, a lot more like a pool hall than a bar, and it had filled up with more people since he'd arrived an hour ago. Heading toward the pool tables in the back, he scanned the room for the tall woman he'd seen in the parking lot. He'd guessed right; it was Emily. She was sitting at the table with Jace and Adam, laughing at something Jace said. A dark-haired woman was sitting next to Jace, tucked up under his arm. That must be his wife, Vivian. Jace had told him earlier in the evening how he'd met her. Vivian had been studying the elk that had overrun Jace's ranch, and then had discovered an endangered salamander. She hadn't been Jace's favorite person in the beginning, that was for sure.

If they went from that rough start to the laughter Wes saw in their eyes when they smiled at each other, maybe there was a scrap of hope for him and Emily, too. Looking at her from across the room, he sure wanted there to be hope. Her long hair gleamed like tarnished gold in the light of the lamp that hung over the table. She was wearing a pretty lace top and fitted jeans tucked into brown cowboy boots. Her smile was wide and genuine and lit up some part of his heart he'd forgotten about over the years. Now he remembered. This was how it had felt when he fell for her the first time. Like there was no one in the room he wanted to see, no one else he could focus on but her.

A hand clapped him on his shoulder, startling him out of his daze. Caleb was grinning at him with a knowing smile. "You okay there, Wes?"

"I'm fine, yeah." Wes noticed the petite woman with long brown hair holding Caleb's hand. Maya Burton. Wes remembered her, serious and smart, from high school. Caleb and Maya had been a couple until senior year, right before Wes left town. There'd been a terrible accident then, with Maya driving and Caleb's sister killed. The accident had shaken the whole town up.

But somehow, here they were, together. Caleb had mentioned earlier in the evening that he and Maya were married, after many years spent apart after that accident.

Caleb turned to his wife. "Maya, do you remember Wes from high school?"

"I do. Nice to see you again." Her glance seemed to appraise him. "I hear you're working with Emily?"

"For the week. Hopefully longer if I don't mess up too badly."

"Was that your brother on the phone?" Caleb had been with him when Wes had taken the call.

"Yep. Calling from London."

"You have a brother?" Maya looked incredulous. "I never knew that."

"We were separated in the foster care system," Wes explained.

"Wes raised him," Caleb said. "He was telling us about it earlier this evening. That's why he left Shelter Creek so suddenly. To go take care of him."

Maya's brows rose. "I had no idea. Good for you."

"Thanks," Wes said. "He turned out okay."

Maya motioned toward another couple approaching them from the bar. "Wes, this is Aidan Bell and Jade Carson. Aidan has a ranch south of town."

Wes was tall, Caleb was tall, but Aidan was taller, with striking white-blond hair. He nodded down at Wes. "Great to meet you. Nice to have another veterinarian in town."

"Good to be here." Wes left it at that. He didn't want to keep explaining that he was on trial and possibly leaving soon.

"And Jade is a firefighter," Maya explained. "You might know her older brothers. Travis was just a year behind us in school."

The name sounded vaguely familiar but Wes couldn't place him. "Sorry, it was a long time ago."

"No worries," Jade said. "I remember you. I was a freshman. You were one of the cool seniors."

Wes smiled, just grateful she didn't say, *You were the foster boy who ran away.*

"Let's go see if we can find a seat." Caleb led the way to their table, holding Maya's hand the entire way. Wes followed them, an uneasy feeling in his stomach. Was he nervous? To see Emily? That didn't make much sense. They'd just spent the whole day working together.

Emily looked up when he got to the table. "Hi, Wes."

"I didn't know you'd be here tonight." He slid into the chair next to hers and immediately felt like he belonged there.

"I didn't, either, until just a few minutes ago. I blame Maya and Vivian here, for keeping me out way past my bedtime."

Jace introduced Vivian, who smiled at him kindly. "Welcome back to Shelter Creek."

"It's good to be back." He glanced at Emily. "I hope this isn't too much time spent with your employee."

"It's fine. Plus, you're not really an employee. You're…" She faltered as if she couldn't find a word for him.

He offered her a few choices. "Useful? Essential? Helpful? Life-altering?"

She grinned at his teasing. "You're Wes," she said. "Just Wes."

Whatever that meant.

It was strange to be with her in a social

setting. Luckily, Adam was there, too, so he and Emily weren't the only ones not coupled up. And then a guy named Liam showed up. He was married to Trisha, whom Wes had met at the vet clinic on his first day. Turned out Liam had grown up on a ranch outside Houston, so they had plenty to talk about. It felt good to hear a true Texas accent again.

Eventually, Wes noticed that Emily wasn't drinking. "Can I buy you a beer?"

She eyed his barely touched bottle with longing but shook her head. "I don't drink much. I have to be able to drive if I get a call later tonight."

"I'll be your driver if that happens," he offered. "I'm not much of a drinker, either. I've only had a few sips all night." He'd never had the time or luxury to develop much of a taste for alcohol.

"Are you sure?" Emily glanced at the bar. "I sure would love a cider. It's been a long time since I had one."

"I'll get it for you." Wes stood and when she looked like she might protest he added, "Not a bribe. You can still fire me guilt-free at any moment."

Her smile wrapped him in the warmth of

their inside joke. Wes headed for the bar with his head high.

Even though they weren't there as a couple, Wes felt like it when he returned to the table with Emily's drink. While she sipped her cider, they chatted with Liam about Texas and his new ranch here in Shelter Creek. When Caleb and Maya challenged them to a game of pool Liam declined, so they decided to play in teams. It was Wes and Emily against Caleb and Maya.

"You know we're in trouble," Maya told Caleb as she picked up a pool cue. "These two are medically trained. They sew animals up. They give shots. They're very coordinated."

"Yeah, but they weren't in the Marines," Caleb reminded her. "I have good aim."

"Where does that leave me?" Maya said, eyeing the table.

"You're tough. You never give up," Caleb said, and kissed her on the top of the head.

Emily racked the balls. "Who wants to start?"

"Wes should break. He's new in town," Caleb said.

"Go Texas," Liam called from where he was leaning against a wall to watch the game.

Wes wasn't sure he should be representing Texas here. He hadn't played much pool. His life hadn't really involved a lot of leisure time. More like work and more work to make sure he and Jamie could get the education they wanted. He lined up his cue and thankfully managed to scatter the balls and get a striped one in the side pocket. Emily gave him a smile that made him feel way more capable at this game than he really was.

They played for ten minutes, pretty evenly matched, but somehow Wes and Emily pulled ahead. Wes couldn't remember a better night out. Every time they sank a ball, he and Emily high-fived. She was laughing, her cheeks flushed. Her eyes sparkled when she looked at him. She was different from the serious, hardworking daytime Emily, and Wes liked seeing this side of her. Especially when he called the corner pocket, sank the eight ball into it, and she flung her arms around him for a quick hug.

It was all he could do to keep it casual, to return the brief embrace and act like it meant nothing, that they were just two colleagues having a fun night out. In reality it meant everything. It wasn't just that she was a beautiful woman, it was that she was *Emily.* His hope, his dream. She was smart and brave and funny and he wanted this. Nights like this, hanging out with friends, with other couples, and with newly divorced Adam who was leaving now because he had to go relieve the babysitter.

But he couldn't have it just because he wanted it. Wes still had so much to prove to her. As the game ended, he busied himself putting their cues away, joking with Caleb and Maya. No way could he let on that this night meant anything more to him than a casual gathering of friends. If he scared Emily off, he'd lose everything he wanted.

Back at the table, she picked up her purse. "That was really fun, but I have to get home. Knowing my luck, I'll get an early-morning call."

Wes's protective instinct kicked in. She wasn't used to drinking and she'd had a lot of cider. "Let me drive you."

"I live pretty close by. I can walk."

"It's February. It's cold out there."

She shoved her arms into her black wool coat and rolled her eyes. "It's almost March and I have a coat."

Wes couldn't keep from teasing her. "Stubborn, much?"

"Fine," she huffed. "You can drive me. All five blocks."

They said good-night to everyone and walked out into the night air. It was just after ten but it felt later to Wes. They'd had a busy day and he wasn't much of a night owl.

"This night is beautiful," Emily said. She raised her arms to the stars as if she were trying to touch them. "It's not *that* cold. How about you walk me home, instead of driving me."

A walk under the stars with Emily? "Sure."

They strolled down the sidewalk, side by side.

"Where's Rex tonight?"

"Home with his toys, watching *Animal Planet*."

She laughed. "I wish I could see that."

"You're welcome to come by and visit him anytime. I think he likes you."

She was silent and Wes cursed himself for stepping across a boundary he should have seen. She didn't want to come by his house. She hadn't wanted him to come back into her life when she'd first seen him less than a week ago.

"Thanks for letting him hang out at work."

She glanced his way. "I'm impressed. He's so well-behaved. Even when we go out to a ranch or stable."

"He's been going out on calls with me since he was a puppy. He knows the ropes."

They seemed to be walking farther out of town. The streetlights had ended and the only light was from the stars arched over the open field around them. "Where do you live, exactly?"

"Having second thoughts about walking me? See, I knew it would sober you up." Emily gestured around them. "I like the peace and quiet out here. I rent an old farmhouse right at the edge of town. It's got a few pastures and a barn. One of these days, when I have some time, I'm going to get a horse or two. That's why I rented it."

"How long have you lived there?"

"About five years."

"You rented a place for horses five years ago and you still haven't gotten a horse?"

She shrugged. "You've seen my work schedule. Plus, I got involved with the wildlife center. I help Maya bring injured animals in for care, I'm involved in their rehabilitation plans and their release… That on top of my regular work keeps me very busy."

Wes was silent, thinking about it. They'd both kept themselves busy all these years. He out of necessity, she out of choice.

"What was it like?" Emily put a gentle hand on his forearm for a brief instant. "All those years raising your brother. Were you lonely? How did you get by?"

He was silent, unprepared for the shift in topic, not sure how much he wanted to say.

"I don't mean to pry. You don't have to answer if you don't want."

"No, I want to. It's just a lot of years, you know?" Wes tried to think about how to sum up so much time. "At first it was really scary. We got to Houston and had nowhere to stay, we didn't know a soul and we had to stay under the radar. I was so worried someone would take Jamie from me and send him back to our uncle."

"That must have been terrible."

"I was pretty stressed. But I found work at restaurants. A lot of those businesses don't ask questions as long as you're willing to do the dishes and clean the restrooms. Once I was able to earn some money, some of the panic went away. But it was touch and go for a long time, figuring out how to pay the bills, and how to make sure no one caught on that I didn't have true legal custody of Jamie. It was such a relief when he turned eighteen and we realized we'd made it."

"I can't imagine," Emily said. "What a journey. You must be really proud of what you've accomplished."

"Sometimes," he admitted. "But mostly I'm just glad to have those days behind me."

They'd reached a driveway with a well-lit house at the end of it. "This is where I live," Emily said.

As they walked down the driveway, Wes studied the house. In the porch light he could tell that it was a simple box shape, with a peaked roof and old-fashioned, paned windows. "It's funny, but all these years, I pictured you living with your parents."

"Are you kidding? I'm thirty-two years old. That would be weird. This way I can visit them and keep an eye on them, but I get my own space."

"Keep an eye on them? Is everything okay?"

"My dad had a heart attack last year. He's doing well now, but I like to get over there and help out whenever they decide to take on some big project around the house."

They'd reached her porch steps. Wes looked at her in admiration. "So you run the vet clinic, you're the veterinarian for the wildlife shelter and you take care of your parents. Do you ever have a day off, just for you?"

"I had tonight off," she countered. "And it was fun. I'm glad we ran into each other." She went on tiptoe and kissed him softly on the cheek. "Thanks for walking me home, Wes."

His hand went to the spot she'd kissed him, almost unable to believe it had happened. "My pleasure. See you tomorrow."

Wes watched her jog up the steps and open her front door. When she waved goodnight and disappeared inside, he started back to the bar, resenting the night air for cooling the spot where she'd kissed him. A spot touched by hope and possibility. Emily wasn't the same Emily he'd left. There was so much more he wanted to know about her. But now he knew what her warm kiss felt like on a cold night. And he knew that no kiss had ever meant so much, or felt so good.

CHAPTER TEN

EMILY LIFTED HER head from her pillow and flopped back down again with a thud. She tried again. *Thud.* Her alarm was buzzing, so she groped for the nightstand and managed to find her phone without lifting her head to look. She hit the button to snooze it and sank back into the silence.

Why was she so tired? Images from the night before percolated through her mind. She'd had a glass of cider at the bar, and she rarely drank. It had been fun but she hadn't felt safe driving, so she'd walked home with Wes. He'd been funny and sweet and he'd told her a bit about what he'd been through. And then she'd kissed him.

Emily sat bolt upright in bed. She *kissed* him? Images flooded back, of his face shadowy in the dim porch light, the bristly feeling of the stubble on his jaw brushing her skin before her lips made contact with his cheek.

What was she thinking? The man was technically her employee. He was auditioning for a job with her and she'd *kissed* him?

Heart thumping in her chest, Emily shoved the covers off and ran for the bathroom, splashing cold water on her face and pulling her hair back in a ponytail. It was getting late, she had to get to the clinic, but she had to talk to Wes first. In moments she was dressed. Grabbing her car keys and an apple from the bowl on her kitchen counter, she set off down the road to collect her truck from Dex's parking lot. It wasn't until she was in her truck, driving into town, that she remembered. She had no idea where Wes lived. She must have his address at the clinic but she didn't have it with her now.

Emily pulled over to the side of the road, put her forehead to the steering wheel and closed her eyes. It wasn't just that she'd kissed Wes. It was just a kiss on the cheek, after all. Nothing too offensive. No, the worst part was that after she'd kissed him, she'd wanted to kiss him some more. Was she really such a fool? This man had walked away from her and never looked back. Never made any effort to reach out and let her know he was okay.

She'd kept her heart locked away ever since, and now, just because he'd come back into town, she was going to risk him shattering it one more time? What was wrong with her?

All this time she'd imagined that Wes's leaving had made her tough, strong, immune to falling head over heels for any man. He'd been back in Shelter Creek for less than a week and he'd proved her wrong.

She couldn't be this weak. She had to get stronger. When people wanted strength, they worked out, or practiced a sport, and their muscles grew. She just needed to practice being immune to Wes. If she worked at it every day, pretty soon it would be second nature.

She'd have to wait to talk to him at the clinic. But since she was out of the house and it was still early, she'd get some coffee at the café and maybe something sweet to nibble on, as well. Though it was going to take more than caffeine and sugar to fix the mess she'd made last night.

By the time Emily got to the clinic, Wes's truck was already there. He'd been making a point to arrive well before eight, as if to show her how seriously he took the job. He'd be the absolute perfect employee if he wasn't Wes.

Taking a gulp of her coffee to bolster her courage, Emily climbed out of the truck and went inside. Lily was already at her desk and Emily tried to mimic the bright greeting her receptionist offered. She read the messages Lily handed her, but nothing sank in. She was useless. She wouldn't be able to think about work until she talked with Wes.

She found him in the back, going over the files of the clients scheduled for today. He glanced up at her as she walked in. "One of the Hendersons' sheep had quadruplets last year? Is that the sheep we're seeing today?"

"Good morning to you, too," Emily said. "And yes, that's the ewe we're checking on at eleven." She eyed Wes warily. He didn't seem upset about the kiss. That was good, but she still had to make things right.

Rex sat up from his favorite spot in the corner and wagged his tail. Emily went to say hello, shaking his paw and running her hands over his fluffy ears. "You ready to go, big guy?" she asked the dog. "We've got a lot of clients this morning."

Molly, her head technician, was working

today and she emerged from one of the exam rooms. "Wes, the early bird, has most of those files memorized, I think."

"Good morning, Molly." Emily glanced at Wes. So he'd charmed Molly, too. Lily had already made a point of pulling Emily aside yesterday to tell her how much she liked him. "Are you okay holding down the fort until we get back here after lunch?"

"No problem," Molly said. "I just have a few nail trims coming in, a flea inspection, stuff like that. Dan will be here in an hour to help me out."

"Great. Call me on my cell phone if you need anything. Wes, want to bring those files?"

Wes loaded them into the portable file box and whistled for Rex. Emily followed him out the back door and around the building to the parking area. Before he opened the door to the truck, she put a hand on his arm to stop him. "Can we talk for a moment?"

"Of course." He motioned for Rex to go explore and the dog obliged, skirting the parking lot to mark it as his personal territory. "What's up?"

Emily launched into the speech she'd prepared while she drove here. "Last night I made a mistake. I'm so sorry. I should never have kissed you. That was a terrible choice on my part. I promise it won't ever happen again."

"Ever?"

Was it her imagination, or did he look a little disappointed? "You work for me. It is completely inappropriate. I didn't even ask your permission. I feel awful."

"I don't." He was smiling and that sparkle in his eyes… Was he laughing at her? "I liked the kiss."

"Okay, good. I'm glad." Wait…he'd liked it? For a moment she forgot what she needed to say as the memory of his warm cheek under her cool lips resurfaced. *Nope*. She could not go there. "I'm very relieved that you're not upset. I can promise you that I will keep things strictly professional from now on."

"No more kissing?" Wes shrugged. "Okay. If you say so."

"Great. We're clear, then." This had been easier than she thought. Thank goodness. "I'm truly sorry. I think it was the cider. I'm not a big drinker."

He leaned back against the truck and folded

his arms. "Are you sure that was the only reason?"

"Of course." Emily couldn't quite meet his gaze, so she looked at his shoulder. He was wearing a plaid flannel shirt with a mix of blue and beige. Why *had* she kissed him? Because the stars were out and she was tipsy and he was being sweet and funny? Or because he was Wes and kissing him felt as natural as a sunrise or the starlight or the crickets calling in the fields around her house.

"Do you normally kiss people after you've had a drink?" He was smiling now, that teasing glimmer in his eyes.

"No!" She cast around for a reason. Any reason that didn't have to do with the way she'd felt drawn to him, or how much she'd wanted to kiss him again. "I think I got caught up in what you were telling me. About caring for your brother. About all the hardships you've endured. I'm so sorry you went through all that."

His smile faded and the spark in his eyes went out. "That's not necessary. I don't want pity, Emily."

"I wasn't pitying you, I just felt..." She

trailed off. The way she'd explained herself...
it did sound like pity.

"We're not all born in a perfect town, to
perfect parents, with the family business
waiting for us when we grow up," Wes said.

Emily took a step back. "You say that like
it's a bad thing."

"It's not bad. But don't feel sorry for me
because I had to make my own way. That
doesn't make me someone you should pity. If
anything, it should be something to admire.
But how would you know? You've had everything handed to you."

What did he know about how easy or how
difficult she'd had things? "That's not fair,
Wes. Nothing has been handed to me. I've
worked hard for everything I have. I work too
much. You've said that yourself."

"That's a choice you make. When you live
like I did for so many years, you don't have
that choice."

"Wait, so you don't want me to pity you,
but now you're bringing up your hard life to
make me feel bad about mine?" Emily put
up her hands to stop the mess she'd made.
"It doesn't matter why I kissed you. All that
matters is that it won't ever happen again."

She pulled her keys out of her coat pocket and unlocked the truck. "If you still want to work with me, we'd better get started."

Wes called Rex, who jumped into the back seat of the cab. As they drove out of the parking lot, Emily stole a glance at Wes. He was looking away from her, out at the misty morning. She'd blown that conversation. If she was going to work with another veterinarian, she'd better work on her people skills. Though Wes hadn't exactly helped them have a smooth chat.

It didn't matter. There would be no more kisses. From here on out their relationship was strictly professional. And if that thought caused a pang of regret, well, she was used to feeling regret when it came to Wes Marlow.

EMILY WAS QUIET on the drive to their first client and Wes didn't try to make small talk. Out his window, the coastal fog was clearing, revealing faint patches of blue sky. A seasonal creek rushed down through the winter-green hills. Those sights would usually bring comfort. But not even the three horses galloping along the hillside could sweeten his sour mood.

When Emily kissed him last night, he'd

taken it as a message that maybe what he'd suspected all these years was true. They were meant to be more than each other's first love. He'd thought of that kiss as he fell asleep last night, and again upon waking up this morning. It had felt like hope.

But now he knew what that kiss had been about. She pitied him for what he'd gone through. He wanted those hardscrabble years where he'd kept himself and Jamie afloat to be a source of pride, not pity. He wanted that kiss to be about the future, not just a reflection on his sorry past.

But it wasn't just the pity that got to him. Emily had thrown a mirror up into his face and he didn't like what looked back at him. Ego. He had to admit the truth to himself. He'd come back here not just because he loved the town and the picturesque landscape, but because he'd wanted to present Emily with this new successful version of himself. He wanted her to fall in love with the man he'd become. Returning here had been all about how *he* felt, and what he needed. He hadn't stopped to think about what Emily might need.

Maybe what she needed was for him to

back way off. He'd shown up, begged for a job, and she'd graciously given him a chance. Then she'd kissed him and he wanted more. But he couldn't bend her to fit this dream he'd carried all these years. He couldn't show up here and demand that she welcome him. What she needed was someone to help with her work. She didn't need him to make her busy life more complicated.

Rex leaned forward from the back seat and nuzzled his arm. Wes rubbed his ears. His dog was way too perceptive.

His pride had made him lash out at her just now. That shamed him more than her pity. It wasn't her fault she was born to the loving, supportive family she had. Just like it wasn't his fault that his parents had gotten so sucked into drugs they forgot they even had kids.

"We're here," Emily said as she turned the truck up a gravel drive. Wes could see the ranch house in the distance, perched on a flat saddle between two hills.

"Nice piece of property this guy has out here."

"His name is Bobby Tillman and he's quite a character. He loves those Renaissance fairs where everyone dresses up in costumes. He's a good man…just a little different." Emily glanced at him over Rex's furry ears. "We'll be okay, right? We can be professional with each other?"

"Of course." That she even had to ask annoyed him. He'd really blown it. "I'm sorry, Emily. I got defensive. I said things back there that were plain unkind."

Emily sighed. "We both messed up, I guess. Let's just try to do better going forward." She parked the truck near a weathered barn. The red paint had worn off in places but the yard around it was neat as a pin.

A man came out of the barn. His long gray hair hung in a ponytail down his back. He waved to Emily and called out. "Welcome, fair veterinarian."

Wes glanced at Emily, who shrugged and whispered, "I told you he was a character."

Wes put Rex on a leash and they walked toward the barn.

"And who is this fine beast and the young man he has on his leash?" Bobby held out his hand and Rex sniffed politely.

"This is Wes. He's working with me this week. And this is his dog, Rex. Do you mind if Rex joins us?"

"If he's well behaved, he's welcome." Bobby smiled warmly at Wes. "You're a lucky man, apprenticing with the best."

Apprenticing? Wes glanced at Emily, but she didn't correct him. Fine. He could be an apprentice. He sure felt like one when it came to dealing with his feelings about her.

"Good to see you again, Bobby," Emily said. "Let's take a look at that cow you were concerned about."

"I'm pretty sure it's mastitis. Her udder is swollen on one side." Bobby led the way into the barn, where a big black-and-white Holstein cow was standing in a bed of thick, clean straw. Emily knelt to look at the udder. "That looks painful. She needs an antibiotic to start."

"I can get it." Wes went back to the truck. When he returned with the medicine, Bobby was telling Emily about a Shakespeare play at the community theater in Shelter Creek.

"Ah, fine apprentice. You've brought the elixir."

Wes grinned. "Something like that."

Emily administered the medication and turned to Bobby. "If this doesn't have her up and moving and a lot more comfortable by first thing tomorrow, call me right away. There are a lot of ways to treat mastitis, and if it's really taken hold we'll have to try some other steps."

"Will do, fair Emily, will do. Thanks for getting out here on short notice."

"Of course. Can't let this pretty girl suffer."

Bobby cleared his throat. "I hate to trouble you with anything else, but do you have a minute to look at a horse?"

Emily's brows went up in surprise. "A horse? I didn't know you kept horses."

"I don't. But I found one on the road early this morning. It's in pretty sorry shape. I suspect someone dropped it out here to be rid of it."

"Oh, no." Emily frowned. "Let's take a look."

Wes grimaced. This was a part of his job that never stopped hurting. Abuse and neglect were always tough to face. He put a hand to Emily's arm. "Are you all right with this?"

The look on her face had him instantly regretting his protective gesture. "Of course I am."

They followed Bobby around the side of the barn to a corral built along the back of the building. Standing inside, its head buried in a pile of oat hay, was the sorriest horse Wes had seen in a long time. It was a paint horse and it must have been beautiful once. Chestnut and white splotches covered its starved body. Ribs, hips, spine, every possible bone was protruding out from its gaunt frame. It looked up from the pile of hay and regarded them with startling blue eyes. Normally they'd be gorgeous, but on such a mistreated animal the pale eyes added an eerie touch.

"It's a mare," Emily said. "The poor thing. Good choice, Bobby, to just offer oat hay."

"I figured it isn't much used to eating, so I'd better avoid anything too rich."

"Exactly." Emily opened the gate and stepped into the pen, motioning for Wes to follow. "Come with me." Then she turned to Bobby. "Wes has a real talent with horses. They love him."

Wes tied Rex's leash to a post by the barn and the big dog flopped down in the dust for his first nap of the day. Wes stepped inside the corral. The horse's head instantly came up high, and its ears went flat back. "Hang on." He put a hand to Emily's arm. "I'm not sure I'm the person for this. She might be afraid of men." He turned to Bobby. "How'd you get her in here?"

"I just walked behind her. She didn't want anything to do with me, so she went right up the driveway. Once she saw the hay, she was happy to go into the corral."

"She may not even be used to people," Wes said. "If you want to approach her, Emily, be careful."

Emily nodded and Wes left to go stand with Bobby outside the corral. Once he was gone, the mare's head came down and her ears tilted forward a bit. She looked at Emily with more curiosity than fear. Emily held out her hand and the horse backed away.

"Turn your back to her," Wes advised. "Look like you're doing something else. If there's a problem with her, I'll yell *run* and you hightail it for the fence."

Emily looked at him with doubtful eyes. "You're sure?"

"It's what I would do. She needs to know that you aren't going to come at her. Or demand anything from her."

"Okay. If you say so." Emily turned her shoulder away from the horse. The mare backed away a few paces, but her ears were forward now. She was still frightened, but she wanted to find out more about Emily.

"Just stay there and let her come to you. I think she's interested." Wes kept his voice quiet. Just loud enough for Emily to hear.

Bobby had his hands together as if he were meditating, or saying a prayer. He was a character, but he actually had the right idea. This horse needed to feel some peaceful energy right now.

The mare took a step toward Emily and blew out a loud, stressed breath. But her ears stayed forward and she took another step. Then another.

"Almost there," Wes murmured.

Emily's face was lit with nervous excitement, a half smile tilting her mouth as she looked at Wes. "It's so tempting to turn around."

"Be patient. If you can get her trust, we can help her. And boy, does she need help."

Just then the mare reached out as far as she could without committing to taking a step closer to Emily. Her nose made it to Emily's hair. Her breath loud, she snuffled Emily's shoulder, then her ear. Emily stood as still as a statue, her eyes on Wes.

"This is going really well," Wes said. "Let her sniff you for a few more moments and then turn around very slowly."

Emily waited for a few more nuzzles, then carefully turned around. The mare snuffed at Emily's chest, her arm and her cheek, then seemed to decide that her visitor was okay. She put her head down and took another mouthful of hay.

"Put a hand slowly onto her shoulder." Wes's heart was growing in his chest. This was the magic, watching trust bloom where none had been before.

Emily reached out a tentative hand and placed it on the mare's shoulder and left it there while the poor animal continued eating.

"Good job." It had worked. Wes breathed a sigh of relief. "I think you've got some horse whisperer inside of you, too."

"Amen," Bobby murmured.

CHAPTER ELEVEN

UNDER THE MARE'S hide was a tiny bit of muscle and a whole lot of bone. Emily tried to keep the tears in her eyes from spilling over. She was a vet, she should be able to keep her emotions in check. But something about this horse, the level of mistreatment it had endured, the starvation… She swallowed hard. She couldn't fall apart right now. This animal needed her, perhaps more than any creature she'd ever met.

"Easy, girl." Emily ran her hand over the mare's withers, then slowly down to the top of her foreleg. An old scar marred the chestnut hair there—perhaps a barbed wire cut that, without proper treatment, had healed badly.

The horse lifted her head and Emily took a step back to give her some room. She held out her hand, knuckles curled, and waited. The mare cautiously nuzzled her hand and Emily studied her face. It was mostly white, the chestnut reserved for her cheeks and forelock. Both her eyes were blue, the pale mottled skin around them vulnerable to sun damage. "Can you see okay, with that fancy face?" Slowly Emily knelt and picked up a fist full of hay. Stepping back from the horse, she raised it slowly, lowered it, moved it left and then to the right. The mare's eyes followed the hay.

"You can see up close, at least." She offered the hay and the mare reached out with her lips to delicately remove the oats at the end, giving Emily a peek at her teeth. "You're not very old, are you?"

She circled the mare carefully, looking for cuts and other injuries, but didn't see any. Her hooves were unshod and had grown long. She'd need a hoof trim as soon as possible. Though when would that be? She seemed half wild. Someone needed to gentle her.

Emily let herself out of the gate and walked over to where Wes and Bobby were waiting. "She's beautiful. She looks to be about six or seven years old, maybe? But why would someone treat her this way?"

"Could be anything," Bobby said. "Maybe someone couldn't care for her anymore."

"Her mane and tail are matted and there are ticks on her belly and legs." Emily said. "We need to get those off, but there is no way she's going to let us do that right now." Her mind was racing ahead. If they could fatten the mare up for a few days and make sure she was healthy enough, maybe they could sedate her. Then they could take care of the ticks, her hooves, and anything else she needed.

"She likes you, Emily," Bobby said. "Given some time, she'll probably let you help her out."

Wes was watching the horse through the fence. He turned to Bobby with a thoughtful expression. "I know you don't keep horses, but do you have any other animals around here that might be able to bunk with her? Horses are herd animals and this one has been alone too long. Another animal might show her that she's safe now."

Bobby tapped restless fingers on his denim-clad thigh. "I don't have ponies or donkeys or anything like that. But we could try Rosalind and Beatrice."

"Who?" Wes glanced at Emily, a brow raised. But she didn't know who Rosalind and Beatrice were, either.

"My retired ewes," Bobby said. "Their lambing days are behind them. They just lie around and eat, and produce some nice wool in the spring."

"Those are some pretty grand names for sheep," Emily said.

"Oh, I don't know about that. Sheep have all kinds of dignity when you get to know them. Besides, I name all my sheep after Shakespeare's characters."

Of course he did. If Bobby found a time machine, he'd set the dial for bygone times without a second thought.

"Let me go get them. Hang on." Bobby jogged to an old green truck parked nearby. He jumped in, got the engine sputtering to life and drove off down a dirt track leading east. Soon he was out of sight.

"You weren't joking when you said he was a character," Wes murmured.

"He's a really special guy. He does amateur theater, he raises sheep, he goes to Renaissance fairs and speaks like someone from back then, too. Shelter Creek has its fair share of interesting folks, but Bobby is one of the nicest, and the oddest, for sure."

They walked over to the fence to observe

the mare. "You should take her," Wes said. "She wants to be your horse."

Emily stared at him. "Did she whisper that to you?"

He laughed softly. "No, I could just tell from her body language around you. She feels safe with you. That's the most important thing for her right now, to feel safe."

"I can't have a horse, Wes. I work all the time."

He nudged her gently on the arm with his elbow. "Hire me, and you'll have a lot more free time. And you need it. No one should work as much as you do."

He had a point. If she asked him to stay another month, she could get him settled into the routines of her practice. He was certainly capable of taking cases on his own and she could actually do something besides work. The thought was a little unsettling. She'd done nothing but work for so long that she wasn't quite sure who she was without it.

"When I dreamed of getting a horse I didn't imagine one that was such a fixer-upper."

The mare seemed to understand her words. She put her head up, oat hay hanging out of the side of her mouth, with the most indignant expression on her face. Then she walked a few steps toward the fence and stuck her nose through the slats to poke at the hand Emily had placed there.

Wes laughed softly. "See? She chooses you."

Emily reached out and stroked the mare's soft, mottled nose. Her pale eyelashes dipped over the bright blue of her eyes. "You and that fancy face of yours. You're a charmer, aren't you?"

"I think you have a name for her, too." Wes smiled when she glanced at him. "Fancy Face. Fancy for short."

Emily smiled. "It does seem to fit her. Hi, Fancy. Do you like that name?"

The mare tossed her head, turned and went back to her hay pile.

"She probably feels like if she lets that food out of her sight for long, it will disappear," Wes said.

The sound of an engine reached them and they turned to see the green truck puttering their way. Bobby parked, hopped out and gestured to the back. "Rosalind and Beatrice, at your service."

Two ewes looked at them balefully from their thick bed of straw in the back of the

truck. One had a white face. Bobby introduced her as Beatrice. The other, Rosalind,
had a black face.

"You're right," Emily said. "These two look
quite dignified."

"They might be just what Fancy needs,"
Wes said.

"Fancy?" Bobby looked puzzled.

"We named her while you were gone,"
Emily said. "I hope that's okay."

He shrugged. "Personally, I was leaning
toward Ophelia. But Fancy will do. It's not
Shakespeare, but it's a good horse name." He
smiled. "Besides, I have a feeling this is your
horse, fair Emily."

"That's what I just told her," Wes said.
"And I'm pretty sure Fancy agrees."

"I don't have time for a horse," Emily repeated her earlier protest.

"Let your apprentice here take on a little
more responsibility," Bobby said. "I'm not
sure I've met anyone who works as hard as
you. As the Bard said, 'Like as the waves
make toward the pebbled shore, so do our
minutes hasten to their end.'"

"That's kind of depressing," Emily told him.

"Nay, it is simply a reminder that time is

passing. Don't put off the things you dream of for too long." Bobby smiled at her, kindness creasing extra lines around his eyes.

"I'll think about it," Emily said. "I will. But it's a big responsibility. Fancy deserves someone who can help her heal."

Wes and Bobby exchanged a glance that Emily chose to ignore. She couldn't take on a horse right now. She'd already taken on Wes. "Let's try her with these sheep. But I think we should put out a separate pile of hay for them, well away from Fancy. Wes pointed out that she might be worried about the availability of food."

"Good idea, apprentice. Come with me to get some hay?"

"Sure." Wes grimaced at Emily as he walked by and mouthed, *Apprentice?*

She shrugged and laughed quietly. Bobby was good for tough, serious Wes. He should learn to laugh at himself more often.

Once hay was piled on the other side of the corral from Fancy, Bobby let the sheep in. They went straight to their hay and started munching, totally incurious about the horse in the pen. Fancy was interested in them, however. She left her meal and walked toward them. For a moment Emily thought there might be trouble, but the mare just snuffed at the ewes and settled down to share their hay.

"Look at her ears," Wes said quietly. "They're floppy and relaxed. She's glad to have some company."

"I'm glad Beatrice and Rosalind can be a comfort," Bobby said.

"Can you keep Fancy for a few days?" Emily glanced at her watch. "We have to get going, but we'll come back and see how she's doing. Maybe tomorrow she'll be comfortable enough for us to get those ticks off her."

"I'll keep an eye on her, and make sure she and the gals are treating each other well. Farewell until tomorrow, fair Emily and Apprentice Wes."

Back in the truck, Wes turned to her. "Why is he calling me your apprentice?"

Emily laughed. "I have no idea. I guess he thinks you're learning from me. Though when it comes to horses, I think I'm more of the apprentice."

"You have a great touch with horses," Wes said. "Don't sell yourself short."

Moments like these, when Wes said kind things that warmed her from the inside out, made it hard to maintain the professional distance Emily had promised them both this morning. But she had to. Staying neutral with Wes was a muscle, she reminded herself. She just had to keep flexing it. Practice makes perfect. She nodded in response to his compliment and started driving. Just move along, nothing to see here. She wasn't going to get personal with the handsome vet riding next to her.

As they neared the main road, Emily's cell phone rang. She slowed to a stop and answered. It was Maya. "Hey, what's going on?" She glanced at Wes and mouthed, *Sorry.*

"What's your schedule like today? Is there anything that can be moved?"

"We have a few routine vaccinations coming up. I can move them if we have to."

"I hate to do this to you." Maya's tone was apologetic, but Emily knew her well enough to hear the excitement there, too. "Apparently there's an injured bald eagle out at Long Valley Preserve. I don't know much else about it. Someone saw it flopping around in one of the ponds. Want to help me catch it? Vivian's not feeling well and Trisha is too pregnant."

Emily glanced at Wes. "Want to catch a bald eagle?"

"What?" He looked alarmed, then shrugged. "Um…sure?"

"Okay, Maya, we're in. Let me call Lily and have her reschedule our next two clients. We'll meet you at the parking area in Long Valley."

"See you soon." Maya hung up.

Emily called Lily to let her know about the change of plans. Then she turned to Wes. "So, this is the part of the job you haven't seen yet. And it doesn't have to be your responsibility at all, if you don't want. When we find injured wildlife, I usually reschedule clients so I can help out."

"And your clients don't mind?"

"People in Shelter Creek are pretty aware of what it takes to preserve wildlife, thanks to Maya's work with the wildlife center. They don't mind, though sometimes it can get tricky if we have a wildlife situation and a domestic animal emergency at the same time."

"You mean you haven't learned to clone yourself yet?"

Emily laughed. "Not yet." Then she started up the truck again and turned right at the main road instead of left. "Come on, Apprentice Wes. I'll teach you how to treat an injured eagle."

CHAPTER TWELVE

LONG VALLEY WAS west of Shelter Creek, just off the road that led out to the coast. It was surrounded by steep green hillsides. Getting out of Emily's truck, Wes could see a board-walk, which led out into the valley and kept visitors above a series of meadows with a stream that meandered between a couple of ponds. "I don't remember this from when I lived here before."

"It was private property then," Emily said, rummaging behind the driver's seat. She pulled out an old blanket. "Jace Hendricks bought this land when he moved here."

"This is where Vivian found the salamanders?" Wes grinned. "He told me about that. Not a great way to start a relationship."

Emily laughed. "I didn't know Vivian as well back then, but I hear it was pretty much fireworks between them at the beginning. They're happy now, though."

"I guess we don't all get things right at the beginning of a relationship," Wes said, reaching into the cab to scratch Rex's ears.

If Emily heard him, she didn't let on. "This valley is also an important fall sanctuary for tule elk. It's their only water source at that time of year. And apparently bald eagles live here, too, which I never realized until Maya called just now."

"So what do we do if we find this eagle?"

Emily reached across to the glove compartment and opened it to reveal a pair of binoculars. She took them out and draped the strap around her neck. "We're going to observe it and try to figure out what's wrong. If we need to bring it in, we'll try to use this blanket to subdue it. I'm sure Maya will bring a crate in case she has to bring it into the wildlife center." She grinned at him. "Have you ever held a chicken?"

"I spent a lot of time working on ranches. I know my chickens."

"When did you work on ranches?"

"In the summers. Our neighborhood in Houston wasn't very safe. I didn't want Jamie running around in the streets getting in trouble while I worked. So I got a job at a dude ranch outside

San Antonio one year and they let me bring Jamie along. He did chores right along with me and we'd get good, home-cooked meals, a paycheck and a place to live away from the city during summertime. We went back every year after that. It's where we learned to ride, and where I realized I could understand a lot about horses by watching them closely."

"There's so much I don't know about you." She sounded kind of disappointed.

"Ask me anything. I'll tell you. I've got no secrets to keep from you now." He winced. Why had he said that? Why remind her, again, of how he'd left her, and how his whole life with Jamie had been a secret for so many years?

"Back to chickens." She moved their conversation back to safer ground. "Holding an eagle is just like that, only they're a whole lot bigger. You have to keep its wings down against its body or you're going to get smacked hard. And you have to hold its legs together so it doesn't shred you with its talons. And watch out for its beak, too."

"So it's not really anything like holding a chicken," Wes teased.

"It's like holding a huge, angry chicken who will do anything to get away."

"All right, then." Wes glanced around the valley. "This wasn't what I was expecting from my workday."

"Working in Shelter Creek is rarely boring," Emily said.

"I'm realizing that. Here I was thinking I'd move here and retreat into a quiet, uneventful life." Wes winked at her. "I was as wrong as a rainstorm in July."

"It's so strange when you talk Texan," Emily said. "I don't know if I can get used to it."

Wes tipped the brim of his hat and gave her his best Texas drawl. "No, ma'am, I guess you won't."

"Stop!" But she was laughing and he loved that he could do that. That he could get a little silly and bring that out in her.

"Yes, ma'am." Then he dropped the drawl, because Maya would be here soon. "I'm going to get Rex out of the back seat so he can get a little fresh air. Luckily, the fog's still thick around here, so we can leave him in the car for a bit."

"Good idea. This is one appointment he

can't join in on. No dogs at the wildlife preserve."

Wes hooked Rex's leash to his collar and let the dog out. He took him along the side of the road, away from the boardwalk, jogging with the big dog to help him work off his energy. He needed the run, too. This day was a roller coaster. He'd woken this morning convinced that he and Emily were going to rediscover the feelings they'd had. Then she'd told him how much she regretted the kiss and they'd argued. Then there was the Shakespeare-obsessed rancher, the poor abandoned horse and now an eagle? All these years he'd thought of Shelter Creek as a rural dreamscape. A place where he would finally live the quiet life he'd always wished for. But he wouldn't call this day quiet. Far from it.

When they got back, Rex was panting and ready for his midmorning nap, and Maya was there, unloading a plastic animal carrier from her truck. "Aren't those usually for small dogs?" he called to her.

Maya waved the crate in his direction. "Dogs…eagles, you name it, we crate it."

Wes grinned and gave Rex a drink of water. When he put the dog in the truck, Rex immediately flopped down on the back seat with a doggy sigh of contentment.

"That dog has two speeds," Emily said. "Run and flop."

"Pretty much." Wes grinned. "Thanks again for putting up with him."

Emily smiled. "If he didn't have such fuzzy ears, I might not. They're therapy ears."

He couldn't resist the opening she'd offered. "A little therapy might do you some good."

She put her hands to her hips. "I'll sure need it after spending this week with you."

Maya was watching them with a small smile playing on her lips. "Are you two done with the witty banter? We should get going."

"Sure." Wes double-checked that the windows were rolled partway down. "Be good, boy."

Rex lifted his head as if it weighed several pounds, then flopped it back down with a sigh.

Emily walked past him and gave him a mock glare. "Therapy? I think I know a cowboy who could use it a lot more than me."

Wes winked at her and offered to carry the crate for Maya. She seemed happy to give it to him, though he caught Emily rolling her eyes. That woman had such a chip on her shoulder about independence. What was wrong with him carrying the crate? He had to be at least two feet taller than Maya. It made sense for him to carry it.

There was nothing unusual at the first pond. A great blue heron picked its way through the shallow water at one end, probably hoping to spear itself some brunch. They continued on the boardwalk to the second pond. Emily stopped and put her binoculars up to her eyes, scanning the far shore. "There it is," she whispered.

Wes squinted to see where she was pointing. It took a moment but then he saw it, huddled in the shallow water at the far side of the pond. It had one wing stuck out and one folded in and its head was just barely above the water.

Maya borrowed Emily's binoculars and watched the eagle for a moment. "This is tricky," she said quietly. "We really don't want to go around the left side of the pond. That is known salamander habitat, and since it's almost spring, they might be out and about.

That means we have to go around the right side to get to the eagle."

"So we're hiking through that marshy area." Emily's mouth crumpled into a grimace. "It's going to be wet and muddy. Wes, you're under no obligation to do this."

Wes glanced down at his fairly clean jeans and tan suede work boots. "I wish I'd brought some waders, but these will have to do."

Maya flashed him a grateful smile. "I like your attitude. And with three of us, we have a much better chance of grabbing the poor guy if he tries to get away."

"How do you know it's a guy?"

"The males are smaller than the females," Maya said. "This one isn't that big, but it's got all its adult feathers."

Emily took the binoculars back and peered through them again. "Maya, I think it might have been in a fight with another eagle. It looks like it's missing feathers, and I can see a spot that might be a puncture wound on its shoulder."

"That sounds like some fight." Wes held out his hand for the binoculars. "Mind if I take a look?"

"They battle for territory," Maya said. "This

valley, with all these ponds, would be pretty attractive for an eagle. It's protected, there's water and they're not that far from the ocean, either. I guess they decided it was worth fighting for."

Wes focused the binoculars on the eagle. Its beak was slightly open, as if it were panting. "It looks really stressed."

"Let's get started." Maya took the crate from Wes and set it quietly down on the boardwalk. From the inside she pulled out a couple of old bedsheets and handed a pink, flowered one to Wes. "The easiest way to catch an eagle is to come up behind it, wrap this around the wings and around its tummy. Hold its talons in one hand while you wrap the sheet around them. That way it will be all bundled up and it can't hurt you, or itself."

"Won't it try to stab me with its beak while I'm wrapping it up?" Wes couldn't really picture how this would work.

"You just have to be careful and do your best," Maya said. "Emily or I will try to be the one to catch it."

Emily grinned at him. "If it comes your way, you'll just have to *wing* it."

"Very funny." Wes handed Emily her binoculars and took the sheet from Maya. He followed the women off the boardwalk and into the soft earth near the shore of the pond. He tried to walk directly in their footsteps to leave as little impact on the land as possible. It was so pristine here he felt guilty marring the landscape.

Maya went into the pond, moving slowly and carefully at a diagonal to try to get on the eagle's left side. Emily turned around and motioned for Wes to go to her right. She was heading along the shore of the pond, straight for the bird. When they were still several yards away, the eagle flapped its wings uneasily. Even though it had its back to them, it must have sensed their presence. They all froze and waited. Wes watched Maya, and when she tilted her head toward the eagle, they started forward again.

Wes had to cross the stream that seeped beneath the grass from pond to pond. He sank in past his boots, gasping as the icy water filled them. There was mud, too, sucking at every footstep. Every step got heavier the more water his boots and jeans took on. Trying not to make sloshing sounds required all his concentration. Glancing over, he saw that Emily was soaked, too. She didn't seem to mind. She flashed him a thumbs-up and a big smile.

They were only a few feet from the eagle now. Its white head was wet and disheveled but still looked impressive, with the huge yellow hooked beak protruding from it. Maybe the males were smaller, but this guy sure seemed big to Wes.

Emily raised her blanket and crept forward by inches. She managed to get right behind the eagle and it still didn't move. She leaned forward, brought the blanket down and the eagle skittered away with a high-pitched screech.

"Get it," Emily gasped as she lost her balance and sprawled into the mud.

The eagle was heading toward Wes, scrambling and flapping its good wing as it floundered in the marshy grass.

Wes held his pink sheet open and walked as slowly and stealthily as he could toward the bird. It stopped struggling, perhaps stuck in the mud. He could see that the side of its white head was streaked with dirt and possibly some blood. Its bright eyes were wide and wild.

Wes tried to calm his heartbeat and let go

of his own adrenaline, just like he did with a frightened horse. "Easy," he murmured. "You're okay."

The eagle folded its bad wing as best it could. Hunched over, the battered bird tilted its head and looked up at Wes with one eerie yellow eye. It was gathering energy, getting ready for its next escape attempt. Wes didn't give either of them a chance to think. He pounced, sheet outstretched, and enveloped the eagle in a gentle bear hug. His hat went flying off as he twisted his body so as not to land on the bird. Instead he landed with a splash on his back in the shallow muddy water, the eagle struggling frantically on his belly.

Wes managed to hold the enormous bird by the wings, but the eagle's talons were bicycling in the air. Stuck on his back, Wes couldn't see exactly where its razor claws were, and no way was he going to feel around for them. "Need a little help, here," he called.

He could hear Emily and Maya sloshing toward him. "Hold on, Wes." Emily appeared in his line of vision, covered head to toe in mud from her belly flop into the marsh grass. Wes couldn't help grinning. "Well, look what the cat dragged in." He gasped as the eagle's beak grazed his arm. "Ouch."

"You're looking a little bedraggled yourself, Wes Marlow." Emily flopped down on her knees next to him, slid her hand along his stomach and managed to get a grip on the eagle's talons. Maya arrived, not nearly as muddy, but soaked to the waist from her walk in the pond. She used her sheet, and the one that Wes had over the eagle's wings, to wrap the panicked bird securely and tuck it under her arm. "Come on, big guy. Let's get you healed up." She started back to the boardwalk, as calm as if she carried eagles around every day.

Wes lay on his back, feeling the icy, swampy water fill the seat of his pants and soak the back of his shirt. The cool, misty breeze prickled over the front of his body. Emily sat in the water next to him, trying to wipe the mud off her face with her equally muddy sleeve. "How are you doing down there?"

He looked up at her pretty, mud-smeared face, framed by the cloudy sky. "Cold. Wet. But hey, I caught the eagle." His heart was racing, and he felt exhilarated to have succeeded. To have had his arms around such an amazing bird.

She smiled. "Well done, apprentice. Do you need some help getting up?"

"Yeah." He grinned up at her. This was all so ridiculous. "I'm pretty sure I'm sinking, actually."

She started laughing—a quiet, helpless, half-hysterical laugh. "I might be sinking, too." Then tears were running down her face, she was laughing so hard. "I'm really sorry, Wes. I didn't think it would be this messy."

Answering laughter bubbled up from his chest, rich and rippling, and he couldn't stop it, either. He lay there in the swamp, eyes on the sky, laughing until he couldn't speak. Eventually he managed to gasp out, "I can safely say that I have never experienced a veterinary practice quite like yours."

That got her laughing even harder. She gestured to the swamp around them. "I don't understand. You find this odd? It's just an average day in Shelter Creek." Then her laughter died down. "Do you think there are snakes in here?"

Wes scrambled to a sitting position, arms flailing. Then he staggered to his feet. He was looking over his shoulder, trying to make sure there were no waterlogged reptiles clinging to his back, when he realized that Emily was still sitting in the swampy grass, laughing even harder than before. "You were messing with me?"

She grinned, totally unrepentant. "I got you unstuck, didn't I?"

His heart slowed down from its wild gallop. "I can't believe you did that to me."

She heaved herself up out of the water and mud, clutching her sodden blanket. "There are a lot more snakes in Texas than there are here. Another reason to love Shelter Creek." She started back the way they'd come, taking big strides to use his previous footsteps. She glanced back over her shoulder. "Are you coming, cowboy?"

He retrieved his hat, the straw covered in mud just like the rest of him. His clothing was soaked and his water-filled boots weighed him down, but his heart felt light. No amount of pond water or professionalism could quench the spark he felt between them. No matter that she'd scared the daylights out of him with that snake comment. He'd follow her onto swampy ground again.

He'd follow her anywhere. Maybe he was a fool, but he was falling head over heels for Emily all over again.

CHAPTER THIRTEEN

WHEN EMILY PULLED her truck into the parking lot of the wildlife center, Wes was already there. After a cold wet ride from Long Valley back to the clinic, they'd gone their separate ways so they could each go home to shower and change.

Wes was leaning against his truck, looking at something on his phone. With one denim-clad leg crossed over the other at the ankle, a clean, brown cowboy hat tilted down, his arms crossed over a different plaid flannel shirt than the one he'd worn earlier, he looked like a picture-perfect cowboy. But he was real and he was waiting for her. Something in Emily's stomach quivered. Butterflies. She wished they'd leave, migrate, go to sleep, anything other than flutter in her stomach. They'd been there ever since she and Wes had laughed until they cried in Long Valley.

She hadn't been able to think of anything since. His willingness to jump in, literally, to wildlife rescue had captured more than that eagle. It had captured her heart. Then, when he'd announced that he was sinking into the marshy ground, he'd got her giggling. And that was it. She was done for. There was no way she wasn't going to fall for Wes Marlow one more time.

The dilemma was twofold. She didn't want to get hurt. She already knew how easily he could break her heart. And she also wanted him to work with her. He was good. He was fun. He clearly loved his work, and he loved animals. He knew when to step forward, like he had with Two Socks. He knew when to step back, as he did earlier today when Fancy didn't want him around. And he wanted to work right here in Shelter Creek.

How could she keep things professional when she was feeling so much?

Though right now, it didn't matter what she was feeling. Trisha had been treating the eagle for shock while she and Wes went home to change. Now Emily had to figure out where it was hurt and how to fix it.

She parked her truck, and Wes looked up

from his phone and smiled. Her butterflies swirled and sailed. She gave him a wave through the truck window and allowed herself a moment to breathe. Her feelings about him were simply that. Feelings. A crush. They didn't mean she should act on them. Nothing had changed since she woke up this morning. She simply needed to practice being immune to Wes Marlow's smile. To get used to laughing with him just like she'd laugh with Maya or Trisha or Vivian.

Though her girlfriends didn't cause her heart to skip a beat when they walked her way.

Emily pushed open the door of her truck and got out on shaky legs. "Hey. Feeling better?"

He smiled, looking almost shy. Had he felt that same connection on the valley floor? "A shower has never felt that good." He ran his fingers over his clean-shaven jaw and gave her a quick wink. "I think all that mud did something nice for my skin, though. How about you?"

"Who needs a spa when you can roll around in a marsh?"

He laughed. "That's what I always say."

Her smile was so big it was hurting her cheek muscles and it was hard to look away from the humor in his gaze. "We better get inside and figure out what to do with that eagle."

"I hope you have a plan. I haven't worked with an eagle before. I was just looking up what I could about it on my phone."

"We've had injured eagles here before and successfully released them back to the wild, so I think we can help this guy out." Emily motioned toward the center. "Come on. I'm excited to show you around. This center is a really important part of our community."

They started for the big glass doors. "Who built it?"

"A friend of mine named Eva first thought of it, back when Maya came home to Shelter Creek. Eva is a friend of Maya's grandmother and they're in a book club called The Book Biddies. The book club members were helping Maya spread the word about how to live peacefully with mountain lions. They got so excited about helping wildlife that they started fundraising for this center."

Wes paused and looked up at the impressive concrete-and-timber building. "A book club got this built?" He looked at her, brows raised. "That's one impressive book club."

Emily laughed. "They're unstoppable. Actually, they've invited some of the younger generation to be part of it, too. Maya, Trisha, Vivian and I are all Book Biddies, now."

Wes grinned at her. "I'd never mistake you for an old biddy. But you always did like to read."

"I still do. But mostly I just like the book club meetings. It's a fun group. They're more like family now."

"Sounds like you've got a great group of friends," Wes said.

"I'm sure you'll get to know them better, the longer you're here in Shelter Creek." She paused by the door to the center, suddenly shy about what she wanted to say to him. "If you still want to stay."

"I want to stay." He glanced at her. "If you don't mind too much. After this morning, when we got so upset with each other, I wondered if I should just go. I never meant to crowd you. Maybe it wasn't fair of me to come back here."

"No!" The word came out much louder than Emily had planned. "I mean, I think you should stay. I think we should keep working together. Would you want to give this trial period another month? At the end of that we can make it a more formal partnership if it works out."

His wide smile gave his answer before he did. "Are you sure?"

Emily nodded. "Anyone who wrestles a bald eagle like that is meant to have this job."

"Well, I hope no other eagle wrestlers show up, because I'm not sharing my paycheck with them."

She laughed. "Good to know."

He held out a hand. "Shall we shake on it?"

"Sure." But when his big hand closed over hers, so warm and sure, she knew this was the wrong way to seal their agreement. She wanted to keep holding on. Instead she pulled away, trying to ignore the way his gaze searched hers intently, as if he, too, had found some deeper meaning in their clasped hands. "Well, it's official now. You'll be my apprentice for the next month."

He laughed outright. "Maybe we could come up with a new title."

"I don't know," she teased. "I think Bobby might be onto something."

"I'll be Apprentice if I can call you Fair Emily."

"In that case, we'll find you a new title. How about Associate?"

He pulled open the door of the wildlife center and held it for her. "I'll take it. I'm happy to associate with you anytime."

Emily walked into the lobby with her butterflies zipping and zooming inside. She'd better get used to them. If Wes kept saying things like that, they might just be here to stay. What had she been telling herself all day? That she had to practice being immune to Wes? That she had to stay professional? They still had a few hours of work left today and she was already failing miserably.

WES WALKED INTO the wildlife center feeling ten pounds lighter than he had this morning. Just a few hours ago he was wondering if he should leave Shelter Creek, and now he'd been offered another month to work with Emily. He'd never had a life where dreams came true just because he got lucky. Maybe the one piece of true luck he'd had was getting sent to live with Emily and her parents in Shelter Creek. Since then he'd worked and saved and struggled for everything he'd ever had. To be handed this chance to keep working with Emily at the moment he was close to surrender felt like a miracle. It felt like a sign. That maybe he didn't have to struggle quite so hard anymore. That maybe he was truly meant to come back to Shelter Creek.

The relief of it had him smiling as he took in the lobby of the Shelter Creek Wildlife Center. It was set up as an interactive museum, with displays about the local wildlife. A young woman sat at the desk, schoolbooks open in front of her. She looked up as they walked in, a bright smile lighting up her face when she saw Emily. "You're here! Have you come to help the eagle?"

"Yes, we have," Emily answered. "I didn't know you were working today. What happened to school?"

"They had some big teacher meeting this afternoon. They let us go early. I figured if I had to study, I might as well do it here and answer the phones while I'm at it."

"You're the best. Wes, this is Carly. She's Jace and Vivian's niece. Carly, Wes went to high school with us. He's a veterinarian and

he'll be working with me for the next month
or so."

"Jace mentioned you. A real Texas cowboy.
Welcome back to Shelter Creek."

Wes tipped his hat to her. "Great to meet
you, Carly. It's real nice of you to volunteer
here."

"I love it," Carly said. "I want to study bi-
ology like Vivian and Maya."

"Sounds like a great plan." Wes liked this
kid. And what was it about this town that created such strong, smart women? Here was
another one in the making, getting ready to
run circles around the next generation of men
around here.

"They're all in the back with the eagle."
Carly pointed toward a door in the back of
the lobby. "Good luck with it. It didn't look
happy when Maya brought it in."

Emily led the way. The door opened onto
a hallway that led to several different closed
doors. Emily pointed them out. "Those are
storage rooms, a small lab, long-term care
for wildlife and there's a meeting room, too."

Everything was spotless and new. Large
photos of wildlife were framed on the walls.
"Did you take these, too?"

Emily nodded. "They're some of the animals we've rehabilitated. Except that bunny. That's Peanut. He lives here permanently."

"Peanut." Wes followed her through a door labeled *Hospital*, shaking his head at the cute name. In the center of the room, Maya, Vivian and Trisha stood around a metal table working together to treat the eagle. Maya had it securely in her arms and Vivian had its feet wrapped in a towel. Trisha was feeding it something brown from an enormous syringe. Whatever it was, the eagle was gulping it greedily. "What's it drinking?"

"A mixture of electrolytes and protein," Emily said. "It will help get his body back into balance."

"Hi, you two," Trisha said quietly. "Wes, once it feels better we'll give it some real food. But right now we just need to stabilize him so we can look at his wounds."

"Wes, will you help me prep the surgery?" Emily pointed to an exam room off to the side. There was a big metal table with surgical lights over it.

"This might be nicer than what you have at the clinic," Wes said.

"Right? Lucky for this place, people in California love wildlife, and many of them have a fair amount of money. We're the only wildlife center in the county and a lot of folks have been really supportive of our mission." Emily reached into a cabinet and pulled out a couple of pale green surgery gowns. She handed one to him. "Let's put these on."

Trisha, Vivian, Maya and the eagle came to join them. "Speaking of which," Trisha said, bustling to disinfect the table. "There's a fundraiser for the center this Saturday night, Wes. A big, fancy party. We're all going and you should come, too. Especially because you're the hero who took a dive in the mud to save our national bird."

Wes glanced at Emily. She hadn't mentioned it, but big parties probably weren't her thing. Helping animals was what made her happy. Part of him wished he could just stand aside and watch her work right now. She was a sight to behold, so calm and focused on their upcoming task, obviously used to leading this team. But he was also looking forward to assisting in his first wildlife surgery.

"Trisha, can you handle the anesthesia?" Emily was studying the eagle carefully. It was restless in Maya's arms, occasionally reaching its beak up to try to bite her face.

"I like how much energy he has," Maya said, moving the bird lower so it couldn't reach its target. "He's getting feisty."

"Good," Emily said. "That means he'll do well in surgery. Trisha, will you please take a quick look in the binder over there and see what we gave the last baldie we had in here?"

Trisha flipped through the records in the binder. "Got it." She scrubbed her hands, pulled on a gown and gloves and went to get the anesthesia machine ready. Emily and Wes scrubbed up and put on caps, masks and gloves.

"All right. Maya and Vivian, here we go. Can you lay him down?"

"One, two, three," they counted, and as if they'd done this many times, they laid the poor eagle on its side all in one motion.

Vivian put the anesthesia cone over its bedraggled white head and Trisha adjusted the readings on the machine. "Here we go, big guy. You're going to take a nap while we fix you up."

The next hour passed in a flash as Wes and Emily searched the eagle for injuries. There were two puncture wounds on its abdomen and a slash to its leg that they cleaned and bandaged. Emily examined its wings and pointed out the missing flight feathers that had grounded the bird in the pond. When they'd finished up, Vivian and Maya moved the eagle to a cage in the hospital room, where it could begin its recovery.

"What will happen with those flight feathers?" Wes slipped off his surgical gown, cap and mask and threw them in the basket Trisha provided. "Those wounds aren't horrible. It should be fine in a few weeks if there's no infection. But the feathers won't grow in until after it molts."

"It's a problem." Emily turned to Maya. "Do you think you and Trisha can call around to other rescue groups?" She looked at Wes. "If we can exactly match those flight feathers, we can graft some on. It's called imping. The grafted feathers will stay until he molts, then he'll grow new ones of his own."

"That's incredible." Then Wes remembered. "I think I read about this once, in a book about falconry."

"Exactly. It's an ancient practice," Maya said. "Most wildlife centers and zoos with bald eagles that can't be released to the wild will save their flight feathers when they molt, so rescue centers can use them for imping."

"I'll call around tomorrow," Trisha said. "Once this guy's feeling a little better, we'll give him another exam and write down all the feathers he's missing. It would be great to get him flying again soon."

Wes glanced at the clock above the door. "Emily, we'd better get back to the clinic. Our window of time is just about up."

Emily glanced at the clock and gasped. "That went by fast. Maya, Trisha, Viv, I'll come by and check on our eagle friend at around six this evening. But call me if you notice any problems when the sedative wears off."

"Trisha's a pro at this," Maya said. "But we'll call you for sure if we notice anything unusual."

They said goodbye to Carly on their way out and walked toward their trucks. Wes was quiet, thinking about the eagle and everything it had been through today. Emily nudged him gently with her elbow. "What did you think of your first eagle rescue?"

"It was pretty great. I can see why you like

working here." Wes didn't have the words for it, really. "It feels kind of like an honor to help a bird like that."

"Wildlife work is so immediate," Emily said. "That eagle probably wouldn't have made it through the night like that, unable to fly." She glanced at her truck. "I guess we should get back to the clinic. But speaking of rescuing things, can I ask you something?"

"Sure. Go ahead." Anything.

"What do you think about that horse we met this morning? I can't stop thinking about her."

Wes grinned. "Fancy Face? I think you two have a special bond. And now that you're going to let me work with you some more, maybe you'll have a little free time to spend with her. If you let me take some cases on my own, that is."

Her brow furrowed. "There's really no reason why you shouldn't. Your references all rave about what a great vet you are." She paused and smiled. "You can take all the cats."

He started laughing. She was so funny when he least expected it. "You don't like cats?"

"I don't dislike them. They can be very sweet. But when they come in to see me, they're so scratchy."

"Scratchy?" Wes gaped at her. "You were just handling an eagle with giant talons who I'm sure would have loved to scratch you to bits."

"That's different. He was just scared. Cats are…I don't know…they always look so satisfied after they scratch you."

"I think you're taking the cats a little personally." Though now that he thought about it, she was right. Some cats did look pretty smug after they took a swipe at you. "I'll take over the cat appointments, for a while, at least."

"But here's the thing. I'm not even sure how we can transport Fancy Face to my property. She's so scared. But we need to do it soon. I checked my email from my phone earlier and I had a note from Bobby, saying he has plans to go visit some relatives next week and he's worried about leaving the horse there. He has someone coming by to take care of his sheep, but a half-wild, skeletal horse wasn't in their plans."

"If we can bring the sheep in the trailer

with us, she might be okay," Wes said. "Let's go up there tomorrow and check it out."

"I might ask if Caleb can come with us. Maya's husband? He's really good with horses. He has this horse named Amos that he rescued and trained. Plus, he has a big horse trailer."

"Sounds like the guy for the job."

"Will you help me out? Tell me how to work with her? I can pay you, if you want. A horse-whispering fee."

"You don't need to pay me." A flicker of frustration had him shaking his head. "Last time I checked, we were getting to be friends, right? I'm not going to charge you money for something I'd be happy to do for any of my friends."

She pressed her lips together as if she were trying not to say what was on her mind. "That's great. I'm lucky to be your friend, then." She pulled her keys out of her pocket and jangled them between her fingers. "Let's get back to the clinic. We have so much to do."

Wes climbed into his truck, wondering if he'd said something wrong. She'd seemed kind of downcast for a moment there. He shook his head, started the engine and headed for his house to pick up Rex. When the dog bounded out the front door to greet him, Wes knelt down for an enthusiastic doggy hug. "Women," he muttered to Rex. "I will never understand them."

Rex sat and offered him a paw to shake. Wes took it. "Thanks for the sympathy. Come on, buddy, let's get back to work."

CHAPTER FOURTEEN

EMILY DROVE UP to Bobby's ranch with Wes by her side. It was a cool day, the breeze sending small clouds scudding across the sky.

"It's not the best day to transport a horse," Wes said. "This kind of weather tends to make them a little hyper."

"That's reassuring," Emily said. "Maybe if we can't get her haltered and into the trailer we can just keep her here. I can come up and feed her while Bobby is away."

"It's an option," Wes said. "But let's try this. Caleb is bringing a horse along. A really old, placid one, apparently. Maybe having a buddy to ride with will help Fancy out."

Caleb's truck and trailer were already there when they pulled up to the barn. They spotted Caleb leaning on the fence, talking with Bobby. Emily parked her truck and they got out. "Thanks for helping us out today, Caleb," she called.

The big man regarded her with a slight frown. "That horse is a mess, Emily. You sure you know what you're doing?"

"Yup." Emily stuck her chin out in defiance. She'd known Caleb forever. He was like a big brother to her. "I'm going to feed her up and give her a nice place to live."

"With sheep," Caleb said. "We already loaded them in the trailer."

"You won't miss Beatrice and Rosalind?" Emily turned to Bobby.

"I know you'll take good care of them for me." He grinned. "What better place to have those old girls stay than with the local veterinarian?"

"I'll make sure they're happy, I promise." Emily glanced toward the corral. "How's Fancy doing?"

"She won't let us near her," Caleb said. "Is she even halter broke?"

"We're going to find out." Wes held up the soft blue halter they'd picked up at the feed-store earlier today.

"Let's go see if we can get it on her." Emily turned to Caleb and Bobby. "Maybe give us a little space to work with her? She seems to be afraid of men."

"That's fine, fair Emily. We'll stay here. You and your apprentice can try your luck with the mare."

Caleb glanced from Emily to Bobby. "Apprentice?"

"Don't ask," Emily said. "Thanks so much, Bobby. Wish us luck."

"Fare well and Godspeed," Bobby said.

Emily and Wes walked to the corral. Fancy was there, pacing nervously. "Maybe they shouldn't have loaded her sheep already," Wes said. "She looks like she's missing them."

As if in reply, Fancy let out a loud whinny, then waited. Sure enough, Rosalind and Beatrice bleated back to her from the truck.

Emily looked at Wes in surprise. "They bonded already."

"That's good. She might be a lot easier to trailer if she feels that strongly about those sheep." Wes looked over the fence at Fancy. "Go on in there like you did yesterday. Stand with your back to her again. Give her a minute to settle and I bet she'll come up to you. When she does, pet her nose and her face. See how she reacts."

Emily let herself into the corral. Fancy went to the far side, paced back and forth and called to her sheep again. Emily stood still with her back to the mare and spoke to her softly. "Hey, girl. You want to go see your sheep? Come on over here."

The quiet words seemed to get the mare's attention. She slowed her pacing, then stopped. When Emily glanced over her shoulder, the mare was watching her, ears forward.

"Just wait," Wes said quietly. "You've got her interested."

Emily waited and eventually heard the shuffle of the mare's hooves in the dust. Then her pink nose came up and brushed Emily's ear. Forcing herself not to react, Emily waited until the mare came closer, to stand beside her. Only then did she slowly reach up to pet her face. Fancy was so striking, with her white forehead and blue eyes. Her cheeks were chestnut under all the dust that permeated her coat.

"Slowly hold up the halter," Wes said. "Let her check it out."

Emily raised it up and Fancy sniffed it. The mare shook her head up and down a couple times but didn't walk away. Emily lifted the halter and put it alongside the mare's face and ran it along her neck. The horse didn't flinch.

"Doing great," Wes coached. "I think she's been haltered before. Go ahead and slide it slowly up her nose, but don't buckle it yet."

Emily did as she was told. Fancy backed up a step, then stopped. Emily waited, heart pounding, and slid the halter a little higher. Finally she had it under Fancy's chin. All that was left was to buckle it. Easing the strap behind the mare's ears, Emily buckled it by her cheek.

"Perfect," Wes said. "Now attach the lead rope."

Emily lifted up the rope and Fancy backed away, ears back.

"I don't like that," Wes said. "Someone probably hit her with a rope at some point. Try again."

It took twenty minutes and a few treats, but eventually Fancy allowed Emily to attach the rope to the halter. Once it was on, she seemed to decide that it wasn't a threat. She walked out of the corral with Emily and they started toward Caleb's trailer.

Caleb was there, standing with a reddish-brown horse. "This is Newt," Caleb said. "He'll show your girl the ropes."

He led Newt up the ramp and into one of the stalls in the large trailer.

"Come on, Fancy, let's follow Newt," Emily said.

Fancy dug her hooves in when she saw the trailer ramp. Wes suggested treats, but Fancy was too nervous to care about them. They tried loading Newt in again and having Fancy walk behind him. Nothing worked.

Emily tried not to let her frustration show. The mare would pick up on it and it would make thing worse. Suddenly Fancy whinnied. The sheep answered, and the mare charged up the ramp to be with her friends.

"I told you fair Beatrice and sweet Rosalind would work their magic," Bobby said.

Emily looked at Fancy, quietly munching on hay next to the sheep. "They can all ride together?"

"It would be better if we keep them separate," Caleb said. "Let's move the sheep to the other side of the partition. The mare will still be able to see them."

"I'll do it," Emily said. Carefully she approached the sheep and shooed them toward Caleb. He maneuvered them into the section of trailer right next to Fancy and shut the metal door behind them. The mare immediately put her neck over the partition to snuffle at her sheep buddies. Satisfied that they were close by, she went back to eating.

Outside the trailer, Emily breathed a sigh of relief. "Caleb, we'll meet you at my house." Emily turned to Bobby. "Thanks again. Please come visit them anytime."

"I will. After my vacation. Best of luck with your horse, fair Emily."

"Have a great trip."

She and Wes got back in the truck and followed Caleb as he slowly drove the trailer down Bobby's driveway. "Thank you," Emily said. "For helping me figure all that out."

"I'm not sure I was much use. That horse only responds to you and two ewes."

She smiled at his wordplay. "Well, I had no idea how to get the halter on. Or what to do when she was scared of the rope."

"Glad to help. That's what friends are for, right?"

"Speaking of friends," Emily said, "I have a question." She'd been meaning to ask him ever since Trisha had brought it up yesterday, but it was so awkward. "That benefit tomorrow night. For the wildlife shelter? Do you want to go? Pretty much everyone you know in town will be there."

She shouldn't care what his answer was. They'd established that they were friends, but that didn't change the fact that she was feeling so much more.

"Can I pick you up and take you there?"

She glanced his way. "We don't have to do that. I was going to go with my parents. We can just meet there if you'd rather."

He shook his head. "I walked out on our prom. Let me do this right. I'll come pick you up. I'll treat you the way I should have treated you back then." When she didn't answer he added, "Come on, Em. Think of it as amends."

"I don't need amends." She didn't know what she wanted, but not that.

"Then how about two friends, going to the party together?"

Emily turned onto the main road. "Sure, that would be fine." She wished that she could be content with Wes as just a friend. The more time she spent with him the more she wished for something more.

"We'll have something to celebrate," Wes said.

"What's that?"

"You've finally got yourself a horse."

Emily smiled. "That's true. And I've wanted one for a long time now."

Wes shot her a lethal grin from under the rim of his cowboy hat. "See? Aren't you glad I showed up? I'm making dreams come true."

She burst out laughing. "Don't get ahead of yourself, there, cowboy."

He was unrepentant. "I know my arrival in Shelter Creek threw you for a loop, but I think you're going to be glad I showed up."

Emily watched the road and tried to ignore the smile that wouldn't leave her lips. She was already glad. That was the problem. If he left again it was going to hurt, and she didn't want to hurt anymore.

CHAPTER FIFTEEN

"WEAR THE BLACK DRESS," Emily's mother said, sipping her tea as she sat in the armchair in the corner of the guest bedroom. Emily had brought her clothing over to her parents' house to get ready, since she'd originally planned on going to the benefit with them. Her mother was already dressed in a sequined top and flowing black pants, the contrast striking with her white hair.

"It's frumpy." Emily tossed it aside. Then picked it up again. "Or is it?"

"Emily Fielding," her mother said. "You know less about clothing than anyone I know."

"I wear jeans and T-shirts every single day," Emily wailed. "I have no idea if any of these dresses look good on me."

"How about the one you wore to Trisha's wedding?"

Emily picked up the pale blue flowing sundress. "It's pretty, but I don't think it's quite right for a dressy evening benefit."

"Why are you so worried? I don't think you've ever been this worked up about clothing before."

She probably should have mentioned something earlier. "Wes is picking me up. He's taking me to the benefit."

Her mother set the teacup down on its saucer with a clank of china. "Wes? Oh, my goodness!" Then she settled back in her chair again. "Well, I can't say as I'm surprised. You two always did have a strong connection."

"It's not like that. I thought it would be a good chance for him to get to know more people around Shelter Creek. If he's going to be working with me, people need to know who he is."

"Ah. I see." Her mother pressed her lips together as if she were trying not to laugh.

"It's professional," Emily insisted. "He also helped save an eagle this week. So he has his own personal stake in the wildlife center now."

"He saved an eagle? How?"

Emily told the story of Wes lying in the mud with an eagle on his stomach. When she'd finished, her mother was dabbing tears of laughter from the corner of her eyes. "Oh, my goodness, that boy is tenacious, isn't he? Good for him. Are you glad he came back to Shelter Creek?"

"I think so," Emily said. "It seems to be going well." She wasn't actually sure that was true. Everything seemed to be changing between her and Wes. From floundering and laughing at the edge of the eagle pond, to cracking her up while they were driving to see clients, Wes had become, once again, the person who made her laugh the hardest. The person who seemed to understand what she was thinking. The person she could be most herself with.

Maybe they could be good friends. Years ago they'd started out that way before things turned romantic. Perhaps that friendship was what had survived after all their heartache. And if they were friends, it didn't much matter what she wore tonight.

Relieved, Emily grabbed the black dress and went into the bathroom to put it on. It fit better than she remembered, with a scoop neck and cap sleeves, a nipped-in waist and a full skirt. Emerging from the bathroom, she twirled in front of her mother.

"Oh, it's perfect," her mom said. "I'd forgotten it was so pretty on you." She stood up. "Hang on. I've got just the thing to go with it." She left the room in a cloud of sweet perfume.

Emily stepped into the pumps she'd purchased for her vet school graduation and quickly grabbed the edge of the dresser for support. Had these always been this high? She took a few tentative steps, hoping muscle memory might kick in. Slowly she found her balance and paced around the room, gaining some confidence.

Her mother came back in. "You look beautiful. And this will help." She fastened a single strand of rhinestones around Emily's neck. "Understated, but it goes so well with that dress. Now, please, please, *please* let me put your hair up?"

"I don't need my hair up," Emily protested.

"You are my only daughter, and my only child and you've almost never let me play with your hair. It will look so elegant." Meg picked up a strand and eyed it disapprovingly. "Especially because the ends are so dry. When was the last time you had a trim?"

"I have no idea. There was a night a few months ago, at book club, where Monique insisted on snipping the ends off." She smiled at the memory. "Maya and Vivian held me down in a chair. They were convinced I'd run away screaming halfway through."

"That book club of yours sounds quite rowdy."

"You should come sometime. Half the women are your age or older."

"That's very sweet of you. But I'm not much of a reader." Her mother sat her down in the chair and went into the bathroom, emerging with a brush and a handful of bobby pins. "Now hold still while I make you perfect."

Fifteen minutes later, Emily was seated at the dining room table sipping a glass of white wine her mother had poured. Her dad was pacing alongside her, looking dapper in a dark suit and tie. "I can't believe Wes Marlow is taking you out on a date." He pulled a handkerchief out of his pocket and dabbed at his brow. "Why am I so nervous?"

"Because our daughter rarely dates?" Her

mother glanced at Emily in alarm. "Have you dated *anyone* since high school?"

"Of course I have! There was that guy Matthew in college, and Pete, also in college. And there was this guy—"

"I'm not sure I want to hear this." Her father stopped pacing and slumped in his usual chair.

"Dad, I'm thirty-two years old. Of course I've dated."

"But never like this. Going to a fancy dance. Leaving from our house. It's like prom all over again."

"Except I never went to prom," Emily reminded him.

It *was* like prom all over again. When the doorbell rang, her father insisted on answering, shaking Wes's hand and ushering him into the dining room.

Wes looked so handsome in his black suit, with his crisp white dress shirt and tie that Emily suddenly got nervous. Especially when he handed her a box with a bracelet of flowers. "A corsage?" She stared at him in surprise. "I wasn't expecting this."

"I figured I've owed you one for a long

time." Wes gave her a wry smile. "You don't have to wear it if you don't want."

Her mother took the box from Emily. "That's much prettier than an average corsage. Well done, Wes."

"Here," he said, stepping forward, "let me put it on." Meg opened the box and Wes slipped the corsage around Emily's wrist and tightened the band so it wouldn't slide off. When he'd finished, his gaze met hers. "You look beautiful, by the way."

Emily's skin heated. "Thank you."

"What a lovely gesture, Wes," Meg said. "Now, before you go, I need photos."

"That's okay, Mom, really." Emily wanted to sink through the floor. She felt like she was a teenager all over again.

"I was deprived of prom photos when you kids were in high school, so I get to have them now," her mother insisted, laughing. "Plus, this is a historic moment with you two reunited and all dressed up."

"Come on." There was laughter in Wes's eyes when he looked at her. "You look amazing. Let's get a couple photos. It can't hurt."

"You all have lost your minds," Emily

grumbled, but she let Wes pull her gently into the living room.

"In front of the fireplace, please," her mother said, suddenly the photography expert. She had her phone out, ready to go.

"Okay, what are traditional prom poses?" Wes put an arm around Emily's shoulder. "Like this?"

When did he get so strong and tall and warm? It was all Emily could do to keep from stepping closer, so she'd be tucked right up against him.

"Now, Wes, do that one where you stand behind her," her mother ordered. "You know, and I take the photo from the side? That's classic prom, right?"

"A little more sideways," her father advised.

"This is getting embarrassing," Emily complained.

"It's nice," Wes murmured in her ear. "I just wish we had some real prom photos to compare these to."

She didn't want to think about that night. She'd been so very sad. "One more pose," she told her parents. "We don't want to be late."

Her mother waved her hand in the air. "Wes, spin her around, like you're dancing."

Wes obliged, raising his hand so Emily could twirl around in a circle. She couldn't help laughing, it was so ridiculous. Wes finished the turn by pulling her in close as if they were really dancing together and Emily bumped right into his chest. His arms went around her to make sure she didn't fall and she looked up at him as he was laughing down at her. It was perfect. Emily froze as every cell in her body said, *This. I want this. Always.*

What was happening to her? She stepped back and turned to get her wrap, only then noticing how quiet the room had become. Wes was gazing at her intently, as if he'd felt something in that moment, too. Her parents were looking at each other, apparently having a telepathic conversation.

"Right. We'd better get going." Emily threw her wrap around her shoulders. "It will break Maya's heart if we're late. I bet she can't wait to present Wes, the great eagle rescuer, to all the major donors who will be there tonight."

Wes grinned. "You're right. I'm practically the guest of honor. Let's get going." He turned to her parents. "Meg, Tom, thank you for trusting me with your daughter tonight. We'll see you in a few minutes at the party." Then he offered Emily his arm and she took it and they hightailed it out the door.

"Sorry about that," Emily said as he handed her into the passenger side of his truck. "I had no idea my parents were going to have a nostalgia attack."

He closed her door and got in the driver's seat. "I thought it was nice. Silly, but nice." He reached out a hand and touched her corsage with a fingertip. "We get to have the prom we never had before. That's not a bad thing, is it?"

With his dark hair and his charming smile, he looked like some kind of old-time movie star. Cary Grant or Gene Kelly, but with a touch of James Dean. Why not let this be their prom? She'd be the girl with the most handsome date, that was for sure. "No, it's not a bad thing." She held out her hand and made a show of admiring her corsage. "In fact, I plan to enjoy it."

"I'll make sure that you do."

The fundraiser was being held in an old mansion just off Main Street that had recently been converted into an event space by a couple of sisters who'd inherited it from their uncle. Emily hadn't been inside yet, and couldn't wait to see it. Wes found parking a block away, thankfully. Emily didn't think she could walk much farther than that in her sky-high heels. He offered her his arm and she gratefully accepted. She wouldn't ruin this night by falling off her heels and sprawling onto the sidewalk.

The venue was magical. The Hobart Mansion was resplendent in its new paint and landscaping. Lights blazed on the porch and garden, and tiny white fairy lights lined the porch and the outdoor patios.

When Wes and Emily climbed the steps and walked into the entryway they were met by Maya, who looked beautiful in a simple red silk dress. She gave them each a hug and immediately brought them to a silver-haired man standing in what must have once been the front parlor. Now it was empty of any furniture except tall cocktail tables and a bar in the corner.

"These are my fellow eagle stalkers, Mr. Van Durst. Emily is the one I told you about who tried to catch it and missed."

Emily raised a sheepish hand. "Yes, that's me."

Mr. Van Durst raised his glass. "You look

so elegant, it's hard to imagine you lying face-
down in the mud."

Emily glanced at Maya, who gave her an
exaggerated shrug and mouthed the words
major donor behind the portly man's back.
"Well, yes, we go the extra mile to help wildlife around here. Even if it means a nosedive
into the mud."

"And this—" Maya moved back in view of
her major donor "—is Wes Marlow. He is the
veterinarian who actually caught the eagle."

Mr. Van Durst raised his glass in a toast
to Wes. "You saved a living, breathing sym-
bol of our great nation, Wes. You should be
very proud."

"Always happy to help out the wildlife center. Have you been interested in wildlife for
a long time, Mr. Van Durst?"

Emily listened, astonished, as Wes made
impeccable small talk. He got Mr. Van Durst
chatting about his hobbies, his family and his
knowledge of birds. Eventually Emily spotted Monique, Eva and Priscilla, her fellow
Book Biddies, motioning to her from across
the room. She excused herself and went to
join them.

Priscilla took her hand as soon as Emily

walked up. "Is that Wes? Oh, my goodness, Emily, he is handsome."

"And making a major donor very happy, bless his heart," Eva said. The wildlife center had been her idea, and she worked tirelessly, when she wasn't at her art gallery, to raise money for it. "And yes, he is handsome. How are you two doing, Emily?"

"Things must be going well if you came here together tonight," Monique added.

"I think we're becoming friends again," Emily said. "I asked him to keep working with me for the next few weeks to see how it goes."

"Always so practical." Priscilla patted her arm. She'd been Emily's third grade teacher. "Even when you were little."

"Practical has its place of course," Monique said. "But I'm not sure it matters when it comes to that handsome veterinarian." She raised her perfectly groomed eyebrows and shook a finger at Emily. "Don't forget to have fun."

Just then Wes shook hands with Mr. Van Durst and came toward them. "Sorry about that, Emily. I think I made a mistake asking that gentleman about his birding hobby. He had a lot to say."

"No, trust me, you did great." Eva reached out to shake hands with Wes. "I'm Eva, founder of the wildlife center. You're my new favorite person. Mr. Van Durst is thinking of funding our aviary."

Wes smiled. "Well, I hope he does."

"How's your running going?" Monique chuckled at the confused look on Wes's face. "I own the beauty salon in town. I see you jogging by with your dog."

"Oh. Nice to meet you—"

"Monique. Nice to meet you, too, Wes. Emily has told us a lot about you."

Wes grinned at Emily. "Nothing too terrible, I hope."

Emily widened her eyes at Monique, trying to get her to settle down. "I simply mentioned that we were working together."

Monique gave her a wink. "Why don't you two find yourself a drink and some appetizers? Go enjoy yourselves. You don't want to waste your evening chatting with a bunch of old biddies like us."

"The Book Biddies," Emily explained to Wes.

"Your book club." He smiled at all the

women there. "Nice to meet you." He turned to Priscilla. "I don't think we've met."

"Priscilla Axel. Emily's third grade teacher."

Wes grinned. "I bet you could tell me some fun stories."

"Monique is right," Emily said. "Let's go get a drink."

Wes laughed. "Okay, no third grade stories, I guess." He offered Emily his arm. "Excuse us, please, ladies. It was very nice to meet you. Enjoy the evening."

As Emily sailed off on Wes's arm, she glanced at him in open admiration. "Where did you get these formal manners?"

"Waiting tables." He smiled down at her. "Many, many tables. Now, do you really want a drink?"

"I don't know." Something inside her was reckless tonight. "The last time I had one, I kissed you when I shouldn't have."

"Then we definitely need to get you a drink." Wes snagged a champagne flute off a passing waiter's tray.

"Wes!" Emily burst out laughing when he handed it to her.

He took it back. "Just kidding. How about

we share it and raid the buffet, as well? I didn't eat dinner."

"Me, neither," Emily confessed. "I was frantically trying to find a dress to wear."

He gave her an admiring glance. "You found a good one. You look incredible, Emily, you really do."

Her pulse raced at his soft words. "Thank you."

They headed to the buffet, loaded their plates and found a quiet room off the back of the house that seemed to be an old conservatory. There were big glass windows and lemon trees growing in pots. A couple of wrought iron chairs and an ornate table made it a perfect place to eat.

"This food looks delicious." Emily bit into a tiny cucumber sandwich with cream cheese.

"Small portions, though." Wes held up a tiny puff pastry with a microscopic amount of bacon on top.

"I guess we should have eaten before we came." Emily took a sip of their champagne, relishing the bubbles as they slid down her throat. "So what do you think of your first week in Shelter Creek?"

He looked at her in mock alarm. "It's only

been a week? I've met a million different residents and their livestock, I almost lost my dog, we've gotten in a couple of arguments, we saved an eagle and you just adopted a rescued horse. We've played pool, I got a kiss, we decided not to kiss and now we're at this fancy place, eating tiny bits of food." He flopped back against his seat. "I thought I was heading to this little town for some peace and quiet. I think I must have picked the wrong spot on the map. Are you sure this is Shelter Creek?"

Emily's face hurt from smiling by the time he was done. "I don't remember you being this funny," she said.

"I was too busy trying to be cool to make a lot of jokes back then. One thing I learned, raising Jamie on such a tiny budget, was any fun I wanted to have, I'd better figure out how to make it myself."

"I like that about you," Emily said. "I think I've gotten really serious these past several years. I've been so focused on work, and trying to fill my father's big shoes, that I forgot about having fun."

"We need to find you some fun, then. Yet another reason I'm glad you want me to keep working with you. When I'm with all those cats, you can take a day or two off a week to do something nice."

She selected a stuffed mushroom from her plate. "Why are you so eager for me to work less?"

Wes picked up the champagne glass and fidgeted with it, swirling the liquid in the glass. "I hate that I made you unhappy back then. I just want to help make you happy now."

Emily swallowed her mushroom in a single gulp. "You feel sorry for me?"

"No." Wes set the glass down. "How could I feel sorry for you? You have an incredible family, a great group of friends and a veterinary practice that, if anything, is too successful. You can barcly keep up."

"That's true." In the dim room, with just the two of them, Emily finally admitted the truth. "I'm so tired. I know that if I don't get help with my practice, I'm going to burn out. It's too much."

"No one can keep up with that amount of work. And here's what bothers me. I remember the girl you were and I see the woman you are now. I can tell how much you still love horses, photography and, apparently, plunging into swamps in pursuit of injured eagles. I want you to have time to be you, in all those different ways. You're a great veterinarian. But is that all you want to be?"

Tears were welling up in her eyes and that was a disaster because she'd put on mascara tonight. She dabbed at the corner of her eyes with a cocktail napkin.

"You're crying?" Wes looked worried. "I'm sorry. I get my boot wedged in my mouth when I'm around you."

"It's not that. It's that you're being so nice." Why was she getting so emotional? People were nice to her all the time. This was Shelter Creek, after all.

"Oh." Wes picked up his chair and scooted it next to hers. "It's a good kind of cry." He draped an arm over the back of her chair and patted his shoulder. "You can cry right here if you want."

She smacked him gently on the spot he'd indicated. "I'm not *that* teary." But she rested her head on his shoulder for a moment and leaned into him. How long had it been since she'd let anyone carry any of her weight?

His arm came around her back. "This is how I wish it could be," he murmured.

Emily wished it, too. But could she let herself fall for him again? The bliss of being close to him like this gave a hint at the pain she'd feel if he went away. He said he was back here to stay, but was it true? She pictured the simple silver promise ring he'd given her, the summer before senior year, still tucked away in the back of her jewelry box at home. The twining silver strands were supposed to represent the way their lives would weave together. He'd had a good reason to leave, but still, that ring represented a promise he hadn't kept.

"Hey," Wes whispered. "I hear music starting up. How about we go dance? This is our prom, after all."

"I'd like that." Emily stood and straightened her dress. She didn't want to think about broken promises or wishes that came with risks. She just wanted to enjoy this night with Wes and not worry about what it meant. He held out his hand and she took it, relishing the feel of his fingers wrapped tightly around hers. They made their way through the crowds, stopping to say hello to the people they knew, until they finally found the source of the music. A big band was playing swing music in the vast ballroom, and couples were filling up the parquet dance floor. "Do you know how to dance like this?" she asked.

"Nope," Wes said. "We'll just have to make it up." He took her in his arms and they swayed to the music, keeping their feet in time with the quick rhythm. Being in his arms was exactly what she needed, the rippling, rocking music making it impossible not to move. "Look at us." Wes lifted his arm so she could turn under it. "We're dancing."

"We make a good team, don't we?" Emily said when he pulled her back in close.

Wes grinned and spun her around. "I agree. You're my perfect partner. Thank you for giving me the chance."

Eva danced by with the owner of the one law firm in Shelter Creek and gave Emily a knowing smile. "Looking good, you two," she said before her partner whirled her away.

"Those ladies in your book club seem like they know how to have fun," Wes said.

Emily smiled at him. "Yes they do. Stick around Shelter Creek long enough and they'll drag you into some of their antics." She glanced around. Vivian was dancing with

Jace on the other side of the dance floor. Trisha was sitting at a cocktail table with Liam, Annie Brooks and her husband, Juan Alvaro. Jade and Aidan were sitting at another table, talking with Caleb. The dance floor was packed. Everyone had come out tonight to support the wildlife center.

Just then Emily caught sight of Maya hurrying toward them, cutting through the chaos of the dancers, a serious look on her face. Wes must have noticed it, too, because he stopped abruptly and tightened his arms around Emily, as if he could protect her from whatever had put the tears on Maya's cheeks.

"Emily, it's your father. He's having trouble with his heart again. An ambulance is on its way."

Emily clung tightly to Wes as the room lurched around her. "Where is he?"

"There's a small room near the front door. Let me show you."

Wes kept a supportive arm around Emily's back as they followed Maya through the crowd to a lounge across from the parlor with the bar. Her father was slumped in a love seat, his tie loosened. Her mother was pressing a damp cloth to his forehead. The fear in her eyes chilled Emily to her bones. She put a hand on her mother's arm. "Did you give him aspirin?"

"Yes, honey. Dr. Corbin is here tonight and he's been helping us out. He'll be right back. He's just on the phone conferring with dispatch."

Her father waved Emily over and she knelt at his side and took his hand. "You look so pretty. I'm sorry to ruin your prom night."

"No, Dad, don't worry about it." Emily could see beads of sweat at her father's temple but his hand felt cold and clammy. "We've had a great prom, haven't we, Wes?"

"Absolutely." Wes knelt next to her and put his hand over hers and her father's. "Don't worry about a thing, Tom. I can hear the ambulance now. They're going to give you the help you need and get you all fixed up again."

Wes was right. The siren was getting louder. Her father put his free hand over Wes's. "You take care of my girls, okay? If something happens to me, you'll look out for Emily and Meg?"

"I will always look out for them," Wes promised him. "But I know nothing is going to happen to you. The doctors sorted you out last time and they're going to do it again."

The ambulance stopped out front and, mercifully, cut its siren. Two paramedics bustled in with a stretcher. They helped her dad stand and loaded him on, ignoring his grumbling that he didn't need a stretcher and could walk on his own. Emily took her mother's hand. "Do you want me to ride with Dad?"

"No, I'll go." Her mother squeezed her fingers tightly. "He'll just give everyone a hard time if I'm not there."

"We'll follow you," Wes told her. "We'll see you at the hospital."

Wes kept a firm arm around Emily as the paramedics lifted her father's stretcher and carried him to the ambulance. Emily watched as her mother climbed in after him. She leaned on Wes, grateful for his support. Her legs were shaking. Her hands were shaking.

"Take some deep breaths," Wes murmured in her ear. "Try to stay calm. There is a lot doctors can do to help people with heart trouble. Have faith they'll be able to fix whatever is going wrong."

Emily hung on tightly to his words and his strength as he wrapped his suit jacket around her shoulders and walked her to his truck.

CHAPTER SIXTEEN

EMILY TWISTED THE handle of her purse between anxious fingers as Wes pulled into the parking lot of the hospital in Santa Rosa. He found a space in the crowded emergency room parking lot and reached for her hand, stilling her fidgeting. "It's going to be okay. Your dad is a tough guy."

She wanted to believe him. But she couldn't stop one thought from taking over all others. "He's already had surgery. That was supposed to take care of everything. What's gone wrong?"

"Doctors aren't perfect. Maybe they missed something. But that isn't a reason to panic, okay? Let's just take this one moment at a time. Your dad is getting help right now. That's what matters."

Wes was right, she had to stay calm. But a voice in her head kept asking, *Why now? Why again?*

"Come here." Wes held out his arm and she unhooked her seat belt and snuggled in under it. His other hand crossed her body to pull her close. He was warm and solid and he smelled delicious. Emily let herself relax her cheek against his chest. How long had it been since anyone had held her like this? Only now, with Wes to lean on, did she realize just how long she'd been alone. He brushed his lips over the top of her head. "I've got you, Emily. And I won't let you go until you tell me you've had enough."

There might never be enough. She knew that now. Wes had captured her heart when she was sixteen years old and despite her efforts, she'd never broken free. Emily tightened her arms around him and closed her eyes, inhaling his strength, the calm center of him. This must be what horses felt around him. That deep knowledge that as long as this man was here, everything was going to be okay.

"We should go in." She reluctantly let go and pulled his suit jacket more closely around her shoulders.

He nodded, still looking at her intently. "You're the strongest person I know, Em. You can do this." He got out of the truck and came around to her door. When he opened it, he offered his hand and she took it. His firm grip on her fingers, his calm presence reminded her that she had to be strong. She had to be steady to support her father and mother.

The neon light of the emergency room lobby cast everything in stark, cool reality. This was where life and death happened and she didn't know which one her father might face.

"Remember, your dad got help right away." Wes let go of her hand to put his arm around her shoulders and pull her into his side for a reassuring squeeze. "I'll bet the doctors will fix him right up."

Her mother was huddled in a blue plastic chair in the far corner of the waiting area. She looked up when Emily and Wes approached, and dabbed at the corner of her eye with a tissue. "He's doing okay. He stayed conscious through the whole ride. They're giving him some tests right now."

"Oh, thank goodness." Emily sat next to her mom and put her arms around her. "That's good news."

"Yes, it is." Her mother's voice grew more

brisk. "And I'll have a few words for him when this is over. He took on way too much in the garden today, insisting on digging up some beds for early planting."

Emily released her mother from her embrace. "Mom, please call me next time. I can do that kind of stuff for him."

"And I'll be happy to lend a hand anytime." Wes sat on the chair next to Emily. "He doesn't need to do those projects by himself."

"That's very kind of you both." Meg gave a little shiver. "I just hope he's going to be okay."

"I'm sure he will." Emily repeated what Wes had said to her earlier. "Dad is a tough guy." She put her hand over her mother's. "You're cold."

"A cardigan sweater isn't quite warm enough for an ambulance ride," Meg said. "But I'll warm up."

Emily glanced down at Wes's jacket, wrapped around her shoulders. "Mom, take this. I rode here in a heated truck."

Wes stood. "I'll go see if I can round up a couple blankets."

Meg smiled faintly. "Weston Marlow, you've grown up to be quite the gentleman."

He smiled at her. "I learned any good manners I have from you."

Emily draped the jacket over her mom's shoulders and watched Wes walk over to the front desk to speak with the receptionist. Her mother squeezed her hand.

"He's become a lovely man. You two looked so gorgeous together tonight. I'm sorry your special date was spoiled."

That was so like her mother, to worry about Emily's evening even when she had a more serious concern to contend with. "Please don't worry. We had a nice time and now we're happy to be here to support you and Dad. Where else would we be?"

"I know, of course you should be here." Her mom sighed. "I just want you both to be happy. And it seems like you could be happy together."

Emily sat bolt upright as her mother's words sank in. "Mom! We're not dating. We're just...I don't know...making peace with each other. And considering working together. Tonight was just..." She trailed off. It had felt awfully romantic. "Tonight was just us trying to become friends again."

"Well, it seems like you are starting a nice friendship, then."

Wes was walking their way with two pale blue blankets. "These don't really match your outfits," he said, handing one to each of them. "But they'll help keep you warm while you're waiting. Also the woman at the desk says there is coffee downstairs. Can I get you both a cup?"

"That would be really nice," Meg said. When Wes left, she turned to Emily with a gentle smile. "I understand that you are just friends, but a lot of people would say he's quite a catch."

"I'm sure he is, Mom, but I don't think he's my catch. No matter how nice he is now, I keep thinking about how he didn't ever get in touch with me. How can I be with someone who so easily went fifteen years without knowing if I was okay?" She helped her mother arrange the blanket over her lap. "I want something like what you and Dad have. You've always been so happy together. I want to be in love like that."

Her mother pressed her lips together and patted Emily's hand. "Honey, that's what we have now, after decades together. It wasn't always like that. Certainly not in the beginning."

"What do you mean?" Emily had heard the story of how her parents met, at a dance in San Francisco. It all seemed very romantic.

"Well, we met at a dance, as you know. But your father lived here, in Shelter Creek. He was only at that dance because he was visiting his cousin Martin at the time. After we met and spent the whole evening dancing together, I left on a cloud, convinced I'd found the man I'd marry someday."

"And that's what happened, right?"

Her mom shook her head. "Not exactly. It turned out your father already had a girl-friend, and it took him a while to decide that he wanted to end it with her. I didn't hear anything from him for a few months."

"That scoundrel!" Emily put an arm around her mom. "He should have dumped her immediately and married you."

"That would have been nice. But we lived far apart. It made things complicated. And the woman he was dating is a lovely person. It was hard for him to end things, even though he felt strongly that I was the one for him."

Emily nodded, trying to reconcile this fickle

young man with the steadfast father she knew now. "Who was this woman?"

"Your friend from book club. Kathy Wallace."

"Kathy?" Emily gaped at her mother. "No way."

"He broke her heart, I'm afraid." Her mother's cheeks flushed a little pink. "You can see why I don't accept your offers to attend that book club."

"But it was so long ago," Emily said.

"I think it would be easier if Kathy had married. But she never did. I've always wondered why."

"Well, now you've got me wondering, too." Emily gave her mother a gentle nudge with her elbow. "Thanks for that."

Her mom's attention had drifted. A doctor came through the doors and into the waiting room. Meg reached for Emily's hand. The doctor looked around and then called out someone else's name. Meg let out a long, shaky breath.

"It's okay, Mom. I'm sure someone will tell us something soon."

"I know. It's just that five minutes feels like an hour when I'm sitting here. Anyway." Meg squeezed Emily's hand once and then let it go. "All I'm saying is that just because a relationship starts out complicated, doesn't mean it isn't right. Sometimes people have things they need to figure out first."

Emily eyed her mother skeptically. "So does that mean you jumped into Dad's arms the moment he finally called you?"

It was good to see the hint of mischief in her mother's smile. "Are you kidding me? I made him wait a few months more before I'd go out with him."

This was a side of her mother Emily had never seen. "You took revenge."

"There was some of that, yes. But more than that, I had to make sure I'd forgiven him for disappearing like that. If I hadn't tried to understand why, and forgiven him, what was the point of even trying to date him?"

"Ah." That was the lesson here. "Have *you* forgiven Wes for running away? For worrying you and Dad so much?"

"I think so," her mother said. "Now that I know why he left, it all makes more sense. But I think there's a difference between us. I wasn't angry with him for leaving the way he did. I was worried and afraid for his safety, but I wasn't angry. I think, for you, his leaving hurt more because you were young, and you were in love with him."

Of course her mom knew. She'd probably always known. "Yes. I was. And I thought he loved me back."

"I'm sure he did." Meg nodded toward Wes, who was approaching with two steaming paper cups. "And from the way he looked at you tonight during those photos, I'm pretty sure he still does."

Emily's stomach twisted into even more knots. "I don't know. It's so complicated between us."

Emily's mom pulled out her phone. "I'm going to text these photos to you. You take a look at them. It sure looks simple to me."

Wes arrived with the coffee. "They actually had a café cart open, so you're spared that stuff that comes out of the vending machines." He handed Emily a cup. "Cream and one sugar for you. Meg, I didn't know your preference so I got you coffee with cream the way you used to like it."

"And I still do. Thank you, Wes."

"Mrs. Fielding?"

They all froze. Emily's mother rose, coffee

cup clutched between both hands, her blanket falling at her feet. "That's me."

The young woman in purple scrubs smiled. She had black hair pulled back in a ponytail and flawless skin. "I'm Dr. Adams, the cardiac surgeon. Your husband is going to need a stent put in tonight."

"Will he be okay?"

Emily heard the quaver in her mother's voice and moved close to put an arm around her.

"He should be fine. He has a partial blockage in one artery, but thankfully, we can fix it. He's just going to need a lot of rest for a few days. And I'll be recommending some physical therapy, as well. I have some forms for you to sign and then I'll bring you back to see him briefly before we get started." She looked at Emily and Wes. "I'm sorry, but we're only allowing your mother to visit right now. We want to start prepping for the surgery as soon as possible."

"I understand." Emily gave her mother a hug. "Tell him we're here and we love him."

"Of course, honey." Her mother kissed her cheek. "I'll be back soon."

Emily sat in one of the chairs and watched

her mother and the doctor walk away. "He's going to be okay."

Wes sat down next to her. "That's great news. The best news, really. Sounds like he'll be up and around in a week."

Emily sat up a little straighter and took a sip of her coffee. "I just hope his surgery goes okay. That doctor... How can she be a cardiac surgeon? She's so young."

Wes laughed, a sound so unfamiliar in the emergency room that several people turned to stare.

"What?" Emily stared, too, wondering what had come over him.

"I know this woman, and she's one of the best veterinarians I've ever had the honor of working with. But some people judge her because she's a young woman."

"Oh." Nothing was funny about this situation, but Emily couldn't help smiling. "I guess I'm a hypocrite."

"Or just very worried about your dad. Which is understandable." He put his arm around her shoulders to give her a comforting squeeze. "But that young doctor will do just fine, I'm sure. Maybe even better than an older one because her training is so recent."

Emily leaned her head on Wes's shoulder and closed her eyes. His spicy cologne was a relief from the antiseptic hospital smell. "I'm really glad you're here with me tonight."

"I want to be here for you, and for your parents. I wish I'd been here for you all those years after I left."

"Me, too." Emily toyed with the edge of her blanket. "It was hard when you left. Everyone was worried about you, and so was I. But I was also really hurt. I was so crazy about you, and you just walked away."

"I knew my leaving would hurt you. But I was so worried about Jamie. My whole focus was on getting him to safety as fast as possible. I guess it helped to know that even if you were sad for a while, you were safe and loved. I trusted that with time, and the support of your family, you'd be okay."

Maybe it was the quiet of the mostly empty lobby, or their stark encounter with mortality this evening, but she finally asked the question she'd wanted to ask for years. "Weren't you sad at all to leave me?"

He kissed her hair gently. "I was very sad. I would lie awake in bed at night, after Jamie fell asleep in my arms, and remember everything we did. I'd go through all our conversations. I'd imagine your smile and it would help me fall asleep. But I'll be honest. There was a big part of me that always felt unworthy of you. I was this poor foster kid, and your family's charity project. I told myself you'd be better off without me weighing you down."

"You never weighed me down, until you left without a word."

"I hate that I hurt you. But what if I'd told you what was going on? I'd have needed you to keep it a secret from your parents. You were so close to them, and we'd already been sneaking around, trying to avoid telling them how we felt about each other. I didn't want to give you one more secret to keep."

Emily nodded. She understood. She might not like it, but she understood. This was what her mother was talking about. Understanding. Maybe even forgiveness. "So, are you going to stick around this time? Keep working with me?"

He looked down at her with a warm smile that would have made her knees weak if she'd been standing up. "Of course I'll stay. For as long as you want me around."

Wes pulled her in closer and Emily closed

her eyes, praying that her dad would be okay, that his heart would stay strong during surgery, that the young doctor knew what she was doing. But she also threw in an extra prayer that her heart would be safe, too, because like it or not, she was falling back in love with Wes.

CHAPTER SEVENTEEN

SHOVELING MANURE WASN'T usually Emily's favorite chore but today the simple task, combined with the clear, crisp morning, was exactly what she needed. The sun was reflecting off the dew-covered leaves of the bay trees near Fancy's shelter. The roof steamed in the warm sun after the chilly night. Even the grass blades sparkled emerald green.

It was Sunday. A blissful Sunday with no emergency calls so far. And last night Wes had gone out on a late-night call for her. How luxurious to lie in bed while he dealt with a lambing issue. She'd thought it would be harder to let go of control, to let him start taking some calls on his own. It had given her a twinge of anxiety but mostly it was just a relief to sleep the night away.

Fancy must have finished her alfalfa. The rich, green, leafy hay was her favorite part of her meal. The mare, less skeletal now but still quite thin, saved her simpler oat hay to nibble on throughout the day. Now she wandered over to sniff the wheelbarrow.

"Hey, girl, are you ready to do some walking this morning?" Wes had suggested that she take Fancy on a short stroll down the path that led from her property to a fire road that ran out over the hills away from Shelter Creek. The farrier was coming by to trim the mare's hooves in an hour, and the more relaxed Fancy was, the better the process might go. A walk would help the mare burn any excess energy.

Not that poor Fancy Face had much to burn. In the nine days that she'd lived here with Emily, she'd mostly wanted to eat and laze in the sun. Occasionally she'd follow her sheep, Beatrice and Rosalind, around as they grazed the grass that grew just beyond the fence. She also seemed to enjoy the time Emily spent with her. After some skittishness, she'd accepted the soft brush Emily used on her coat. Eventually she'd let Emily pull the ticks off her, too. With her coat clean and her mane and tail untangled, Fancy was starting to look like a horse with a chance at a happy future.

Fortunately, the local farrier was a woman, since Fancy still didn't seem to trust men. Jayna was experienced, calm and confident. She just might convince Fancy to let her get near her hooves. Emily sure hoped so. The poor horse had to get them trimmed down. The length was interfering with her gait when she walked.

Fancy came closer and snuffed at the handle of Emily's shovel. Then she took a step closer and raised her nose to blow hay-scented breath on Emily's face.

"Well, aren't you the sociable one today." Emily reached up to smooth Fancy's forelock. "That's good, because you're going to get your hooves trimmed. Then you'll be able to walk better. Aren't you excited?"

Just then Emily's phone buzzed. Fancy backed away a few steps with a snort, her ears forward as she studied the phone Emily pulled from her back pocket. Emily's heart jumped when she saw her mother's name.

"Mom, what's up? Is everything okay?"

"Everything's fine," her mother said. "Don't worry."

Don't worry? Her dad had been home from the hospital for less than a week. Of course

Emily worried. The surgery to insert the stent had gone well, but the surgery he'd had last year had gone well, too. And then they'd almost lost him again. "How's Dad this morning?"

"Doing just as well as when you were here yesterday. Thanks again for doing our grocery shopping for us."

"Of course. Anything I can do, Mom, I'm happy to help. Please just ask."

"Well, I'm asking now. Your father and I would love it if you would come for an early supper tonight."

"Sure. That will be fine."

"And I was wondering if you'd like to ask Wes to join us?"

"Wes?" Would she? This whole week since he'd been so sweet and supportive in the hospital, they'd never once mentioned the connection they'd shared. Instead they'd been circling around each other, acting like cordial colleagues. But Emily watched him whenever she was sure he wouldn't notice. She loved the way he listened so carefully to clients, the gentle way he dealt with animals, his capable hands and agile mind. She'd spent the week coming to terms with a fact she couldn't refute. She was in love with Wes. Completely. Again.

"He was such a help that night in the hospital. We'd really like to thank him personally," her mother said.

"Sure." Emily couldn't say no to that. "I'll invite him. He's stopping by soon to try to help get Fancy's hooves trimmed."

"Your father and I can't wait to meet that horse."

Emily watched Fancy, who'd wandered off to investigate what the sheep had been served for breakfast. "It's better you haven't met her yet. She still looks pretty thin. If Dad had seen her last week, it might have made his heart even worse than it already was."

"You've done a lovely thing, rescuing that poor animal," her mother said. "Now, text me and let me know if Wes can come to dinner with you."

"Will do. Talk to you soon." Emily put her phone back into her pocket. Would Wes want to come? It seemed as if he'd been avoiding her this week. Did that mean he regretted letting himself get so close to her? Or was he just trying to give her some space?

Space was good. She wasn't a girl anymore, easily swept along on the tide of her feelings. She had to be more careful now. They'd skated so close to renewing their relationship that night at the party. And at the hospital it had felt so reassuring to be able to lean on him. But he hadn't been reliable when she'd trusted her heart to him once before. Realizing she cared for him, deeply, brought with it a whole new wave of fear. If she cared, he could hurt her again. And she was pretty sure this time the pain would be worse.

She shook her head. Maybe she needed this little walk more than Fancy. She felt jittery just asking Wes to her parents' house. Which made no sense. It was their invitation, not hers. It didn't have to mean anything more than that.

Shoveling up the last of the manure, Emily pushed the wheelbarrow to the manure pile and dumped it. Then she retrieved Fancy's halter from the shed next to the shelter. It was gratifying that Fancy only showed mild interest when Emily approached her. No backing away, no stress. They were developing more trust. Emily slipped the halter on Fancy's nose and slid the strap behind her ears. A quick buckle against the horse's pretty chestnut cheek and they were set.

Their stroll took them on a flat path through tall green grass. Emily let Fancy pull mouthfuls of it to snack on as they walked. The sound of the mare crunching her treat was soothing. The trail smelled like damp earth and there was a hint of salt on the breeze blowing inland from the Pacific.

"This is so pretty, isn't it, Fancy?" The mare glanced at her, but her focus was still on her mouthful of grass. "You can't have much more of that grass, my friend," Emily told her. "Too much and you could end up with a bad tummy ache."

They'd arrived at the spot where the path met up with the fire road. "Maybe someday you and I will ride out there," Emily said, looking wistfully up at the hills. "But for now, we've got to go back." She led Fancy in a circle on the dirt road. Just then a cottontail rabbit darted out of the tall grass, leaping right in front of them as it sprinted to the safety of a nearby bush. Fancy's head went up and she took several steps backward, blowing sharp, panicked breath through her nose.

"Easy, Fancy. Easy, girl." Emily moved

with her, letting the lead rope play out a little, allowing the mare her moment of worry. "Just a rabbit, Fancy Face. Just a little bunny. Settle down." Fancy slowed, and after a few more puffs her breathing quieted, though she still eyed the spot where the bunny had been with suspicion. "We've got a lot of work to do, don't we? Not everything in this world is out to get you." Emily kept talking with Fancy, petting her neck, murmuring soothing words. Soon the horse relaxed and began tugging at the lead rope, hoping to reach a patch of juicy-looking grass just off the road.

"You must be feeling better if you're snacking again," Emily laughed softly and led Fancy back up the path toward her pasture. "You just have to learn to trust me. I know someone hurt you before, but that doesn't mean anyone is going to hurt you again."

Her own words echoed in her ears. She stopped and Fancy stopped, too, regarding her with mild curiosity in her pale blue eyes. Wes had never meant to hurt her all those years ago. He'd been frantic to save his brother. There was no reason to believe he was going to hurt her now. "I guess that applies to me, too, doesn't it?"

Fancy snorted and lowered her head, rubbing her forehead against Emily's shoulder as if she were nodding. Though she was probably scratching an itch.

"Okay. We both need to work on our trust issues. Agreed?"

Fancy finished her scratching and Emily led her back up the trail.

WES PULLED INTO Emily's driveway and parked his truck. From here he could see her down by Fancy's shed, brushing down the mare's white and chestnut patches. Once Fancy was healthy and at her ideal weight, her coat would be breathtaking. Right now it was dull despite Emily's brushing. It would take a while for nutrients to build up in the horse's deprived body. Poor mare. Who would treat an animal that way?

They'd probably never know. Wes had checked the bulletin board at the feedstore and the online listings, as well. No one had posted a notice that they were looking for a paint horse. That was a relief, because no way would Emily be willing to return Fancy to whoever had starved her like that.

Emily was protective of her practice, her

father and her horse. Wes loved how she stood up for those she loved. He wanted to be one of the people she felt so fiercely about.

But he'd figured he'd better back off this past week. She'd needed space to focus on her father. Tom needed rest after his surgery, but resting wasn't his strong suit. Wes figured it would take both Emily's and Meg's willpower to get him to take it easy after the surgery. Plus, Emily needed to put her energy into bonding with Fancy. These first days were crucial to laying a foundation of trust between them.

Wes got out of the truck, conscious that there was more to it than that. Last weekend he and Emily had taken a couple of steps closer, first at the benefit, and later at the hospital. He'd stayed there all night, holding Emily close, tending to Meg, as well, until they got word that Tom's surgery was a success. But Emily needing his support in the hospital didn't necessarily mean she wanted him closer in real life. She'd been cool and professional at work. She hadn't suggested they spend any extra time together.

Longing echoed through his cells. He loved her. He knew that with all his heart. But he could wait. He could give her space to figure out her feelings. Even if it didn't come easy.

He made his way down the path to where Emily stood with Fancy. He couldn't help noticing how cute Emily looked in her worn jeans, dusty boots and a simple blue T-shirt. Wes stopped a few yards away from her. "Hey, Emily. How is she this morning?"

She looked over at him and smiled her greeting. "We took that walk you suggested. She did fine. Got a little scared by a rabbit, but she calmed down pretty quickly."

Wes nodded. "Honestly, it's not a bad thing. The more she experiences things like that, the more she'll realize that nothing bad happened as a result. The next time she sees a rabbit, it might not be so traumatic."

"I hope so." Emily smiled lovingly at her horse and ran a hand down Fancy's nose. "There are a whole lot of bunnies around here, pretty girl."

"Maybe you could introduce her to that rabbit they have at the wildlife center."

"Peanut?" She looked thoughtful. "That's not a bad idea. Peanut is so calm, she'd be a good introduction to bunnies."

"The farrier isn't here yet?" Wes was here

to advise them about ways they might keep Fancy calm if she had a bad reaction to getting her hooves trimmed. He sure hoped he wasn't needed. The poor horse *had* to have the trim.

"She should be here any minute. Thanks for coming by."

"Anytime."...

"Do you want to try to say hi to Fancy? I want her to get over her fear of men."

"Give her time." Wes took a few steps forward. He'd stopped by a couple times this week to offer Fancy a carrot or just stand near her fence and have a chat. Last time he was here, she'd walked over and snuffled his ear, knocking his hat off. It was progress, but he didn't want to push her. Just like with Emily, he was trying to show Fancy that he was here to be supportive and kind, and didn't expect anything in return.

Watching the horse carefully, Wes could see her tense. "How about if you untie her? She'll be more comfortable with me approaching if she knows she can get away."

Emily undid the rope and held it in her hands. Wes walked toward them and stood nearby, a couple feet away. He turned sideways so he wasn't facing the mare directly. "Let's just talk for a moment. How is your dad doing this weekend?"

"Good. My mom called and said he was hoping for a family dinner tonight. They want you to join us."

Warmth washed over him. He wanted to belong to this family. Especially to Emily, but with Tom and Meg, too. Maybe he was greedy, reaching for way more than he deserved, but there it was. "I'm honored to be included." He looked at her more closely. "Are you okay with that, though?"

The color that rose on her cheekbones reminded him of the way the sunset had turned the clouds pink yesterday evening. "Sure. Of course." She ran her hand down Fancy's neck. The mare was settling down now, getting used to Wes's presence. He took a step closer, still keeping his body turned a little away from the horse. Emily smiled at him. "You kind of look like you're trying to sneak up on her."

He grinned back. "I just don't want her feeling like I want something from her. She has to decide to come to me in order to feel more powerful and less afraid."

"She looks pretty relaxed now."

Good. That was the plan. "Did you have fun with your friends last night?" She'd mentioned that she was going out with her Book Biddy friends. They'd read some book about women and wolves and were going out to howl at the moon.

"It was hilarious. We took a walk and we howled a bit, but then we realized that the official full moon wasn't until tonight. And then Kathy stepped in a gopher hole and twisted her ankle. And Eva was getting all artsy on us and trying to take these nighttime photos, but no one would hold still for long enough."

Wes laughed softly, not wanting to startle Fancy. "It all sounds very Northern California."

"You mean women don't go outside and howl in Texas?"

"Hey, maybe they do. I never thought to ask."

Her blue eyes shone with laughter. "It was pretty silly. But we had fun. How about you? Did you ever reach your brother? You mentioned yesterday that he wasn't returning your calls."

A ripple of worry stirred in Wes's stomach. "He left me a message last night. I was asleep when he called and I guess I'd turned my ringer down at some point. He said he's doing fine. But that's about it." He shook his head. "I don't know if I'll ever stop worrying about him. I guess this is what a lot of parents feel, too. I just want him to be happy and settled and I have this gut feeling that he's not."

"Maybe he's just trying to find his footing in a new job and a new city," Emily said. "He could be out trying to meet people, or putting in extra hours at work. There are a lot of reasons he might not be calling you back as often as you want."

"You're right." Wes tried to let her words sink in and soothe. "I guess I had to be so vigilant for so long, it's hard to let go."

Just then Fancy's curiosity got the better of her. She took a step toward Wes, then another, and explored his T-shirt with her nose, blowing horsey breath all over him. "Hey, girl." He kept his voice quiet. "Nice to see you, too." Slowly he lifted a hand and placed it on her neck. She didn't flinch but she froze, ears forward, regarding him with intent curiosity in her pale eyes. Wes ran his hand down her neck, brought it back and did it again.

"This is great," Emily said quietly. "She's making so much progress."

"We're proud of you, Fancy Face." Wes moved slightly so he was facing the mare. "You've been through a lot. We're here to help you."

Fancy lifted her head and knocked his hat off.

Wes grinned, stepping back to retrieve it and put it back on his head. "Is this going to be our thing, then? I try to make friends and you knock my hat off?"

Fancy leaned forward and knocked it off again.

Emily started laughing. "She's getting downright sassy."

The rumble of wheels had them both turning toward the driveway. A big red pickup came down the grassy hill toward them and pulled up alongside the pasture. The woman driving leaned out the window, her dark hair woven into braids that hung down past her collarbone. "Hey, Emily," she called. "Gorgeous horse."

"Hi, Jayna. Thanks for coming out on a Sunday."

"No problem." Jayna hopped lightly out of

the cab, clapped a straw cowboy hat on her head and closed the door softly behind her. "Sounds like this poor horse really needed some help." She squinted at Fancy. "She sure is thin."

"I know. She was found wandering up off Simmons Road." Emily motioned toward Wes. "This is Wes Marlow. He's started working with me."

"You're a vet?" Jayna took a few steps toward him and they shook hands. She had a firm grip.

"Yes, ma'am."

She grinned. "And not from around here."

"Texas. Houston area."

"I like your accent, cowboy."

"Are you from Shelter Creek?" He didn't recognize her from high school.

Jayna shook her head. "I moved out here from the Central Valley."

Another transplant. He wasn't the only one who saw something special in this little town.

"Wes is really good with horses," Emily said. "Fancy is still pretty skittish, so I asked him to come by and see if he could give us any tips to make this go smoothly."

"Let's take a look at her," Jayna said.

Emily pulled a carrot out of the back pocket of her jeans. "Want to start with a bribe?"

Jayna laughed. "Sure."

Wes watched as Fancy accepted the carrot. The horse seemed at ease with Jayna. It was definitely men she had a problem with. Jayna ran a confident hand down Fancy's right foreleg and picked up her hoof to examine it. Fancy's ears went back.

"Emily, distract her," Wes said softly. "Talk to her. Pet her head."

Emily rubbed Fancy's nose and spoke to her quietly.

"Do you have any of those alfalfa cubes you mentioned the other day? The ones she liked?"

"In the bin in the cabinet."

Wes went to the cabinet and took the lid off the metal bin. He scooped some cubes into a bucket he found there and brought them to Emily. "Try feeding her one."

Fancy immediately took the cube and her ears relaxed as she chewed. "Good idea," Jayna said as she made her way around Fancy, checking on each of her hooves. "This all looks pretty straightforward. I'll go get my tools."

"You need some help?"

"Sure."

Wes followed Jayna to her truck. She opened one of her back cabinets and pulled out a pair of nippers, handing them to Wes. They looked like huge pliers. She'd use them to trim off the excess hoof, kind of like how people trimmed their fingernails. She strapped on a pair of thick leather chaps to protect her legs and found her rasp, which was basically a giant file. Then she put a small hoof knife in her pocket. "All right, let's do this."

It took surprisingly little time to get Fancy's hooves trimmed. Jayna didn't want to take off too much at once, so she clipped and filed them to what she called a reasonable length. "It's not ideal, but we'll work our way down to ideal," she said.

"Fancy handled it like a champ," Wes said to Emily.

She beamed with pride and hugged Fancy's neck. "I'm so relieved. We're on our way to getting her all healed up."

Jayna was ready to leave, so after she and Emily said their goodbyes, Wes carried the nippers for her and watched as she packed her gear into her truck. "Thanks again for doing

302   SECOND CHANCE COWBOY

this on a Sunday. It's hard for Emily to find
time during the week."

"I know you vets must be busy." Jayna shut
the doors to the cabinets on her truck. "But
if you find some time and you want to grab
a cup of coffee, let me know." She gave him
a flirtatious smile and climbed into the cab.
"See you around, cowboy." She started the
engine, backed up the hill to the driveway
and turned her truck toward the road in one
smooth arc.

Wes walked back to Emily, a bemused
smile on his face. It had been a while since
a woman had made the first move. He didn't
want to take Jayna up on her offer, but it was
flattering.

"What's going on?" Emily had turned Fancy
loose in her pasture and was standing with
her arms folded on the top rail of the wooden
fence, watching her horse. The mare was on
her way to visit Beatrice and Rosalind.

"I think Jayna might have asked me out,
just now." He folded his arms up on the top
rail, too. "She asked me for coffee, whatever
that means."

Emily glanced at him, then quickly looked
at Fancy again. "It means she likes you."

Was he wrong or was there a sharper note in Emily's voice? "That's flattering," he said. "I'm sure it is."

Wes studied Emily as she studied her horse. There was a tightness to her jaw and an intensity to her gaze. Fancy was interesting, but not that riveting. Hope stirred inside, the hope he'd been trying to ignore since last weekend. "I don't think I'll take her up on the offer, though," he said.

"Why not? Jayna's nice."

She was being so casual. Too casual. Wes might not know her as well as he used to, but he could see through this. "She is nice. But she's not you."

Emily looked at him, her eyes widening. So blue. So sweet, with the faint smile lines radiating out. Those freckles scattered across her nose and cheeks. He wanted to know them, to map them like constellations. "I want to be with you, Em. I want to spend time with you, outside of work. But I can back off, if you'd rather."

She shook her head. "I'd rather you didn't. Back off, I mean."

That flicker of hope sparked into flame.

"You mean you'd like to spend some time together, too?"

She nodded. "I would." Her smile widened. "I like spending time with you."

"Well, all right, then." He looked back at Fancy because the grin on his face must make him look like a total fool. "I'm looking forward to that."

"Me, too," she said softly and scooted a little closer to him so their elbows touched on the fence. Wes closed his eyes for an instant, relishing that tiny bit of contact and the words they'd said. Somehow he'd earned a little more of her trust and regard. He'd do his best not to mess that up again.

CHAPTER EIGHTEEN

WES SWALLOWED THE last bite of apple pie and folded his hands as if in prayer. "Meg, that meal was better than anything I've eaten in a long time."

"Even better than your favorite deli sandwich?" Emily, sitting next to him in her parents' dining room, tossed him a sidelong smile.

"Yup."

Meg reached for the pie pan. "I can cut you another slice, if you like."

"I would, but I'd like to be able to fit in Emily's truck tomorrow. We've got a full schedule."

Tom took a sip from the mug of herbal tea that Meg had made for him. "I thought you two were going to start dividing up the cases, so you'd both have more free time."

Wes suddenly found it challenging to meet Tom's gaze. "We were. And I still take more of the cats that come in, since Emily apparently isn't a cat person. But I don't know, I guess we kind of like doing the large-animal work together."

"Really?" Meg leaned her elbows on the table and rested her chin on her folded hands. "And why is that, do you think?" Her knowing smile made it clear that she'd already intuited the answer.

"We like hanging out together." Emily glanced at Wes, her skin turning that sunset pink. "We work well together."

She was so cute when she was embarrassed. But he didn't want her managing this situation all by herself. "We've actually decided that we'd like to spend a little more time with each other away from work, as well."

Meg looked from him to Emily and back again. "That sounds like a great idea."

Tom grinned. "Glad you two are finally figuring things out."

"Well, I wouldn't go that far," Emily said, then glanced at Wes, her brows raised. "I mean, I guess we still have some things to figure out. Don't we?"

It was kind of fun to see calm, in-charge Emily floundering around. "I suppose we do."

There was an awkward silence. Rex and Mavis must have sensed it because the two dogs rose from where they'd been curled up together in the corner of the room and came over to the table. Mavis snuffed underneath for crumbs, but Rex, intuitive dog that he was, pushed his nose into Wes's hand. Wes buried his fingers in his dog's thick fur. "I truly appreciate the way you've all welcomed me back, after the way I treated you. I don't think a lot of people would be as forgiving. I hope I can show you all that I deserve your faith in me."

"You have," Tom said. "You stayed with my family at the hospital. And you've already taken some of the burden off Emily at work. We're glad to know she won't be working every waking moment."

"I don't know about that." Wes couldn't resist teasing Emily a little. "Maybe if I can get her to stop looking over my shoulder…"

"I'm not looking over—" Emily stopped. "Oh. You're teasing me." She smacked him gently on the forearm. "Don't be mean."

"Seeing you two give each other a hard time at the table takes me back in time," Meg said. "Remember the time you made Emily spit out her water, she was laughing so hard?"

Wes grinned at the memory. "She took out the entire salad, if I remember correctly."

"This is getting embarrassing." Emily hid her face briefly in her hands. "Can we talk about something else? Dad, how have you been feeling?"

"I don't know how those doctors do it, but I almost feel normal. Still a little achy and slow, but I'm getting stronger every day." He grinned at his wife. "Meg here won't give me any other choice."

"You're going to heal a hundred percent, Tom Fielding, or you'll answer to me."

"See?" Tom laughed. "She's a bully." But the love in his glance when he looked at his wife contradicted his words.

"It's tough love," Meg retorted. "And self-preservation. I don't want you to scare me like that ever again."

This was what Wes wanted. A love that stayed strong through the hard times. Love that could inspire laughter, even when things were rough. He glanced at Emily, who was watching her parents with a slight smile on her face. She was it for him. He knew that like he knew how to breathe.

"Why don't you two go and do something fun tonight?" Meg glanced at the clock on the stove. "It's only eight."

"We'll stay and help clean up first," Emily said.

"Not tonight." Meg stood, reached over and picked up their dessert plates. "I'll clean up. You two go out on a date."

Wes sent Meg his silent gratitude.

"We've got this." Tom stood, too, and picked up the pie plate. "Me and my heart problems messed up your evening last weekend. Get out of here and forget about work for a while."

Emily looked up at Wes, a question in her eyes.

"I'm up for it if you are." He scooted his chair back and stood, offering her his hand. "Emily Fielding, will you go on a date with me?"

She took his hand and held it tight. "Wes Marlow, I thought you'd never ask." They went to get their coats, Rex at their heels.

As they said goodnight, Meg squeezed Wes's hand. "I'm so glad you two are working things out."

"I don't know how I got so lucky as to have you all in my life a second time. But I won't mess it up, I promise."

Meg patted his hand gently. "You never messed it up. You did what you felt like you had to do. I'm just glad we get to have you in our lives again."

Wes shook hands with Tom, and then he and Emily stepped out into the crisp evening. Rex ran ahead, sniffing his way through the yard. "The rain has stopped," Wes said. "It looks like the clouds have moved on."

Emily looked up at the sky. "I can see a couple stars. Maybe we'll be able to see the moon if the sky clears up a little more." They walked in silence to his truck. Wes opened the back door and Rex settled into the back seat. Once he and Emily were seated in the cab, Wes angled his body toward her and took her hand. "So. A date. What do you want to do?"

"I actually don't know." She looked at him with wide eyes. "I haven't been on a date in years."

He grinned. "What was your last date?"

"A guy I met at a conference in San Francisco. He works for a pharmaceutical company. We had dinner a couple times." Her brow furrowed. "That was a few years ago, actually. I haven't really been focused on meeting someone." She looked down at their clasped hands. "And you? Do I really want to know who you last dated?"

"You mean, did I have some big love or something?" Wes grinned and shook his head. "Nope. That's never happened for me. I dated a few women in college but it never got serious. The last person I dated was a woman in Houston a couple years ago. We both liked to hear live music, so we went to a few concerts together. But it seemed like we liked the concerts a lot more than we liked each other."

"I don't think we can find a concert tonight," Emily said.

"What do you do in Shelter Creek for fun?"

She pressed her lips together before she answered. "I'm going to be honest. I don't think I'm very good at having fun. I've been so focused on work for so long. I just wanted to make Dad's practice a success. I guess there's some pressure that goes along with inheriting someone's life's work."

"Well, I've got a confession," Wes said. "I

don't think I'm that good at having fun, either. I spent so many years trying to make every-thing okay, you know? Trying to make sure I had enough money for Jamie and me to get by, and to get through our schooling. I'm not sure I ever really learned how to relax and just have fun."

Emily leaned close and kissed him sweetly on the cheek. "We never got to follow through on the plans we made, to go to college and vet school together. But maybe we can learn how to have fun together."

He caught her chin with two fingertips. Pulled her closer and brushed a kiss lightly across her lips. He lingered there, his mouth brushing hers, his heart pounding on his ribs. This closeness, her breath, her eyes wide, tak-ing him in, it was what his deepest dreams were made of.

"Fun," he murmured. "I'd like that." An idea rose in his mind and caught at his imag-ination. He straightened and reached for his seat belt. "Are you up for a bit of a drive to-night?"

"Sure. What are you thinking?"

"Trust me?" He knew he was asking for a lot with those words.

"Okay." She gave a little sigh. "I'll trust you."

He started the engine, pulled up a country music playlist on his phone and turned the truck west, heading for the coast.

EMILY GLANCED AT Wes as the winding road neared the coast. "Are we going to the beach?" She could barely see him in the dark cab.

"That's what I was thinking. I sure missed the ocean out here, all the years I lived in Houston. The Gulf Coast is nice, but it's not like this."

Emily looked out her window, wonder slowly filling her chest like helium. There were no streetlights out here, just moonlight that had broken through the remaining clouds to cover the hills around the road with silvery shadows. "This is so beautiful." She'd driven these hills many times at night, on the way to emergencies or making her weary way home afterward, but this was different. She was out here with Wes by her side, and the miracle of it, of them together, flooded her veins with heady, reckless energy. She turned up the music, swaying to the rocking country song she didn't recognize. She wanted more, of this night, of this feeling. She pressed the button to lower her window and let the chilly air flood the cab and blow her hair all over.

"That night air feels good." Wes rolled down his window, too, the wind making his thick hair stand on end. He drummed his fingers on the steering wheel in time to the music and glanced her way with a smile that looked more like an eerie set of white teeth caught up in the moonlight. A werewolf.

Emily laughed and stuck her head out her window. "Owooo!"

Wes burst out laughing. "Are you howling?"

"Howling at the moon. Come on, do it with me."

He was still laughing but he played along, tipping his head toward his window and letting out his own howl.

"Aw, come on, you can do better than that," Emily told him. "Give a real howl. We'll do it together, on three." She counted off. "One, two, *three*." She let out the loudest howl she could muster, feeling all the worries about her father slide out the window with her voice and whip away in the wind. Wes howled, too, loud and long, and then they did it again. This time Rex joined in from the back seat, which had them dissolving into laughter while the husky kept going with a long "owoooooooo!"

They were still laughing, and blasting music like the teenagers they'd been, when Wes turned into the gravel beach parking lot. He glanced her way. "You okay with this date so far?"

"I feel great. Thanks for thinking of this. I haven't been here at night since high school." Not since she'd been here with him and Adam and some other friends one night the summer before senior year.

"Are you serious? You've lived here for so long." Wes pulled up to a big driftwood log at the edge of the lot and parked. He flipped on the inside light.

"I guess it didn't occur to me. It was kind of a high school thing to come out here in the evening." And she hadn't wanted to be reminded of all that she missed about those days with him.

"Well, good thing we're here now. Everyone needs a little moonlight and beach sometimes. I used to drive Jamie out to the coast some evenings after work. We'd have a picnic, throw a ball around and jump in the water. It was cheap fun." He reached into the console compartment and fumbled around, emerging with a small box between his fingers. "Matches. In case we want a fire." Then he reached behind the seat and pulled out a knit cap. "Want to put this on?"

"Thanks." Emily pulled it on and reached for the door.

"Hang on." Wes touched her arm. "Look at me?"

She did, suddenly self-conscious. Her hair was probably a windblown mess after the car ride. She cringed inside as he studied her for a moment, seeming to search over her face with his gaze. He lifted his hand and ran his fingertips lightly along her jaw. "You are so beautiful, Emily. You take my breath away."

He was beautiful, too. No cowboy hat tonight, just thick black hair that fell so straight and sleek over his forehead. Eyes that had seen so much that she'd never know. A deep longing ached in her throat. She wanted to know him, to understand him, to allow herself to sink and disappear into all the emotions rising inside. "Likewise." It wasn't adequate. But it was all she had.

Rex whined and shoved his nose between them. Emily smiled and rubbed his soft ears and the thick fur of his neck. "Are you feeling left out, Rexy? Don't worry. We're taking you somewhere you're going to like a lot."

Wes hooked a leash to Rex's collar. "You ready?"

Emily zipped up her jacket, glad she'd worn her thick parka tonight. A small thrill of exhilaration ran up her spine. How long had it been since she'd been out in the night, just to be there? Not to help an animal or to drive from one place to another, but just to enjoy it? "I'm ready." She opened her door and hopped out, accepting the hand Wes offered when he and Rex came around the front of the truck to meet her.

They followed the small path up the dunes, the wiry grass whispering all around them in the breeze. Then they were up and over, and the moonscape beach and the glimmering ocean opened out in front of them in a beautiful play of mercurial light and shadow. Emily stopped in her tracks and let go of Wes's hand to clasp her hands together. "I'd forgotten how gorgeous this is."

He grinned at her. "I hadn't. I've imagined this for years now."

The dune sloped down before them, conjuring long-ago memories of running and rolling her way down. "Race you to the water?"

Wes didn't wait to answer, just bent down to let Rex off the leash. The husky took off toward the waves, leaping and barking his delight. Wes held out his hand and Emily took it and they went after him, laughing as they ran reckless and stumbling through the thick sand. The night was so clear after the rain. The brightest stars hung like ice crystals in the obsidian sky. The rest were obscured by the full moon's bright halo. In front of them, luminous foam tumbled on the roaring waves.

She'd forgotten how magical the beach could be. She slowed her pace. "Shoes off?"

Wes didn't even answer her, just stopped and reached down to pull off his cowboy boots. He was rolling up the legs of his jeans by the time Emily got her sneakers unlaced. When they were both ready, pant legs rolled as high as they could go, he grinned at her. "You ready for this?"

"Absolutely. But don't forget, the water here is a whole lot colder than Texas."

They jogged to the water's edge, letting the remnants of waves wash over their toes. "I'm not forgetting," Wes gasped, jumping from one foot to the other as a wave raised the water level to their ankles. "Or if I was, I remember now. Man, that's cold!"

"It's freezing," Emily agreed. But it was exhilarating, too. The cold, the night, this man. Rex came charging up, barking his joy, circling around them, oblivious to the freezing water. "Let's run with him," Emily said. "It will warm up our toes."

"Come on, Rex!" Wes took off running alongside his dog. Emily sprinted and soon caught up. They ran at the edge of the waves, so the water washed their feet and then retreated, over and over. Rex leaped and danced in front of them, barking out his elation. Eventually they found a steady pace, the rhythm soothing, their progress slow enough that they could catch their breath and look all around them at the moonlit world. Seagulls nestled in the dry sand near the dunes, probably asleep for the night. A crab skittered on the packed sand ahead of them.

When they reached the boulders at the end of the beach they slowed to a walk, turned around and strolled back, hand in hand. Emily relished the way Wes held her hand so tightly. There was no room for resentment in her mind tonight. Wes had left her behind when they were young, but he'd come back to her as soon as he felt like he could. Right now that was enough. When Wes stopped walking and pulled her close to dance with her in the moonlight, she closed her eyes and let him lead, feeling the cold sand under her toes, the sharp breeze on her skin and the warmth of Wes's body against hers.

"I want to date you." His breath played over the lobe of her ear as he spoke. "I want to dance like this, and hold you like this." He stepped back and looked down at her, stilling their swaying. "I love you, Emily. I think I always have."

His words were as magical and as unreal as the silvery landscape surrounding them. Emily didn't want to think or analyze or remember old hurts. She rose up on tiptoes and kissed him, relishing the way the feel of his lips sent all of her skin tingling. Three words rose straight from her heart to her lips. She raised her hand to run her fingers through his thick hair. "I love you."

She touched his lips and felt his smile under her fingers. She could see it in his eyes and feel it as his arms slid around her back, pulling her into his chest, holding her close, cradling her as if he'd found something precious and new.

And maybe this was new. They were different people now than they'd been back then. Even if Wes felt familiar as she pressed against his chest, he was so much more than he'd been before.

Wes kissed the top of her head and Emily nestled closer. "I think our first official date is a success," he said.

"We're better at this having-fun thing than we thought." Emily tilted her head up so she could look at him. He bent to brush his mouth to hers and smiled against her lips. "We sure are. Who knew?" Then he kissed her one more time and started up their slow dance again. Emily was pretty sure the stars were dancing with them, wheeling in circles and spirals overhead. Or maybe that was just how it felt to be in love with Wes, for the second time.

CHAPTER NINETEEN

"It's so pretty here." Emily leaned over the console of Wes's truck and planted a soft kiss on his cheek. "And it's April. Wildflower season. A perfect time for a stroll in Long Valley."

Wes ruffled her hair, mussing the combination of brown and blond silk that never ceased to fascinate him. "I've never paid much attention to flowers. Except the bluebonnets. Couldn't miss those in Texas."

"We've got our own bluebonnets out here. Though we just call them lupine." She pointed toward the green hills rising around Long Valley. "See all that orange? California poppies."

A white truck pulled up next to them with Maya at the wheel and Vivian next to her in the passenger seat. Emily rolled down her window and Maya did the same. "Are you all ready to say goodbye to Mr. America?" Mr. America was the name their eagle had somehow acquired during his recuperation at the wildlife center.

"We are. He's looking good and ready to go," Emily told her.

"Just so you know, I might have invited a few people," Vivian called from her side of the cab. "It's great public relations for the wildlife center."

Maya laughed. "A few? I think every donor is coming, and half the town. That's why we're releasing him in the late afternoon." She rolled her eyes. "It was most convenient for the public."

"Remember, their donations keep us going," Vivian reminded her. "They've all promised to be quiet. And we're going to film it. Then we can make a publicity video for our website."

Wes saw Emily's mouth quirk into a little frown. "As Mr. America's official veterinarian, I'm going to insist that they stay pretty far back when we release him. I hope they brought binoculars."

"I told them they should," Vivian assured her.

Wes couldn't help worrying. Mr. America needed this to go well. "We did everything we could, right? He'll be able to fly okay?"

Emily turned toward him and put a hand on

his leg. "Don't worry. His punctures healed weeks ago. His grafted feathers really took. He's been flying all over the practice pen. He's ready."

"I guess I feel kind of responsible for the guy, since I'm the one who tackled him out here."

Emily nodded. "This is one thing that is hard about working with wildlife. We don't know what will happen to him once he's free. He could flourish, or he could get in a fight with another eagle tomorrow. We just have to have faith that everything will work out."

Faith. Wes had been working on that lately. He had a diamond ring in a velvet box in his dresser drawer. He wanted to give it to Emily more than anything, to ask her if she'd be his wife. But what if she said no?

He and Emily had been dating for over a month now and every day was better than the one before. They worked so well together, and it turned out they played well together, too. Thanks to Emily's father, they actually had some playtime. Tom had confessed that he really missed working, and he'd volunteered to handle any emergencies that came up if Emily and Wes wanted to venture out of cell phone range on the weekends. That meant they could take Rex on hikes out in the hills on quiet Sundays. They'd also spent countless hours working with Fancy, who was blooming into a healthy, beautiful and trusting horse. And they'd enjoyed many fun evenings hanging out with friends.

Coming back to Shelter Creek had been a dream and an impulse all in one. But Wes was sure now that whatever had guided him back here had been calling him home.

"It's going to be okay, Wes." Emily squeezed his hand. "We did a good thing here. Let's go set our buddy free."

"All right. Let's do it." He opened his door and Emily did the same. They went around to meet Maya and Vivian, who were opening the tailgate of the truck. There was a camper shell on the back, and Wes reached over and helped them lift the rear window.

"Do you want to carry him?" Maya nudged Wes gently with her elbow. "You were the one to catch him, so it seems fitting."

Wes had to clear a lump out of his throat before answering. "Sure." They'd saved an eagle. It was kind of a big deal.

Mr. America had traveled to his destiny in

a large plastic animal carrier. Not the most dignified mode of transport and maybe he resented the indignity, because when Wes reached for the handle on top of the crate, the eagle let out a shrill shriek. The tip of his beak poked through one of the small holes in the plastic, as if he'd like to bite Wes's fingers right off. Emily was right. This guy was healed up, feisty and ready to be free.

Carefully Wes slid the carrier out onto the tailgate.

Vivian handed him a blanket. "Put this around the crate, just in case he gets a talon out of one of those holes. And carry it from the bottom. It's solid there."

Wes grinned. "Now I know why you all are giving me—" he added air quotes "—'the *honor*' of carrying him. The guy's a living, breathing, lethal weapon."

"You can handle it," Maya said. She glanced out to the road. "Here comes the cheering section."

One by one, cars pulled into the small parking area. More parked out on the road, crammed onto the gravel verge. Eventually there were a couple dozen people standing around in the parking lot, most with binoculars and cameras draped around their necks.

Wes recognized many of them. The ladies from the Book Biddies came to greet them, and pretty soon Emily, Maya and Vivian were absorbed in hugs from their friends. Maya's grandmother, Lillian, even offered Wes a hug, which he awkwardly accepted. Trisha and Liam arrived with their little boy, Henry, in tow. Caleb and Jace showed up, too, and Jace had his three kids with him. Wes could see Adam out on the road, directing traffic around all the cars parked halfway out into the westbound lane.

Eva, the founder of the wildlife center and the one responsible for recruiting donations, climbed up onto the tailgate of someone's truck. "If you can hear me, give me a thumbs-up," she called.

There were puzzled faces in the crowd, but they dutifully signaled that they could hear her and gathered around her to listen.

"First, I want to thank you all for coming. Many of you have supported the Shelter Creek Wildlife Center financially, or by volunteering, or both. We would not be here today without all of you."

A few people started clapping but Eva held out a hand to signal for silence. "It's a day for celebration, but it has to be a silent celebration. This eagle, whom we call Mr. America, has been through a lot. He was rescued here in Long Valley after a fight with another eagle that left him with wounds and missing flight feathers. Fortunately, our veterinarian and staff at the center have been able to nurse him back to health. However, this is a stressful day for Mr. A. No matter how excited we are to see him fly free again, we have to stay calm and quiet. Agreed?"

Many hands rose with more thumbs-up signs.

"Okay, then," Eva said. "Let's go set this eagle free."

She hopped down from the tailgate and came over to where Emily, Maya, Vivian and Wes had the eagle. "You all go out first. I'll lead this crowd behind you and make sure they stop quite a ways back from the second pond."

"Sounds good." Maya looked at Wes. "You ready, cowboy?"

"I guess so." Wes draped the blanket around the crate with Emily's help and lifted it from the bottom. He could hear the eagle's talons scraping the plastic, but as he started walking with the crate it seemed to settle down.

"Something good is going to happen, Mr. A," Wes said. "We're going to send you back to your life. Maybe you'll find a mate. Settle down. Have a few kids." He heard a laugh and glanced over at Emily, who was walking beside him. "What are you laughing at?"

"Nothing. You're just cute, that's all."

"I'm thinking Mr. A's plan doesn't sound half bad." He winked at her. "Settle down, build a nest somewhere…"

"Wes!" Her face had that sunset glow he liked to put there. She might be embarrassed, but she was smiling, too, so he smiled back.

"Just saying."

They were coming around the bend to the second pond. "All right," Wes said to Maya. "What's the best way to do this? Please don't tell me I have to dive into the mud again?"

"Hopefully, this should be a whole lot easier," Maya said. "I think we can just put the crate in the grass near the boardwalk." She winked at him. "On dry land."

Wes made a show of rolling his eyes to the heavens. "Hallelujah."

"Come on." Maya hopped off the board-walk and Vivian followed her. They held up their hands. "Pass Mr. A to us."

Wes set the crate down on the wood planks and Vivian and Maya each took an end. Care-fully, they carried it closer to the edge of the pond. Wes and Emily followed behind. Near the shore, they looked back at Eva. She'd stopped the crowd several yards back, where the boardwalk curved around the other side of the pond. The guests would have a great view from there.

Two men Wes hadn't met before set up a tripod and a big video camera in the grass on the other side of the pond.

"It's time," Maya said. "Let's do this."

"Goodbye, Mr. America," Vivian said qui-etly.

"Fly free," Emily added.

Wes sent a silent wish out to the bird that it would be safe. That it would live long and be well.

Maya used the blanket to shield her hand as she lifted the door and folded it back over the roof of the eagle's crate. Then they all walked several steps back again, until they were standing near the edge of the boardwalk.

Vivian got her camera out and focused it on the crate.

Emily reached for Wes's hand and he folded his fingers around hers, seeking her warmth and comfort in this unexpectedly emotional situation. He glanced over and caught her using the sleeve of her free hand to dab at her eyes. He let go of her hand and put his arm around her.

"I know I'm being silly," she whispered.

"No, it's okay. I feel the same way, too." She glanced up at him and pretended to wipe a tear from his eye. He caught her hand in his and kissed her knuckles.

Nothing was happening at the crate. Maybe the eagle was still shaken up from his ride out here. Wes could hear his own heartbeat in his ears, hear Emily shift her weight, rustling the grass under her feet. Was something wrong with the eagle?

Just then there was the scraping sound of talons on plastic, and Mr. America emerged from the crate. He waddled a few paces, so ungainly on the ground, and then glanced quickly from left to right, as if he were trying to get its bearings. Finally he unfolded his wings, flapping them experimentally at first, then with more confidence, until he rose up into the air, caught a current, flew higher and circled over the pond and his crowd of well-wishers.

Fists pumped in a silent cheer as Mr. A circled higher, sailed across the valley and disappeared into the top of a large fir tree on the far side.

Emily threw her arms around Wes. "He's okay. He's probably resting over there, but his flight feathers worked perfectly. He looked great!"

"He sure did. Thanks to you." He looked down at her. "You're an amazing veterinarian, Em. You saved that bird."

There were tears on her cheeks when she looked up at him. "Sorry if I'm an emotional wreck but this kind of thing never gets old. We helped him out and now he has a second chance."

Wes grinned. "I know how he feels. I feel like I've been given a second chance, too."

Emily went on tiptoe and kissed his cheek. "Everyone deserves one."

Vivian approached them, her smile pure elation as she high-fived Emily. "That was perfect. Picture-perfect. He's magnificent."

Maya brought the crate and Wes let go of Emily to take it from her. They all clambered back up onto the boardwalk. Maya threw her arms around Vivian's and Emily's shoulders. "Ladies, we did it again. And Wes, too," she added, shooting him a grin. "You can be an honorary lady."

"Thanks." Wes didn't care what he was. He was just glad that the eagle seemed so healthy and strong.

Trisha came up the boardwalk to join them, Liam behind her holding Henry. She was getting so big her tummy poked out like a basketball. "That was amazing! I'm so proud of Mr. America!" She patted her stomach. "I'm just sorry I'm getting too big to be helpful."

"You nursed that bird during the weeks that he needed it the most," Maya said. "That was the most important part, after Emily and Wes patched him up."

They all walked back to the main group, accepting congratulations from the donors and spectators. Back at the parking lot they said their goodbyes, and then it was just Emily and Wes, back in the cab of his pickup. "That was something special," he said, leaning his head back against his seat and trying to take it all in.

"It sure was." She squeezed his hand. "We're done for the day. What would you like to do?"

"I'd like to go get Rex and take him for a walk."

"You think he's getting tired of watching animal TV?"

Wes started up his truck. "He's only been on his own for an hour or two, but I know he loves it when we're all together, exploring the town."

Emily smiled and put on her seat belt. "Me, too. Let's go take a walk."

THE GRASS WAS wet with dew when Emily stepped out her back door and started down the hill to feed Fancy. It was going to be another sunny day, though it was supposed to rain next week. As much as she loved the sunshine, rain in April was a good thing. There was always the threat of drought in California.

She stopped to pick a small purple wildflower and turned it in her fingers. Last night, after letting the eagle go, she and Wes had taken a long walk with Rex. Then they'd ordered pizza and watched a silly comedy on TV. Snuggling next to Wes on his couch, with Rex nestled against her, had felt like her perfect version of domestic bliss. She'd never thought she'd find that with Wes.

She stopped at the shed and pulled out a couple of flakes of hay for Fancy, then went to toss them through the window of Fancy's shelter and into her manger. She froze, hay in hand. "Oh, no!" She dropped the hay on the ground. Fancy was standing completely still in the shelter, her head down, breathing hard.

Emily ran to the gate and let herself into the pasture. "Hey, Fancy Face." She tried to keep her voice calm despite her racing heart. "What's going on, girl?" She knelt down by the mare's head. Her blue eyes were half-closed, the expression dull. "Okay, you stay here, Fancy. I'm just going to run up to the truck and grab a few things."

Emily walked calmly out of the pasture and then broke into a run. As she climbed the path to her truck, she pulled her phone out of her back pocket and called Wes. When he answered he sounded a little out of breath, too.

"Wes, I'm so worried about Fancy. I'm

pretty sure she has colic. She looks bad. Can you come over here?"

There was a slight pause on the other end of the phone. "Em, I'm so sorry, but I can't."

"Why not?" Emily tried to picture their calendar in her mind. They didn't have any early-morning appointments, did they?

"I talked to my brother this morning. He quit his job."

"Oh. Okay." Emily reached into her truck and pulled out the stethoscope she always kept in the front console. "That's too bad. But Wes, I need you. I know it's silly but I'm kind of panicking. Fancy doesn't deserve this. Can you please come?" Her heart was hammering like a fist on her rib cage as she jogged back toward the pasture with the phone to her ear.

"You know how to handle colic, Em. Just treat it as you would with any other horse."

"That's the thing, I can't treat it like any other horse. It's Fancy and I can't think straight." Emily stopped in her tracks, the meaning of his words sinking in. "You're not coming?"

"I'm heading to London. I'm worried about Jamie. I've got to see what's going on."

"You just talked to him on the phone. Did he sound upset?"

"Not really. That's one thing that has me worried. He was so excited about this job. Now he just quit like it was no big deal."

Emily started down the hill again. "Just call him back. Ask him what's going on."

"He's not telling me anything. He's my brother, Emily. I'm his only family. What if something's wrong?"

"But he just told you that everything was fine, right?" Maybe she was selfish but she didn't want him to go to London. Not now, when Fancy was sick.

Wes ignored her question. "Look, I know this is going to cause some inconvenience at work. There are a few appointments that I'll need you to take for me."

"Can't you leave for London tomorrow?" Now she sounded pathetic. Emily let herself into the pasture and walked to where she could peer into the shelter. Fancy was still there, her head down, her breathing shallow. "I need you, Wes. I'm so worried about this horse."

"I'm sorry to let you down. I really am. But I have to start driving or I won't make my flight. You're a great vet, Emily. You can handle this on your own."

He wasn't coming. He was leaving, right when she truly needed him. Just when she thought it was safe to lean on him. Old hurt rose to mix with the new, pushing tears down her cheeks. "Yes, I *can* handle it on my own, Wes. But you know what? I shouldn't have to."

Emily hung up and shoved her phone back in her pocket, tears stinging her eyes. *No.* She couldn't cry about Wes. She'd shed enough tears over him to last a lifetime. She took a few calming breaths and then approached her horse. She brought her stethoscope to Fancy's side and listened hard. Dread twisted in her stomach. She moved the stethoscope toward Fancy's hip and listened again. She moved it lower, panic shrinking her lungs. There was no noise. No comforting gurgles to show that Fancy's stomach was digesting her food. Fancy definitely had colic.

Emily's skin chilled like she'd jumped into cold water. She walked a few paces away, trying to stay calm. She couldn't handle this by herself, no matter how many times she'd treated horses for colic. She was too worried to think straight.

She called her father, grateful when he

promised to come immediately. She called Annie Brooks, who probably knew more about animals than she did. Maya answered on the second ring and promised that she was on her way. When Emily hung up the phone she fell to her knees, swamped with relief. She was blessed to have friends and family she could rely on. She just wished she could rely on Wes.

CHAPTER TWENTY

THE PLANE TOUCHED down at Heathrow Airport at nine in the morning, right on time. Wes peeled his cheek off the wall of the plane and untangled himself from the scratchy airline blanket. Rubbing his eyes, he pushed up the window shade and stared out at the busy runway as they taxied for the gate. London. The April sky here was cloudy, nothing like the bright blue sky at home. The clouds seemed fitting.

Once out of the airport, hailing a taxi, he saw more of the differences he'd expected. A black cab driving in the opposite lane swooped to the curb to pick him up, with the driver sitting where the passenger should. Hurtling down the busy motorway and then through the packed streets to his hotel, Wes tried to take it all in. The tall modern buildings mixed in with ancient stone facades was a contrast he'd expected from seeing photos, but it still surprised him how small the older buildings looked when there were skyscrapers looming above.

He wanted to be able to turn to Emily and talk about it all. He wondered what she'd make of such a bustling city when she'd lived most of her life in a quiet country town. But now he'd never know because he'd blown it. He'd smashed her fragile faith in him.

But why was it so fragile? He'd been nothing but trustworthy since his return. Was the boy he'd been fifteen years ago still more vivid in her mind than the man he was today?

Wes shifted in his seat and drummed his fingers on the windowsill, relieved when the driver said, "Here you go, mate," and pulled up in front of a hotel with majestic columns rising in ornate splendor from the sidewalk. Wes had picked it off the internet because it was pretty and it looked like he imagined a London hotel should look. If he was blowing his dreams apart for this trip, he might as well enjoy it.

Paying the cabbie with his credit card, Wes thanked him, grabbed his suitcase and headed across the marble lobby to the front desk. While he waited for his room, he admired the graceful furnishings. He'd never in his life stayed anywhere this upscale. He'd had a job washing dishes once, in the kitchen of the Four Seasons in Houston. That was the closest he'd come to this type of atmosphere.

After the clerk handed him his room key, Wes pulled out his cell phone and called his brother's number. Jamie answered on the second ring.

"Wes, you should be sleeping."

Wes grinned. "That would be weird since I'm standing in the lobby of the Waldorf."

"What?" Jamie's voice came out in an astonished croak.

"I'm here. In London. Want to meet up?"

"Of course." There was a pause on the other end of the line. "You flew all the way to London? To see me?"

"Yes, I did. So get your unemployed butt up and ready for some sightseeing. If I have to come all the way around the world to talk some sense into you, I'm going to see this famous city while I do it."

Thirty minutes later, Wes stood on the steps of Saint Paul's Cathedral and watched Jamie jog across the street toward him. His brother looked the same as always, his tall figure familiar in dark jeans and a black jacket. They shared the same thick, dark hair and green eyes, but Jamie's face and frame were leaner and he was a little shorter than Wes.

Wes jogged down the steps to wrap his brother in a bear hug. "Good to see you, bro."

Jamie pulled back, eyeing him quizzically. "Good to see you, too, I think. I can't believe you're here, in London."

"I needed a break from tiny town, USA."

Jamie nodded sagely. "Ah. Things not going so well with the dream girl?"

"Not at the moment." Wes gestured toward the old church. "Come on, let's go inside."

"This old tourist trap?" Jamie grinned. "Just kidding. I'm not that jaded yet. It's all pretty amazing here."

They wandered the church, admiring the lofty stone columns topped with carvings and historical statues. But it was the ceiling that had Wes stopping in his tracks, awed by the intricate mosaic pictures that covered every surface. Biblical figures, decorative panels and mystical animals swirled and interacted, all created with tiny pieces of glass and tile.

Jamie came to stand beside him and pointed up to a mosaic of David as an old man with white hair, leaning his elbow on a table, lost in thought. "He reminds me of you."

"What?" Wes looked at his brother in astonishment. "I'm not *that* old!"

"Are you sure?" Jamie raised his brows skeptically. "Because you've flown all the way across the planet just to scold me. That feels pretty old to me."

"I'm not here to scold," Wes protested. "I was worried about you."

Jamie shrugged. "Well, now I'm worried about you. You seem kind of down."

"I'm fine, but you just quit your brand-new job." Wes couldn't keep much from his brother. "Okay, I'm not totally fine. I may have ruined my chances with Emily."

Jamie took his arm. "Come on. Let's grab a coffee and take a walk. You can tell your little brother all about it."

Outside the cathedral they bought coffee to go from a café and started walking through city streets toward Buckingham Palace. Jamie took them on a route that led along the River Thames. Walking by the water, Wes told Jamie about his efforts to win Emily back. "We got close again, you know? We spent time with her family, we've been training this horse we found, Fancy. She's beautiful. One of those paint horses, with blue eyes." He pulled out his phone to show Jamie a photo and there was Emily, her long hair cascading over her shoulders, feeding Fancy a carrot. "You can see how thin she is still. When a client of ours found her, she was skeletal."

"She's beautiful," Jamie said. "Emily, that is. The horse is nice, too. So why are you here, visiting me, and not there, trying to make everything better with her?"

Wes started walking again. "She doesn't trust me. I needed to come here, to see you, and she got mad. Like I had to make a choice between her and you. She hung up on me."

Jamie took a sip of his coffee and they walked in silence for a moment. When his brother spoke again his voice was gentle, like he was teaching a little kid. "First of all, it probably reminded her of when you left her back when you were young. You didn't exactly handle that well. You never even contacted her."

"No. I didn't," Wes admitted. "But I've apologized so many times. I've done all that I can think of to make it up to her."

"Except sticking around when she felt like she needed you."

Jamie's words hit like blows from a hammer. Wes thought of Emily, trying to handle Fancy's colic on her own. She could call on a lot of friends for help. She wasn't really alone. But still, he should be there. She'd really wanted him there.

"And secondly—" Jamie bumped his shoulder gently with his own "—I don't need you flying here to rescue me. I'm fine."

All the panic that had Wes running for the next flight to London resurfaced. "You quit your job. The job you were so excited about."

Jamie put a hand to Wes's shoulder. "Bro, I'm twenty-five years old. I've got my master's degree in business and I graduated top of my class. I'm going to get another job. I have two interviews lined up already."

Wes gaped at him. "You do? I thought you were just giving up."

"Why would I do that?" Jamie gave him an irritated look that Wes knew well. "Why can't you have a little faith in me? You always treat me like I'm so fragile. Like I'm about to fall apart."

"Those years you spent with Aunt Liz and Uncle Rick—"

"Those years didn't break me, because you came and got me out. And you gave me so many good years to erase the bad ones."

"But we were so poor," Wes said. "Everything was so hard. I could barely provide for you."

"Those years were hard for *you*, Wes." Jamie's voice was firm. "I was in school and I had some pretty great teachers. I was safe and cared for, with a home and food and activities. You gave me everything, and I always felt lucky that I got to live with my cool big brother."

Wes tried to absorb his Jamie's words. He'd tried hard to protect him and make everything okay for him. But Wes had never felt like he'd actually succeeded. His brother had always been someone to worry about, someone to save from the rough edges of the world.

"I think the person who might have suffered the most trauma when I was growing up was you," Jamie said. "You were exhausted, working multiple jobs and never sleeping to make sure we'd be okay. I had it easy. All I had to do was go to school."

His brother was right. Wes had paved the way for him. For both of them. He'd made it work. A weight seemed to lift off his shoulders and drift away into the mist over the river.

"And I'm okay, bro," Jamie assured him. "I'm not going to fall apart just because I quit my job."

"Why did you quit, then?"

"I had a racist, bigoted boss and a bunch of coworkers trying hard to be just like him. If I didn't get out of there, I'd have punched someone."

Wes laughed. "That's the result of your upbringing, in all those tough neighborhoods."

Jamie shrugged. "Maybe. Or maybe you just raised a decent human being who stands up for what he believes in. Anyway, I've got an interview at a really cool financial group that gives loans to small businesses. I think I might fit better there."

Relief had Wes throwing his arm around Jamie's shoulders. "I'm sure you will."

Jamie hugged him back and then let go so they could get around a lamppost. "But if I don't like that job, or I want to shift careers, or even drop everything and travel the world, I don't want you to panic. You're not responsible for me anymore. We both made it through and we're going to be just fine. You can go back to Tiny Town in the middle of nowhere and relax."

Wes looked out over the river. A tourist boat puttered by, the guide's voice a blurry drone from this distance. Big Ben towered over the spires of Westminster Abbey just ahead of them. And Jamie didn't need him anymore.

The freedom was strangely bittersweet. Wes had never resented raising Jamie. He hadn't had a lot of time to sit back and enjoy it, but his role as a big brother and guardian had defined him. It had given him an identity and made him who he was. Now it was time to let that go and just be Wes Marlow, small-town vet.

After witnessing the action and excitement of London, that idea should seem boring. But it didn't. He wanted to see a little more of this great city, but he couldn't wait to get back home.

They'd reached Saint James Park. "Are you ready to meet the Queen?" Jamie asked.

"Is she receiving hicks from Tiny Town today?"

"She's got a special knighthood prepared for you. Something about brotherly love. And horses."

"Come on." Wes tossed his empty coffee cup in a trash can, suddenly jubilant. He'd been worried about his brother for so many years, but now he had permission to let go. He took off running up the manicured path toward the lake. "I'll race you."

"You'll never win, old guy," Jamie challenged and sprinted past Wes toward the lake in the center of the park.

Wes jogged after him, laughing. Jamie was right. They were all grown up, and they were both going to be just fine.

CHAPTER TWENTY-ONE

THE DAY PROMISED perfect spring weather when Emily stepped out of her back door and made her way across the dewy grass toward Fancy's stable. Rosalind and Beatrice were already up and about, grazing in the far corner. Fancy was still in her shelter, standing with her weight on three legs, her back right cocked and resting.

"Fancy," Emily called softly, not wanting to startle the sleepy horse. Fancy was getting stronger every day since her colic scare. It had taken Emily, Maya and Annie hours of walking her after they dosed the mare with medication that day, but the colic had passed. Now, five days later, Fancy was eating well, as if nothing had happened.

Except things *had* happened. Wes had walked away when she needed him. And even if Emily shouldn't resent him for going to help his brother, she did.

Fancy Face looked up with sleepy eyes when Emily approached the window of her shelter. It was early, but Emily had a busy day ahead and wanted to get into the clinic early. Now that Wes was gone, she had so much to do. How had she ever gotten it all done alone before he came to work with her?

The problem was Wes had gotten her used to free time. She'd loved her days off to spend with Fancy, or to help out at the wildlife center, or to take long walks with Rex and Mavis. Now that she'd experienced a more balanced life, it was hard to face the long days of endless work ahead of her. Wes had changed her, possibly for the better. But now she *had* to hire someone else to work with her.

Unless Wes came back. But she'd hung up on him. Would he want to come back? He'd most likely find a way to live near his brother, since Jamie was clearly the first priority in his life.

Would she even want him back? He'd dropped everything, including her, when she was panicking, to go see his brother. It felt like an echo of the past, even though she knew, logically, that it was a totally different situation. But still, his departure felt uncomfortably familiar.

Fancy poked her head through the window in her shelter and nickered at Emily.

"Hey, good girl, you're awake." Emily went to greet her horse, marveling at Fancy's new confidence. The mare stuck her nose right up to Emily's ear and blew warm horsey breath all over her face. She even let Emily run her hands down her face and over her cheeks, and kiss her on her pink, spotted nose. Her blue eyes looked clear and calm. "You are doing so well," Emily told her. "I'm so proud of you."

Emily unhooked the latch on the shed next to the shelter and pulled a couple of flakes of hay off the bale. She scooped a few alfalfa cubes and poured them into a feed bucket. It was a testament to Fancy's new lease on life that the horse tried to grab the bucket out of Emily's hands before she could hook it in place.

"Hang on, Fancy Face," Emily said, using her shoulder to block Fancy's enquiring muzzle. "Or should I start calling you Bossy Pants?"

Fancy backed off and Emily broke up the hay for her, then left the mare to her feast. She grabbed some more hay and brought it out to the metal basket feeder near where Rosalind and Beatrice were nibbling grass. The two sheep were less pushy than Fancy, waiting politely while she shook their hay into the feeder. She ran her fingers through their thick wool. "You two are going to need a haircut soon."

"They're looking good."

Emily looked up to see Bobby by the fence near Fancy's shelter. "Hey!" She waved him over. "Come in and see your sheep."

He came through the gate and strode toward her, his feet clumping in rain boots that came all the way up to his knees. "Fair Emily, good morrow," he said. "And Rosalind and Beatrice, nice to see you ladies, too." Rosalind looked up at her owner, her black face a study in bland sheep-like disinterest. She regarded Bobby for a moment while she chewed her hay, then turned back to the feeder for another bite. "Ah, the unflappable nature of sheep," Bobby said. "It's one of the reasons I enjoy them so much."

"They seem happy," Emily said. "How do they look to you?"

"Blissful," Bobby said. "Out here in the peace and quiet of their own pasture, spending their days comforting their dear friend, Fancy. I have never known two happier sheep than Rosalind and Beatrice."

"You make it all sound so poetic," Emily teased him.

"What is life without poetry, fair Emily?" And then he sobered. "I came by to see how you were doing. I heard your young apprentice has left town."

Emily nodded. "You know he was never my apprentice, right? He's a highly educated, talented veterinarian who was considering working with me."

There was a mischievous twinkle in Bobby's eye, and he tugged once on his long ponytail, a gesture that seemed to be a habit for him. "I am aware of who he is. I also know that he was once your true love but abandoned you many years ago. I figured, after he strode back into town and into your life, that it might be good to take him down a peg or two. Thus, the word *apprentice*." He grinned. "If he returns, shall I continue the nickname?"

"You can call him my apprentice for as long as you like. If he ever comes back." It was a sweet and odd show of loyalty.

"He'll come back, Emily. Or, if he doesn't,

he isn't nearly as intelligent as he pretends to be."

Emily smiled. It was funny who became your unexpected allies during rough times. "Thanks, Bobby."

"You don't need him, you know. You're a great veterinarian. This town is lucky to have you. It would be nice to have a second vet, just so we don't wear you out, but the ranchers around here respect you."

"How do you know that?"

"I keep my ear to the ground."

A funny image of quirky Bobby, roaming Shelter Creek with his head tipped down low had Emily suppressing a laugh. He was such a nice man. "I appreciate that. I really do."

They went to check on Fancy, and Emily was thrilled when the mare let Bobby approach. Fancy even put her nose out to snuffle his curled knuckles. They'd made so much progress with her in a short time. So much of it was thanks to Wes and his guidance. Emily just hoped she could continue to help the horse without Wes around. For a moment she could picture him so clearly, standing by the fence, the brim of his cowboy hat tipped up, while he watched her work with Fancy. How could she go forward knowing she might never see him like that again?

One day at a time. One step, then another. Just like she'd done the last time Wes left Shelter Creek. It wasn't easy but it would have to be enough.

Bobby left for the feedstore and Emily got ready for work, reflecting on the rancher's words. Bobby's visit reminded her that she had a good life here in Shelter Creek, surrounded by people who liked and respected her. After so many years of effort, the ranchers around here trusted her. She needed to focus on her work and on being an active part of this community, and stop worrying about when and if Wes would come back home.

If only her heart didn't hurt quite so much…

"FRED, ARE YOU HERE?" Emily walked toward Fred Corrigan's barn and then stopped. Something was different. The air was clear. Of course it still smelled a bit like cow, but it was so much better than it had been on her last visit. Peeking into the barn, she saw clean floors freshly hosed down. There were no cows in sight. Fred must have sent them all out to pasture to enjoy this sunny, breezy day.

"Can I help you?"

Emily turned toward the voice to see a woman wearing overalls and muddy boots come around the corner of the barn. She had her brown hair in long braids crowned by a floppy pink felt hat that had seen better days. She was pretty, with a sun-kissed face, pert nose and wide blue eyes.

"I'm Emily Fielding. The veterinarian. I stopped by to see how Fred was doing." The truth was, she'd stopped by to distract herself. She had a rare free hour in the middle of the day. Wes would have told her to use it to relax, to run home and visit Fancy or to grab a sandwich with him at the Redwood Deli.

The other woman was looking at her quizzically and Emily realized she'd completely drifted off into her own thoughts. She brought her hand to her forehead. "I'm sorry. It's been a long week. Can you tell me your name again?"

"I'm Greta Corrigan. Fred's daughter."

"You have goats," Emily said. "I've heard of you."

"Greta's Goats. Which has now relocated to this property."

"You're taking over the dairy cattle, as well?"

Greta gave a rueful smile. "As much as dad will let me. He's barking orders from his rocking chair on the porch every time I walk by. That's why I was sneaking around behind the barn just now."

It was the first time Emily had really laughed since Wes left, and it felt good. "I don't blame you. Your father can be a handful." She gestured to the barn. "The place looks so much better."

"We've got a few good hands working for us now. And I run a clean dairy, whether I'm milking goats or cows."

"Well, I was just stopping by to check on things. Last time I was here, I was pretty worried."

"Ah," Greta said. "You're the one who called Annie Brooks and her husband and all the other folks who came to my dad's rescue."

Emily nodded. "I had to do something."

"I'm grateful to you. I hadn't realized things had gotten so bad here."

"It's hard when our parents get older." Emily remembered her father looking so pale in his hospital bed just a few weeks ago. "It puts us in a difficult position."

"Is that the young lady veterinarian?"

Emily turned to see Fred stumping along with his cane. He still wore his cowboy hat and jeans, but Emily could see that his shirt was clean and pressed. Having his daughter home was good for him.

"Young lady veterinarian?" Greta glanced at Emily, a worried expression on her face. "He calls you that?"

Emily nodded. "Good morning, Fred."

"Good morning, young lady. I don't recall phoning you. I hope you're not charging us for this visit."

"No, this is a social call. I wanted to see how you're doing."

Fred stopped in front her. "You're not spying for that meddling Annie Brooks again, are you?"

"Dad!" Greta came to stand beside Emily. "Annie helped you out a lot. And she got me to move back here to help out, too. So please don't give Emily a hard time. She did the right thing, letting Annie know that you were falling behind with the chores."

Fred looked puzzled, like he wasn't used to having his rants contradicted. "Well, I suppose things are looking a little cleaner around here. And it's nice to have my daughter home." He turned to Emily. "Young lady, perhaps I owe you my gratitude."

"I appreciate that," Emily said. "I'd also like it if you didn't call me young lady anymore. You may call me Emily. Or Dr. Fielding, if that makes you more comfortable. But I'm not that young and I spend all my days around animals, so I'm not sure I'm much of a lady, either."

Fred's mouth opened, closed, then opened again. Finally he nodded once. "Okay, then, Dr. Fielding. I'll wish you good day."

He turned on his heel and stumped off, heading for his house.

"Well done," Greta said. "If I've learned one thing about my father, it's that you have to stand up to him, very firmly and very clearly. Once he learns that he can't push you around, he's actually not a bad guy."

Emily nodded, not sure what she thought about that. Fred not might be a bad guy, but she doubted he'd ever be a very pleasant one.

"You know, he was talking about you the other day. He said you got cattle exams and vaccinations done faster than any vet he's worked with. And that you taught him how to manage his pastures in winter so there's less mud and the cattle's hooves stay healthier. For all his 'young lady' nonsense, he thinks you're a great veterinarian."

"That's good to know." And a gratifying surprise. Emily had assumed she'd be sending Wes out here to deal with Fred Corrigan in the future, but maybe it would be okay to handle this place on her own. She always had before, and with Greta in charge, it would be a lot more fun. "I'd better get going. Let me know if you need anything. I don't know if you have a vet you've used in the past, but I'm local and happy to help."

"My vet is out on the coast and a ways south of here," Greta said. "Plus, it will be nice to work with a woman."

"Likewise."

Emily got into her truck feeling better than she had since Wes left. She'd stood up to Fred and helped to get his daughter home. Overall, she'd changed his life for the better. She hadn't let her own resentment of her grumpy client win.

And then it hit her. She might have done well with Fred Corrigan but what about Wes? She stared at the road ahead in dismay. He'd needed to see his brother and she'd overreacted. She'd let her resentment win with him. Shame curled in the pit of her stomach.

She'd known, deep down, that she was perfectly capable of handling Fancy's colic and that she had other people she could rely on. Her quarrel hadn't really ever been about Fancy. It had been about wanting Wes to choose her over his brother. She'd been selfish and caught up in her past hurt, using his situation with his brother to take out her old pain on him.

She needed to put that pain to rest and understand that Wes had come back to her, grown and changed. She had to forgive him for running away when they were young if they were going to have any kind of future together now. If she couldn't trust him, or believe in him, they were both wasting their time.

CHAPTER TWENTY-TWO

WES SET THE bag of pastries and the extra large cup of coffee on Emily's desk at the clinic. Next to it he put the mason jar of delicate flowers he'd purchased at the flower shop yesterday evening when he drove into town. The curving stalks and the pale pink and purple petals reminded him of Emily—pretty, soothing and a little untamed. It was just a small gesture, but he had to start somewhere.

No one else was here yet. He'd made sure to arrive before Lily, even. He had a feeling that Emily would be keeping early hours since she'd been working on her own. Hopefully, they could talk before any of the other employees got here.

Back in the treatment area he found Rex's bed. Someone had shoved it in the supply closet, and Wes put it back on the floor in Rex's favorite spot. Rex rolled over for a belly rub, and Wes obliged. When he'd gone to London he'd left Rex with Maya and Caleb. According to Maya, Rex had slept by their front door every night, waiting for Wes to come get him.

It was good to be back at work. Everything in the clinic was well stocked and neat as a pin, a tribute to Molly's and Dan's constant cleaning and organization. The air smelled like disinfectant. A peek into the hospital area showed Wes that they'd had no overnight visitors.

Once Rex was relaxed and flopped on his bed, Wes pulled up Fancy's veterinary file. Emily had managed to resolve the colic within about five hours, according to the notes she'd written down. Still, guilt kicked Wes in the stomach, making it impossible to drink the coffee he'd purchased for himself. He should have stayed and helped.

"You're here." Emily stood in the doorway to the reception area, holding the coffee cup and pastry bag. "You're here and you brought food."

She was beautiful in her usual jeans and sweatshirt, her hair pulled back in a ponytail. So simple, so natural, so perfect. "It's just a token," Wes said. "An apology. I should have stayed to help with Fancy. I was wrong to go to London when you needed me."

She regarded him with a wary expression in her big eyes. "Your brother needed you, too."

"My brother is a grown man and can take care of himself, as he informed me several times. He doesn't want me trying to rescue him anymore."

"I see." Rex came to greet her, big tail wagging, and Emily knelt to cuddle him.

Wes tried to explain. "I've always worried that the time we spent with my parents, who were pretty unsteady, or the years Jamie spent with my aunt and uncle, would have a lasting impact on him. So when he quit his new job with no warning like that, I panicked. I thought maybe it was a symptom of a breakdown or something."

Emily nodded, still holding on to Rex.

"Turns out I was the one having the breakdown, jumping on a plane for a wild-goose chase in another country. My brother is fine. He simply hated his new job, and for good reason. He's already got a new one that I think he's going to be much happier with."

Emily stood, giving Rex one last pat on the head. "I'm glad that all worked out for you." There was a careful distance in her voice that made him nervous.

"Jamie reminded me that he's a grown man and his choices are really none of my business. I have to let him go. But worrying about him, caring for him, it's all I've ever done." Wes reached for his own coffee, relishing the warm cup in his cold hands. "It's a strange feeling. I don't really know who I am without him to look after."

Emily flipped idly through the file he'd left on the counter. "There are plenty of animals here in Shelter Creek that need looking after."

His heart did a small backflip of hope. "Are you saying you'd hire me again? Because I'm pretty sure I failed my trial period at the end there."

"Maybe I had you on trial for the wrong reasons." She met his gaze then. "I've been holding on to so much old hurt about when you left before. It clouded my judgment when you needed to leave this time. It felt so emotional and so huge, when of course you had to go to your brother if he needed you. Family is important, and he's all you've got."

Wes swallowed hard. He hadn't known what he'd find, coming back here today. He hadn't expected her compassion.

"I've been seeing everything in terms of how it affects me. Or how it affected me when I was seventeen." Emily's mouth tilted into a rueful smile. "I'm not that girl anymore. I can stand on my own a whole lot better now."

"But what if you didn't have to? Or at least, not all the time?" Wes held out his hands, palms up, inviting her to come to him. "I want to stay, Emily. I want us to pick up where we left off. I want to work with you. I want to be with you. Is it possible? Or did I do too much damage?"

She pressed her lips together, looked down and away. Wes dropped his empty hands. He wasn't going to like her answer.

"I'm really glad you came back. I missed you. A lot. So much. But I think I need some time, Wes. One of the things I realized while you were gone is that I have to learn to trust you. I have to believe that I matter to you more than anything. If I don't believe that, and if I can't trust in what we have, it will never work."

It wasn't exactly what he wanted. She wasn't

rushing into his arms. But she was being honest about what she needed. This love between them hadn't broken overnight. It had eroded slowly, year after year, all those years he'd stayed away. Maybe he'd have to build it back up slowly, too. Word by word. Action by action. "I'm glad we can still work together. And maybe still walk Rex sometimes? And work with Fancy?"

She nodded. "I've missed that."

"Me, too."

She looked at him then, and their gazes held. Warmth sparked. There was a promise there. He'd hang on tight to that for now.

Wes took another sip of his coffee. "What's on the schedule today? I'm ready to get to work."

EMILY TUGGED AT the bandanna Wes had tied over her eyes. "This is silly. I'm going to get carsick." The window next to her rolled down and the warm spring air blasted her face. It was one of those May days where California decided it was done with spring and ready for summer. "Where are we going?"

"We'll be there in one minute, I promise."

Rex's cold nose found her ear. "Ugh, Rex, no fair."

"Sit," Wes told his dog, and the nose was gone.

This was supposed to be a normal Saturday. Wes had come over for breakfast on her porch. She liked to make him pancakes. Then they were going to work with Fancy. If there were no emergencies, and their schedule stayed clear, they'd hike with Rex. Maybe after, they'd head over to her parents' for dinner, or meet up with friends.

Wes had been so respectful of her wishes in the month since he'd been home. He was always there, always her friend and colleague, but never asked for more.

Lately she'd been wishing he wasn't quite so respectful. The guarded feelings she'd had when he came back to Shelter Creek were long gone. She wanted more and she thought he still did, too. Sometimes she'd catch him watching her with an intense look in his eyes and wonder if his love and trust had grown as hers had. Or if he wanted to kiss her again as much as she wanted to kiss him.

But how could she move forward? She'd insisted on this distance between them. Did she just sit him down and announce that she trusted him now? That she wanted to date again? That was so unromantic. And what if he didn't want her kisses anymore?

Emily gripped the door handle, grateful to feel the car turning off the road onto gravel. "It's not my birthday and it's not a holiday. I can't figure out why we're taking this mysterious journey."

"You'll find out in a moment. Hang on."

Wes stopped the car. They were in shade, Emily could feel the cool shelter of something, a tree maybe? Wes got out and came around to her side to open her door. He gently helped her out of the car. Turning her around, he untied the bandanna from her eyes. "Here it is."

Emily blinked, trying to adjust to suddenly having vision again. In front of her was a pretty farmhouse that she'd driven by many times, just on the way out of town on the road to Bobby's ranch. She'd pointed it out to Wes once, telling him how much she'd loved the huge porch and the grove of ancient oaks that shaded the house from the summer sun. The property had been empty for a few years now, the owners caught up in some kind of financial problem with the banks.

"What are we doing here?"

"I just thought we'd take a look around."

Look around? It was private property. "Do you know the person who lives here?"

Wes nodded. "Yeah, he said it would be fine."

Rex was already exploring, running in and out of the oak trees, his nose to the ground.

Maybe Wes was thinking about buying it? Emily followed him to the front door. There was a big red bow attached to it, like a wreath. Most likely a leftover Christmas decoration. The thought saddened her for a moment. Someone had loved this beautiful house, spent their holidays here, and now it was empty.

Wes pushed open the door. "It's unlocked," he said.

The inside was gorgeous. Craftsman columns framed the entrance to the living room and dining room. Built-in cabinets awaited someone's china collection. There was a rustic stone fireplace in the living room. The kitchen was simple, with white cabinets and walls.

"What a great house." But it felt strange to

be here, on someone else's property. Emily walked through the mudroom behind the kitchen and out the back door. Beyond the garden she could see a barn and corrals. "There are stables here?"

"Want to check them out?"

"I guess so." Emily turned to Wes suspiciously. "Are you thinking of buying this house?"

Wes grinned, looking a lot like the eager boy she'd known before. "I bought it already. It's mine. What do you think?"

Emily stared at him, struggling for words. "You bought this house?"

"It was a surprise. Are you surprised?"

She clapped her hands to her mouth. "Of course I am. Oh, my gosh, Wes, you know I've always loved this house. But this is a big investment. Are you sure?"

He took her hand. "More sure than I've ever been. Come on. Come see the stables."

Still holding hands, they made their way along a gravel path until they came to the barn. It was modern, with cement floors and sliding stall doors. "This is gorgeous," Emily exclaimed. "You have room for a dozen horses here."

"I'll need a place for my clients to stay while I work with them."

He'd mentioned the other day that he might want to train horses in his free time, but she hadn't realized he was this serious. Wes stopped at a door at the far end of the barn. "This is the tack room. Check it out."

Still stunned that this beautiful property belonged to Wes, Emily peeked through the door at the tidy racks for saddles and bridles. There were cabinets for medicines and blankets. "This has everything." Then she paused as something caught her eye. By itself, in the corner, almost hidden by the door, was a saddle on a wooden saddletree. Goosebumps prickled her skin. "Wait a minute, Wes, how did this get here?"

It was her saddle—the one from the tack shop that she'd been admiring for months. The exact saddle, with its beautiful tooled flowers and the silver thread. "My saddle." She turned to Wes for an explanation. "Did you buy this?"

His smile carved creases around eyes that were lit with warmth and emotion. "Lloyd told me your heart was going to get broken if someone else bought it. I figure thanks to me, your heart has been broken enough. I wasn't going to let it happen again. Plus, Fancy is going to be ready for a saddle soon. You might as well be ready, too."

"I don't know what to say."

Wes dropped to one knee in front of her. "Say you'll marry me. Say that you and Fancy and Rosalind and Beatrice will come live here with me and Rex and we'll make a home together. A life together."

Tears, hot silent tears slid down her cheeks. Emily's hands covered her chest as if she could somehow calm the pounding of her heart.

"I love you, Emily. I've loved you for so long. I've never loved you more than I do today, but I'm going to love you more tomorrow. I know you're learning to trust me. Can you trust me enough to be my wife?"

Emily went to her knees, as well, put her fingertips to the stubble on his cheek and kissed him with all the love she'd kept tucked away behind caution and fear. His mouth was warm, his kiss firm, and he wrapped his arms around her and kissed her back the way she remembered. The way she'd been dreaming of. A kiss that left no questions, no doubts, as to how much he loved her.

Some moments later his lips softened on hers and he pulled back gently. "Was there a yes in that kiss?"

"Yes." It was hard to get words out when there were so many tears. "There was definitely a yes in that kiss. I love you, Wes. I think I always have. But I love the man you've become more than I could have possibly imagined."

He stood, lifting her gently to her feet with him. "Then accept this?" He took something out of his pocket. It was a platinum ring covered in tiny diamonds that sparkled in the sunlight flooding in through the tack room window. Two loops of the diamond band crossed through each other. "They're supposed to be horseshoes. For Fancy. For luck."

The cool metal slid onto her finger. Emily held her hand out, gazing at the sparkling band. "It's absolutely beautiful, Wes. But it's a lot. A house, my saddle…this ring? You didn't have to do all this."

He pulled her in close and wrapped his arms around her. "I've dreamed of a life with you since our first kiss. I need you to know that I'm not leaving you, ever again. This town is home. This house can be home. But most of all, you're my home, Emily. And you have my whole heart. You always have."

Emily held him tight and let the happy tears slide down her cheeks. He was strong and sturdy and he was Wes. Her love. And he was home, to stay.

* * * * *

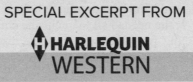
*Can ex-marine Marcos Ramirez settle into ranch life…
complete with a family he never knew he had?*

Read on for a sneak preview of
The Texan's Secret Son,
a new story in Kit Hawthorne's Truly Texas series.

Nina had never forgotten Marcos's face, though close to
eight years had gone by since she'd seen it last. She had a
small square photo of him in her jewelry box, but it was
a memorable enough face without the tangible reminder.
A strong face, but with something oddly vulnerable in
the shape of the lips, the ever-so-slightly dimpled chin.

And the eyes…oh, the eyes. She'd seen them go
through a whole gamut of emotions over the twenty-plus
hours of their first meeting.

Now they were hard and cold as stone.

Eliana had contrived to get him and Nina seated
across from each other. Marcos looked like he'd rather be
anywhere else in the world.

"So, Nina," said Renée, "where are you living?"

"I'm renting a house not far from work. It's small, but
it's on a big lot. Plenty of backyard for Logan to play in."

"Good! Are you all unpacked and settled in?"

"Not even close."

They went on that way for a while, about the move,
the town, even the weather. Renée kept up an easy flow

of small talk, and Nina was grateful. It helped ground her, and right now she needed all the help she could get. She was still reeling from the impact of the discovery that Eliana's brother was actually the Marcos Ramirez she'd known.

At least she didn't have to talk about her fake husband, and no one would ask any awkward questions about him. She had Eliana to thank for that. Clever, coming up with the idea about avoiding the subject because Logan missed his dad so much that he might get weepy if he heard him mentioned.

The irony of the ruse was that Logan's father had been missing all his life, and Logan didn't seem to care one bit. It worried Nina a little, how weirdly unemotional he was about the whole thing.

Really, though, that was only the top layer of a whole onion of irony in this particular situation.

Marcos was the only one not contributing to the conversation. He sat across from her, grim and silent, not even meeting her eyes.

The Marcos Nina remembered was worlds away from this guy. Singing along with the Lyle Lovett track at that San Diego bar. Flashing her that daredevil grin. Pulling her to her feet for a dance. Looking down at her with those gorgeous green-flecked brown eyes, saying, *I, Marcos, take you, Nina, to be my wife…*

Don't miss
The Texan's Secret Son *by Kit Hawthorne,*
available June 2021.

Harlequin.com

HWESTEXP0421

Get 4 FREE REWARDS!

We'll send you 2 FREE Books <u>plus</u> 2 FREE Mystery Gifts.

Harlequin Heartwarming Larger-Print books will connect you to uplifting stories where the bonds of friendship, family and community unite.

FREE Value Over **$20**

**IF YOU ENJOYED THIS BOOK
WE THINK YOU WILL ALSO LOVE**

LOVE INSPIRED

INSPIRATIONAL ROMANCE

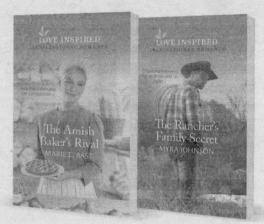

Uplifting stories of faith, forgiveness and hope.

Fall in love with stories where faith helps
guide you through life's challenges, and discover
the promise of a new beginning.

6 NEW BOOKS AVAILABLE EVERY MONTH!

LIXSERIES2021

SPECIAL EXCERPT FROM

LOVE INSPIRED
INSPIRATIONAL ROMANCE

When a young woman is visited by a man from her past,
will her whole life change forever?

Read on for a sneak preview of
Her Small Town Secret *by Brenda Minton*

"There's an incredibly gorgeous cowboy waiting for you in the front lobby. He might be all hat and no cattle, but I'd take him if I wasn't happily engaged," Avery Hammons's assistant, Laura, said, winking.

"Gorgeous cowboy type?" Avery asked after settling her patient's arm back on the bed.

"Avery Hammons, please come to the front desk. Avery, please come to the front desk," a male voice, not one of their staff, called over the intercom.

"Who was that?" Avery asked, leaving her patient's room, Laura hot on her heels.

"My guess is that would be our man, Mr. All Hat. Can we keep him? Please tell me we can keep him," Laura practically gushed.

Avery hurried down the hall of the long-term care facility where she worked, turning a corner and then stopping so quickly that Laura nearly ran into her. "Oh no!"

The cowboy leaned against the counter, the intercom phone in his hand. One corner of his mouth hitched up as he nudged his hat back a smidge. "Honey, I'm home."

No, no, no. Avery stood there in the center of the hall, caught in a nightmare in which Grayson Stone was the star. He was the one person who could—and would—shake up her life and ruin everything. It was what he'd always done. What he did best. He knew how to make her feel beautiful and worthless, all at the same time.

She shook her head, wanting, needing, to wake up and have him gone. She closed her eyes, said a quick prayer and opened her eyes slowly.

"I'm still here," he drawled with a slight chuckle as he set the phone on the desk.

Yes, he was still there. All six feet, lean athletic build of him. He grinned, as if this was all a big joke and he wasn't pushing her life off its foundation. Life had always been a joke to Grayson. The spoiled son of a judge and a pediatrician, he'd always been given everything he ever wanted or needed.

She'd been serious, studious, determined to change her future. She had wanted to prove that a kid from Dillon's Trailer Park could become something, someone.

Grayson was her kryptonite.

Don't miss
Her Small Town Secret *by Brenda Minton,*
available June 2021 wherever
Love Inspired books and ebooks are sold.

LoveInspired.com

LIEXP0521

Love Harlequin romance?

DISCOVER.

Be the first to find out about promotions, news and exclusive content!

Facebook.com/HarlequinBooks

Twitter.com/HarlequinBooks

Instagram.com/HarlequinBooks

Pinterest.com/HarlequinBooks

YouTube.com/HarlequinBooks

ReaderService.com

EXPLORE.

Sign up for the Harlequin e-newsletter and download a free book from any series at **TryHarlequin.com**

CONNECT.

Join our Harlequin community to share your thoughts and connect with other romance readers!
Facebook.com/groups/HarlequinConnection